to Peter and Donna,

with love

Pulp Books is an imprint of Pulp
Faction, PO Box 12171, London N19 3HB.
First published by Pulp Books, 1999.
All rights reserved.

Do What You Want is a work of fiction.
Any character resemblance to people
living or dead is purely coincidental.

A CIP record for this book is available
from the British Library.
ISBN 1901072169

Lyrics from the following songs appear
with permission:

Lipstick on your collar by Lewis/Goehring,
by permission of Anne-Rachel Music
Corp/MCA Music Ltd © 1959.

Thirsty Dog by Nick Cave,
by permission of Mute Song Ltd.

Do What You Want

by

Chris Savage King

I

Jonathan stared at the heap of silver Gaggia instruments in his sink. Stupid machine had never worked properly ever since he'd first got it. He picked up the pieces, threw them down, passed wet fingers through his blond hair, admired his jaw line in the mirror, then shot down the stairs and was off to work.

He'd lost a fortune at poker last night and the pleasure he'd felt at the time had worn down into cash flow anxiety that niggled like a pile of broken chips. They weren't even professionals. Jonathan thought that if he gambled at all he should do it properly. Same with drugs. Definitely. He never touched dope, but he kept smack around.

He was streamlining his life, for good. His skin had flared up again. Some rash, old acne, eczema, something - he couldn't stand bleeding every time he shaved. Must be the diet - clean it up. He could ask Deanna. She was supposed to know about it. Macy's Foodstores weren't the be all and end all but he should use his contacts to the full.

Posies of crimson and mauve flowers were shaken excitedly in his face. He stepped back and saw two tiny hags with sunken eyes, brandishing them. He shouldered through and one of them spat out something, some kind of curse. He hared off, rigid with hate. Some kind of art wank, possibly.

He swung into reception through the revolving doors, ignored the lift man, knocked back a warm espresso, arrived at his floor, looked at Charles, grinned meanly, then jerked his head. Charles was on his mobile. Jonathan nodded curtly and made his way out, down the escalator, its steel walls singing, through the revolving doors, up an escalator, into the dealing room.

He adjusted his tie and hopped into place and held his head back, ready. It was all growls and yips and figures filing, icy blue, onto a screen and murmurs thickening, and Jonathan loosened his collar and felt the sweat around his neck and thought Christ, no one knew, top of the world, it was better than being God: the whole world was here. The figures filed out faster, murmurs accelerated, there was escalation and fall, the figures filed out faster, then it died down, jackets were unfastened, and the morning was in sail.

Jonathan clipped his collar into place and felt his sweat cool and dry on his skin. Charles caught his eye and Jonathan joined him. They polka stepped to the lift door and clapped each other on the back. They filed into the street.

'Safe,' said Charles.

'Yep.'

'Near strangulation.'

'Yep.'

They marched on, overtaking dawdlers, elbowing through

news stands, weaving round sponsored litter bins. Charles spotted a pair of black meshed legs disappearing into a taxi. He leered and grunted. So did Jonathan.

'Ginny last night…' said Charles.

Jonathan turned to him. Charles' face was flooded with triumph.

'Don't tell me then,' said Jonathan. 'Uh? Eh?'

Charles smiled. 'Later,' he said.

Coach lamps were lit. Thick linen tablecloths floated then settled over wooden tables. Vans jerked to a halt at the side of pavements. Buttoned groups of security men carried steel cases. Jonathan and Charles snuck off for a coffee at Minty's.

'Barston tried to make me get him into Vellarco,' said Charles.

'What?' said Jonathan.

'I said 'Fuck off Tony'. Thinks it's '85!'

'Christ!' said Jonathan. 'What?!' They left.

'Wanker,' he added, as they turned a corner.

They swung through the revolving doors, ignored the lift man, stood straight, faces front, going up. They muttered their farewells and crouched over their computers. Jonathan ran his hands all over his face.

He tapped the keyboard hard and light - a series of brief electric shocks - grasping money for a few delicious seconds, then throwing it out and drawing it in again. He leaned back in the chair, talked to his Flexifone, called up information, just to check. By lunchtime he was up £150,000. Soon the silent Malays with tall chefs hats would be round with fancy sandwiches, sushi and cakes, baby bottles of water and wine.

He didn't want that today. He wanted something pure. Calf's liver would do - it slipped down easily, there was no bother with cutting it up. Or oysters.

He stood up and pulled at his lapels, hoping someone would join him. They were fastened into their machines, still. He looked down at his shoes and stamped his feet lightly. He liked to relax alone, anyway. He wanted to be alone today.

He walked into the street, with only his wallet on him, and Maxine's gory mouth reproached him in his head. She'd been at Claire's on Sunday, waltzing around in a chaotic outfit, and coming on slyly to some man with a Renaissance hair-do, parted at the middle and fluffed out at the sides. So he was some kind of a ponce, too. She'd given Jonathan all these dirty looks, but they hadn't exchanged a word.

Three years ago, at Claire's , Jonathan and Maxine had swiped a couple of bottles and sat under one of Claire and Anthony's trees, just to be on their own for a while. Maxine's big, pale thighs had stuck out under a crumpled green skirt, her clumsy boots and daubed make-up making her seem more vulnerable and interesting than when they met up anywhere else. There in a house and garden filled with older people with drab, expensive clothes and well-aired vowels.

'Anthony's got me a job,' said Jonathan.

'What job?'

'In the City.'

Her face hadn't changed, then she smirked. 'The *City*?'

'Yes. *City*.'

'You're going to do it?'

'Yes.'

She had given a throaty laugh. 'What? That's it - what you're going to do?'

'Yes.'

'You don't have to do what Anthony wants.'

'I'm not doing what Anthony wants. It's what I want. I'd like doing that. It'd be really fantastic.'

'That's what you want?'

'Yes.'

'Don't you know what you'd like to do without Anthony telling you?'

'I'd like doing that. Make a packet.'

She'd tried to smooth down her skirt, without much effect. 'How do you know?' she'd asked.

Jonathan hadn't answered.

'I've got to get to work…'

'What work?' he'd said.

'Exhibition soon. '*Pandemonium 1*. Want to come?'

'Pandemonium *what*?'

'*Pandemonium 1* is the name of the exhibition,' she'd snapped.

'Oh that would be Bond Street would it?'

'No of course not.' She'd gathered some energy, pulled herself up, and turned around to gaze at Claire's friends in the distance. 'What these people like…isn't very important.'

'Why are you here then?' Jonathan had said.

'My mum just died. Claire felt sorry for me. She got in contact again. We're related, vaguely.'

'Right,' Jonathan had said, falling silent.

'Y'alright then?' he'd offered, at length.

'Happens to everyone,' she'd added, after a pause.

'Yeah I suppose it does,' Jonathan had replied, 'unfortunately.' He'd nodded to himself.

'It'll happen to you someday. *Pandemonium 1*'s an exhibition with other people. Mixed exhibition. Locally. Mine.'

She'd picked up one of the bottles, and left. Maxine's back had depressed slightly as she'd stumbled back over the grass in her Doc Martens.

He saw Maxine only occasionally now. They avoided sensitive topics.

Jonathan stopped short and looked in a shop window at a display of teapots mounted on black velvet, thinking how no one looked like Maxine, around here. He was so glad of that.

He sat in the bar, relishing its mahogany interior, and the easy deference of the bar staff. Suits surrounded him, discussing serious business. This was what it was all about. He read the FT, slipped the oysters down. They were so fresh and silky. It was how life should be - not cluttered with hoyden painters, or ugly fucking gypsies shoving flowers in your face.

He finished his lunch and pushed the plate aside. A good, thick, white plate, stamped with a coat of arms. He was having lunch with Anthony soon, just to discuss a few things, man to man. He used to be scared of him, but that was such a long time ago it hardly mattered. Anthony was excellent. He had proper values. He and Claire were a fine couple, born rich. Jonathan was honoured to know them.

'Thank you sir,' said the waiter, removing his plate.

Jonathan stared into space, his mouth slightly open.

There was another thing. Daniel was coming back. He was on his way. Claire had said so on Sunday.

He blotted his lips dry. No. And a big NO had been torn from his throat when he looked at the phone and dreamed of Daniel last night. His letters to Daniel in Rome - Christ, his letters. He'd been in a state then, had only just got the job, had been traipsing around too much lyrical art with Claire.

What had he said? Emotional diarrhoea - another complaint he'd got rid of. He was ashamed of them now. And of the couple of late night calls he'd made to Daniel in Rome. Sheer madness.

But he'd better do something - some kind of damage limitation. Get there first, just in case. Lunch wouldn't hurt, especially with someone else there. Because things were different now. Patti - he'd got Patti. Blonde, sleepy, but with beautiful clothes like a girl in an Antonioni movie. Worked in the office, but not too near. Went out for drinks sometimes with their boss. Charles fancied her. Patti's father was something to do with Sotheby's. Patti had three languages under wraps.

Lunch with Daniel wouldn't hurt though, no.

He got out his Flexifone and left a message on Deanna's answering machine. She'd come. He slid a postcard of Montgomery Clift out of his wallet, and scribbled a message to Daniel on it.

He wondered whether he ought to tell them where the

restaurant was, but it was in the phone book, it was well known. What were they supposed to be - stupid? But that was the trouble - dealing with people different from you. You never knew if they stuck to the same rules you did.

2

In another part of town, where the making of sandwiches and money was still a primitive art, Maxine climbed the concrete stairs to the floor above a comic shop where she shared rooms with Lydia, a singer. Her two portfolios had to be manoeuvred to get them around the half landing of the narrow stairway. She flung them down on the bed in her room, went to the kitchen and got a beer from the fridge.

It was Lydia's birthday today, and in the early hours Maxine had cleared part of the kitchen table and laid out her presents: a fuchsia lipstick, a baby bottle of champagne, three neat spliffs wrapped in blue tissue paper, a bottle of the oil Lydia liked to use in the bath, and a postcard of a painting of Maxine's called *Poppies*, with 'Happy Birthday Lydia xxx' written on the back in silver ink. They'd all vanished now. Lydia had just left a sheet of paper covered in ticks and kisses. Maxine smiled, sipped the beer from the bottle, and went into her room.

She was always glad to get back to her room with its smell of turps and all her work stuff. It was usually colder there than outside, but too much warmth would have made the paints turn, and the brushes dry out. She found the slightly damp chill bracing when she returned to it. She and Lydia kept their place just how they wanted it.

Syd, their landlord, who ran the comic shop, was thin-hipped and drank too much, and harboured a slow-eyed curiosity about the two of them neither was in a hurry to discourage so long as the rent was cheap. They had got a car recently - a beat up old Morris that a friend of Lydia's said was a bargain, especially for town driving. Lydia had got third party insurance, which they took to mean 'some friend driving it occasionally'.

Coming back from Claire's on Sunday, Maxine had looked despondently at the flat's bare walls. She and Lydia never did much with the place because they always had better things to do. But it didn't look so bad now. Maxine had met a man with long hands and connections, who had just given her the go-ahead for her first solo exhibition. He'd spent a long time with her, discussing her work and assessing it in hushed, busy tones. They'd sat on the terrace of his gallery, facing a shabby block of flats, and she felt like someone who mattered, at last.

Maxine had also run into Robert at Claire's on Sunday. She'd had her eye on him for a while. She left early so he wouldn't get tired of her, or want her to say any more than she already had done. Claire's and Anthony's area of London, its tall white buildings and bright clean pavements redolent of timid ailments and nursing agencies, and their house with its high ceilings, treacherous polished floors and antique furniture, could only set her off at a disadvantage.

Anthony just gave her the creeps.

She picked up one of the *Poppies* cards and scrawled a message on the back - '*Bloody Marys, then? Anytime you like. M x.*' Then she put it to one side, ready for sending off to Robert some time later in the week.

She heard someone coming up the stairs. Piss off Syd, she thought. It was a boy with a long face and a head like a boiled egg, wanting to see Lydia.

'She's not in,' Maxine said.

'I'll wait.'

Maxine led him into the kitchen, then went back into her room, and slammed the door.

Opening one of the portfolios, she laid out three sketches against the large canvas she was working on. She sat on the floor with her ankles crossed, and cut her toenails with kitchen scissors. She flicked the nail cuttings into a pile in a saucer, rubbing off any dirt that clung to them. She was absorbed in this. She had an idea of putting them into a sculpture.

She got out of a box full of severed dolls' heads and limbs, magazine cuttings, frosted pink false nails, a tattered orange wig, some scraps of fur and a rabbit's foot keyring. She looked at them. She went to the kitchen to get another beer. The boy was still there, staring at a plate of old toast crumbs, a grubby bra and a book called *Killer Women* on the kitchen table.

There was only one bottle of beer left in the fridge, and what was left of the vodka was just for her and Lydia.

'Why don't you go and sit in Lydia's room?' she said

brightly, 'she wouldn't mind!'

'I'll have to go in a sec,' he replied. 'I'm double parked.'

'You could try the *Macrobiotic Speedline Café*.'

'Who?'

'Lydia works there. So do I.'

She was pretty sure Lydia wouldn't be there, but it would get rid of him. She tore Lydia's message in half and drew him a map in brisk, hard strokes on the back of it.

'There,' she emphasised a line, 'some people get confused.'

'Thanks,' he said.

'What's your name?'

'Paul.'

She started working again. Later, she heard Lydia bang the door, and come in with some others. They went into Lydia's room and plugged in their guitars. She and Lydia never interfered with each other when they were working.

They started playing and Lydia started singing. They were making so much noise Maxine's concentration hardened. An hour later when they were on an up and cooking so good, she returned to the larger canvas and felt them drive her efforts. It was coming through the walls.

She heard them leave. Lydia - lipsticked, perfumed and silly - wandered into her room because the door was open. She draped her arms around Maxine's neck, and her shoal of black corkscrew curls fell over Maxine's face. Lydia kissed her on the cheek.

'Hello my darling thank you for my lovely pressies.'

'You liked them?'

'Yes I did.'

'You had them?'

'Quite a bit. You nearly finished?'

'Yeah,' said Maxine. 'And the gallery's going for it. *Done.*'

'See?' said Lydia. 'Told you.'

They'd consulted the Tarot about it last week. Lydia jumped off Maxine and saw the saucer of nail clippings.

'You going to paint them?'

'No,' said Maxine.

'Anything to eat?'

Maxine got up and stretched, and put her socks on.

'Frozen tempeh, carrots, that leftover tofu tart from Tuesday.'

'We ought to get rid of that soon.'

'Yeah.'

'You want to go out then?'

Maxine put her shoes on. 'Yeah.'

Round the corner they ordered their usual - tiny, flaky shrimps and slithers of vegetable in such blistering chilli sauce it made their eyes water. Lydia, on a health drive, once, said this cleared the system and prevented colds. She and Maxine had a few scuffed books on alternative medicine. They liked to dabble in it, so long as it didn't involve any effort or sacrifice.

The lantern light in the restaurant made them look slutty. The lamps were dim and dusty because the place mainly served the takeaway trade. The family that ran it were used to having Maxine and Lydia in, so they ignored their intimacy and talk, and got on with their own business - that night, shifting a load of small packages, and getting their children off to bed.

'So…' Lydia said, 'solo in Southwark.'

'Happy Birthday!'

They clinked their glasses and laughed. She'd ask Jonathan anyway, Maxine thought. He looked so pleased with himself on Sunday. She still hadn't forgotten the postcard he'd sent her after she had laughed at him for going into the City, all that time ago. A particularly mashed cubist Picasso and a very nasty message on the back of it:

> *Your hovel is filthy, fetid and stinks,*
> *Full of manky fruits*
> *And draughts.*
> *Stuff your paintbrushes and other stuff up your*
> *cunt, shithead*
> *I hate your fucking guts*
> *Love Jonathan*
> *PS. Is this a poem? Is this art then?*

She had definitely had it with him.

'Robert turned up at Claire's on Sunday.'

'Dreamboat?'

'Yeah. Seemed to go alright.'

'What's he do?'

'Architect.'

'Any work?'

'Some.'

'Ohh!' Lydia breathed her cigarette smoke through clenched teeth. 'Bet he wears nice undies…'

'Yeah, well fingers crossed…' Maxine looked up and Lydia's face was pursed to laugh. 'I just get a good feeling off him…yeah, *really*…'

'Like Piers van Damme?'

'Better than him.' Maxine pushed her coffee aside. 'Piers didn't wear undies, as I recall.'

'It was a bit of a mystery that…'

'What? No knickers?'

'Piers Vee Dee. You know. He sat in a room - everyone else became suicidal.'

'I thought it was quite a fascinating quality.'

'Yeah, I know you did,' said Lydia.

It had been disastrous. Maxine didn't want to think about it. It wasn't as if Lydia's choices were so brilliant. There had been the aptly named Wally, whose chief source of income turned out to be bag snatching, who came on to all of Lydia's friends. Augustus had seemed like a plum choice at the time, until his fiancée had popped round for a chat.

'Funny isn't it? Marcus has all those ideas about a new *Macro* building, then I meet Robert…'

Lydia pulled on her cigarette and looked at Maxine hopelessly. 'You really think he'll pull that off?'

'Why not?'

'Because it's Marcus. He's always got *ideas*.'

'Don't have to write if off already do you?'

'I'm not,' said Lydia. 'I was just wondering…'

Maxine fiddled with a matchstick in the ashtray, slinking back into her own privacy.

'The Drachma still paying up?'

'They've threatened to cut our dates down,' said Lydia, 'but it's not serious. They've paid the £200. And I've got another advert.'

'Someone called for you today - Paul.'

'It's okay. He came back later.'

'Is he…?'

'Just the new pianist.'

Just as Maxine thought. He didn't have the aggrieved look of most of Lydia's boyfriends.

'Sounded good tonight though,'

'Yeah - well we'll see,' said Lydia. 'Our tapes are still out.'

'I saw Deanna in town today,' said Maxine.

'Oh yes?'

'With a Spanish woman.'

'She a new girlfriend?'

'Suppose,' said Maxine. 'They were just having lunch, but you know…they said they'd come to Southwark.'

'What's the girlfriend's name?'

'Don't remember,' said Maxine. 'I wrote it down for the invites.'

'Working in food's a funny thing to do,' said Lydia. 'It'd put you off.'

'It's not like just serving at the *Macro* is it?'

'No,' said Lydia. 'You'd be more involved with it somehow, all the processing, knowing what goes into the stuff. Yuk.'

Hanging contentedly over their cigarettes, happily established as central in their orbits, Maxine and Lydia mused in silence until their eyes moved incidentally, then inexorably, towards the clock.

'Time?' said Maxine.

'Right,' said Lydia.

They smacked down two fivers, and left.

They crossed the main road, heedless of the traffic that had gathered snarl and speed since it got darker, a rubbish bin spilling into the gutter, and a crowd getting restive at the bus stop. They were intent on one purpose and there were few more determined sights than Maxine and Lydia heading to the 24 hour shop, at ten to eleven. They had an arrangement with the manager. It was just best to get there before his prices went up.

3

Claire held a vase in her manicured hands and stared out of the window into the trees. It was very quiet, and very green, and if she looked hard enough she could see the silvery lake.

She was at home with a slight migraine, and Anne, the cleaning woman, was in hospital - something to do with her legs, or maybe her knees. So Claire, while she was recovering, thought she would clean some china.

She rubbed it with a pot of facial cream, and cleaned it with a rather good astringent she'd bought at great cost at a department store some time ago. She hadn't used it on her face for long - it was rather abrasive, and a great deal of fuss. But it did a remarkably thorough job on her china. For her face, she stuck to oatmeal soap.

Her answering machine clicked on. I'm ill, she thought. Let them talk into the machine.

'Oh hi there Claire, it's Daniel - in Rome still (short chuckle). *Line's nice and clear though isn't it?'*

Claire sighed, put a piece of china down, and picked it up again.

'I've talked to Priscilla. She said to come in next week. Sounds

great! Uh - just what I wanted (pause). Really looking forward to it. I don't know if you know anything about this, but I - um - asked her to send a job description. She just sent a load of brochures...'

Claire stared fixedly at a spot on the wall.

'They were nice brochures. Shakespeare, Greek Art, and...uh...other things. Yes. So I'll see you then. (Long pause). Bye then!'

Poor boy, thought Claire, pressing the button that erased all the messages. She didn't know if this little job helping out her old school-friend Priscilla at an Arts Centre would be much good. But Daniel couldn't spend his entire life marching people around cathedrals.

Jonathan seemed to be coming into his own. He was so charming in his pride in his work. On Sunday he mentioned he was trying to improve his languages, and sometimes played tapes on his Walkman for the purpose. He could not decide between Italian, Spanish, Portuguese, or Intense French Revision. Claire said he really ought to focus, else he would not make much progress in any of them.

One would hardly guess, and of course no one would ever know, that Jonathan was the son of an old secretary of Anthony's. The parents lived an insular life in Dorset these days. They never visited - thank God - best for Jonathan. It occurred to Claire that all the business with childbirth might have been worth it, had she produced Jonathan. And yet she was already an aunt to Maxine, the daughter of a distant cousin of hers. Very distant. Dead now. Maxine - her very own black sheep! She seemed to be wholeheartedly devoting herself to the creation of ugliness. She wondered if Maxine would get along with Robert. No matter. *Amour fou* was one of Claire's favourite tropes in art and literature.

Claire of course had been assailed by a familial chorus years ago. She'd watched childbirth come back into fashion with trepidation. But there were limits to how far she would go purely for the sake of form. Anthony had never been bothered. So Claire had dropped hints about a defective reproductive system - a common enough complaint in women of her class, and for all she knew, quite possibly true.

Her china finished, Claire sighed again, and supposed she had better go into work. Else poor Jadine would have a nervous breakdown, and of course, there was Deanna later. She picked up her cashmere coat, added a coat of lipstick, and dabbed her face meticulously with beige powder.

She arrived at the office - a Georgian building in a square, a little like her house, but smaller and more central. She gave a forced smile to the receptionist, and moved into the part of the building with the most light.

Claire's office with its walnut desk, bay windows and bottles of sherry and whisky in cabinets, carried the old lavender smell, harshly preserved, of a world in which sherry in drinks cabinets and bay windows figured as essentials in life. Jadine banged away at her Apple Mac in what used to be a quite roomy stationery cupboard. Claire buzzed Jadine.

'Did we manage to sort out those little problems?'

'Yes,' said Jadine.

'Good,' Claire cut her off.

The proofs for *The English Writer and the Italian Countryside* had arrived, with a note from the designer: 'the author's still written too many words - more cuts please - need more white spaces!?'

Claire smiled. The designer was right. It was pleasing prose, but still got in the way of the book's overall style. The pictures of the Victorian jugs for another book looked better than the set she'd sent back last week. She supposed she ought to chase up her gardening authors. She had to think quite hard to tell them apart.

Deanna arrived clutching brightly coloured folders, wearing a pleated skirt, a polo neck, square looking shoes, all set off with a leather jacket. Her shiny bob was artfully contained by a headband. She looked like the most gorgeous of school prefects.

Claire had first met her when she was a recipe checker for another of Claire's books - *Recettes de Volaille Choisies de ma Vieille Tante Paysanne*. She now worked for Macy's Foodstores, involved in producing fast food.

Deanna was romantically involved with a rather argumentative schoolteacher called Paula. They seemed to get along. Paula was a good soul, and intelligent, Claire thought, though not what you'd call a good advertisement for it.

Claire liked the way Deanna's tough fingers gripped the pen, as she made scurrying notes on Claire's comments on chapters. She handed Claire some menu cards.

'I know it sounds a bit naff,' said Deanna, 'saying product this and product that, but the company insists.'

Claire nodded. Deanna's eyebrows went up in the middle

in a quite delightful way.

'I've made the instructions pretty clear, you know - some people don't know what you mean when you say 'reduce' the sauce, and all that...'

Claire smiled. This was, presumably, what the board meant by burgeoning markets. Everyone cooked these days.

'Well that all seems in order. They actually look rather good.' Claire threw her arms back then leaned forward. 'And how are *you*?'

'I'm fine,' said Deanna. 'I did another synopsis, for another book, my own.' Deanna handed Claire a folder. 'Thought you might like to have a look.'

Claire opened the folder, took the top sheet out, and held it at a distance.

'*Under An Hour*,' she read out loud. 'Interesting.'

Then she put it back, shut the folder and smiled. The publisher's budgets were already over-stretched.

Jadine went out at lunchtime, and Claire glided into her office. She picked up an oily piece of paper which had presumably held a pizza, and a sticky, empty bottle of pineapple juice, with her fingertips. She dropped them into the bin. 'Now that's better isn't it?' she said, to the absent Jadine. She put the dictionary from her office strategically close to Jadine's computer. Pity you couldn't get girls like before, bright but unambitious girls, fresh out of University, who wanted to work at something nice. Girls you could have conversations with.

Claire returned to her office and dictated a letter:

'Best paper, Jadine. Top of the cupboard behind you.

Address in the folder. Let me have it back sometime. Dear Deanna - that's D-E-A-N-N-A - Lovely to see you today, comma, and delighted to be working together again. We never seem to have much time though - exclamation mark. Paragraph. Would you like to have dinner with me on the 10th? Apparently *Les Quatre Chats* - L-E-S Q-U-A-T-R-E C-H-A-T-S - that's four cats in French, Jadine - is supposed to be awfully good. All best wishes. Etc. Make sure I sign that one.'

Jadine came in with Claire's letters.

'I can spell *'Les Quatre Chats'*,' she said.

'Yes,' said Claire, autographing the letters, 'but *'Don Quixote Geraniums'* is an X - like the book and the ballet - not *'Quick Sauté'*. So take that back...'

Jadine looked at the letter. 'It was the way you said it.'

Claire looked up pleasantly. 'Have you read Cervantes?'

'No,' said Jadine. She looked petrified.

Claire loved these spats. She hadn't read Cervantes herself, but some friend of Anthony's had.

That evening she went to the *Institut Français* to see Doucetêtes's latest - *Les Enfants Deshabillés*.

Its ambience inevitably reminded her of her and Anthony's cottage, in England, which they hadn't visited recently.

She went home. The clock chimed. How her china sparkled! She could tell Anthony was in. She fetched some Chablis, and poured some into two tulip shaped glasses. She lay back in the armchair. She and Anthony always stopped for a glass of wine at 10pm. The study door creaked. Here was her husband. She handed him a glass, and they sat opposite each other. This was what their marriage was all about - unspoken agreement, mutual accord.

4

As soon as Daniel got back to London he knew he'd made a mistake. Rome's constant sunshine and routine work now seemed all that he wanted. At Heathrow, he held a suitcase over his head to squeeze through the barrier, and a woman shoved him out of the way and said, 'Excuse me, I'm busy.'

In Italy he'd found it fun sometimes to pretend to be French or Spanish. Now he was back home he thought he'd pretend to be Italian.

'*Mi scusi, cara bella,*' he bared his teeth at the woman.

'Bog off,' she said, then pulled her coat firmly around her.

He watched her as she charged through the exit doors, and swum in a pleasing idea of himself as a lecherous foreigner. He was still anonymous until next Monday morning. Buying up his entire Duty Free consignment wasn't excessive.

The tube train rattled on and he was spookily transplanted into some prewar backwater. No one here ever did bother to install high speed railways. All the stations along the way looked like great big toilets. He felt oddly energised, and excited at new prospects. He wanted to be in the thick of things, instead of skimming over surfaces. He fixed his gaze on a menacing advert for mouthwash. Understanding every word of a language wasn't always an advantage.

Daniel glanced at the book of a very still woman next to him: 'In Mauritius we make love in other ways...', he read, and wondered if this was true. In Rome he'd had a brisk run of sex with tourists and locals, much of which he'd honed into anecdotes while it was still in progress. Now he was back home, he had an urge to do it with someone he wanted to talk to.

He thought of Jonathan. He'd thought a lot about him in Rome. An improved version featuring Jonathan had been grafted over most encounters. Jonathan's stilted letters, and his say-nothing late night phone calls, held promises that could only be delivered in the flesh. Maybe they could get something going - even have an affair. They had more in common far apart than in previous meetings. There would still be a vast difference between their incomes and status, of course. Daniel decided that if it didn't work out, he would blame it on that.

In a Rome bar yesterday they'd played *Mony Mony*, which instantly recalled the basement jukebox in a holiday camp. Daniel went down there as a child because there was safety in numbers. Lots of older girls - boys didn't get you on your own. He remembered standing in front of his mother by the swimming pool, holding his wrist behind his back to hide a Chinese burn. She'd sat up in a deckchair, wearing a floral swimsuit, still splashed and laughing, having been chucked in the pool. By the same pool at a quieter time, while everyone got dressed for dinner, he'd had footballs slammed into his eyes and was ducked until he choked.

He'd decided then to get far far away as possible, to a place where people didn't do terrible things to each other. There was nothing anyone could do to him he couldn't run away from now. In Rome, it didn't matter what anyone did - there was no one around who would notice.

His teenage years were uneventful - he'd stayed in and washed his hair most nights, with one of his mother's towels round his head, and a stack of Cilla Black records. He was glad his new boss was called Priscilla. It was like the fulfilment of a very old dream.

He had always fancied working in the arts, but never got interviewed. Now the job had just come up, and it all seemed very simple. Claire would have to regard him as some kind of equal. Maxine couldn't sneer at him for liking the wrong art works. He would have a special authority, now he was working in it. Overall, the job would settle a lot of overdue scores.

He got out an Italian novel he was already halfway through. He thumbed it, broke its spine, then stared at himself in the window. He wondered if having a heart-shaped face was really an advantage. His hair required an urgent service. In Italy, he had been determined to read only Italian, with the result he hadn't read very much of anything. He stared at the Italian words, and couldn't connect with them. He stuffed the book down the side of the seat - it was already obsolete.

It was his stop. He walked past an electrical shop, covered with rusted grids, a couple of shops he couldn't remember, now closed down, and a front garden where pink hollyhocks shot past bent 'For Sale' signs, as if overjoyed at having gained supremacy.

An old neighbour was picking up rubbish in the front and putting it in a carrier. He racked his brain to try and remember her name.

'You back then?' she said.

'Yes!'

'Your friend left Thursday.'

'Great.'

A police car screamed across the main road. The neighbour looked in its direction.

'Lively at the moment, here,' she said. 'You look brown. Got all your presents I see.'

Daniel laughed.

On his mat ('Welcome') there was a cheque book he'd ordered, a flyer for delivery pizzas and a Montgomery Clift postcard. He turned it over. Jonathan. Lunch would be a start. He smiled at the wary civility of Jonathan's handwriting.

There was a flat Telecom envelope, which he re-addressed to his lodger, and a brown envelope from the Council. He threw that in the bin. In the hall, his lodger's stuff had been packed into a load of cardboard boxes that would fall apart if anyone attempted to move them.

He cradled the phone by the window. Jonathan's answering machine rustled, then bleeped four times, then blurred, then rustled out something unintelligible. He phoned Deanna, whose line was engaged. He called Maxine, who yelled her delight at his return. They should have a drink, or something, she said.

'Tomorrow?'

There was a burst of laughter at the other end.

Maybe Tuesday week, but she'd have to confirm it.

'How d'you find England now?'

'It's different and the same. They deliver pizzas to you!'

'Yeah, they do that,' she said. 'But they're a bit various. Sometimes you wish they hadn't bothered.'

'Really...'

'They've phased out Toblerone boxes too...'

'Christ!' said Daniel.

'And all the chocolate bars are an ice-cream...'

'Right...' said Daniel.

There was a pause, then both of them spoke at the same time.

'I was...'

'I was...'

'You teaching English again?' Maxine said.

'No, another job. Claire helped out.'

'Oh,' she said, 'oh, *really*? Where's that?'

'Arts Inc.'

'Oh,' she said. 'Oh.'

He phoned his parents and said everything was fantastic, then sat on the sofa, smoking a crushed Camel. The sofa felt damp. He went to the kitchen. There were teabags but no milk. There was half a bottle of cider in the fridge, so he started on that.

He put on some baroque music, with its hints of cunning

progress, then felt intimidated and depressed. *Another One Bites the Dust* was his next carefree choice. He danced in front of the mirror, checking various angles. He went into his bedroom, with an eye to its future use. New duvet cover - white, maybe - why not? - a bedside table with a proper drawer, and a softer light bulb should do it, now he had a career job. He puffed up the pillows and switched the tape to one on which he'd recorded 13 versions of *Fever*.

Four hours later, awash with cider and Valpolicella, stuffed with delivered Napoletana pizza, the TV on with the sound off, and *Elton John's Greatest Hits* blaring out, Daniel suddenly felt better. He found his stash of Jonathan's old letters: '…I suppose I'm fitting in, but sometimes it's difficult to tell…' He felt tenderly disposed, a special confidante, someone who could help.

Almost catatonic, he held a cigarette stock still and stared at his Diva poster while *Don't Let The Sun Go Down On Me* moved into a melodramatic swell. Tears filled his eyes. Jonathan, he decided, during *Candle In The Wind*, was a little bit like Marilyn Monroe, and so was he. So was everyone, really. He put the letters aside and polished off the bottle, and fell back on his bed, hugging himself. Among the torrent of thoughts he'd had when he came back, only one remained, late at night - Jonathan, Jonathan.

5

Robert had been massaging Maxine's *Poppies* postcard under his breast pocket, on and off, for about a week. Every now and then he took it out and looked at it. It was an invitation into another world, a better one. The postcard was unique. It was reproduced so you could feel the quality of the paint under your fingertips. The strongly defined colours, the roughness in the paint, the thick roundness of the shapes - the kinds of qualities he liked to get into his own work. But it was difficult, given where he worked, with open-ended plans that kept chopping and changing, miserly developers, iffy contracts and everything panning out to the level of someone else's idea of good taste.

He felt a cheat, but there was a reason for it. No one built anything of their own until they were forty. If you were going to toe the line then you might as well do it properly. So he was ensconced in a building with long, slender skirting boards, stucco ceilings and gold carpets, with a very well appointed receptionist, and crusty senior partners, and sofas in the reception area as round and cushiony as Maxine's curves. He created parts of buildings that fitted in with others' grand plans. He paid attention to the design details to keep himself interested.

But it was a dead end, and the women he'd been seeing lately were very much like him. They sat in restaurants, discussing their careers, office politics and other issues, and had sex when they weren't strung out. Yet sometimes he saw a girl on the street with a shaved head and a plait springing out of it, and clothes that looked and hung like combat gear for a reserve army, and wondered what they did or knew about that he didn't. The women he'd been involved with tended, in a matter of weeks, to get difficult in the most uninteresting ways. But Maxine wouldn't bother you too much, he thought - she was too preoccupied with herself.

At Claire's it had been the usual thing. He was flattered to be asked, then wondered why he went. When Claire's guests asked him what he 'did', he was strangely dumbstruck. The topic of Prince Charles cropped up and Robert's spirits sunk. He shortly found the talk had been adjusted to the placid admiration of the garden. He agreed, it was a very nice garden, finely landscaped, splendid, yes.

He'd been collared by someone called Priscilla or Prunella, who flirted with him, which was an improvement. Until he saw it was just an exercise. He could have been anyone.

Maxine was being lectured at by some ancient crony of Anthony's, and shot Robert a little wry smile that sent shockwaves to his groin. She backed off from the man, thrust her empty glass into Robert's chest and said, 'Get me another one?'

They'd walked around Claire's china and she said, 'Oh,

these are a nice lot of old pieces aren't they?' He knew what she meant. Like Claire's house and Claire's guests, who knew about things, but didn't have feelings about them.

He was at a loss with Maxine so said what he'd been thinking, about motorway bridges being a form of perfect design - as fluent as an S or a question mark, better than any number of recent buildings.

'I paint, and a few sculptures - some of it's public,' Maxine said. 'I did a painting called *Motorway* quite recently.'

Then she went, but he got the card. First thing that day, he attended a meeting where the clients refused to go ahead unless they cut the budget. He looked at his plans and saw his next batch of work laid out as an arid voyage into mean-minded mathematics. He picked Maxine's postcard from his pocket, and nearly wept over it.

They met up at a basement bar with dark walls, candlelight and low seats. She was showing off the cleavage he'd already imagined, and was wearing some peep-toed shoes that told him she was probably intending to make a night of it. Their heads moved closer together as they talked about David Bartlett films, Richard Rogers, cowboy artists - any old shit - and she ran her fingers over her neck and shook her red, ringletted hair back, so he could get a good look at the goods.

They sipped Bloody Marys and Maxine tapped her feet. It just so happened - what a coincidence - that one of her paintings was on show down the road. Would he like to see it? Course he would.

On the way she explained it was a travelling exhibition,

that she liked her work to go places in lieu of herself, also that she liked exhibiting with others, she wasn't hung up on that romantic artist thing, that artist in isolation stuff, that *male* thing. He thought these great notions.

The building was down a side street, with brick walls, and a hand painted black and white sign like a flag outside: BODY ART. In the entrance, a bulky white plaster male torso, with no head, arms or waist, stood in front of bare red lightbulbs fixed on the wall to flash a message: ARROGANCE IS BLISS.

The place was small, only a couple of rooms. The walls were distressed and the music was heavy metal with a woman's deep voice rasping through it. It vaguely reminded Robert of some punk record he'd owned a long time ago, but the sound was more lustrous.

'They're playing Lydia's tape,' Maxine said.

'Lydia?'

'My flatmate.'

They were all bits of women's bodies, the exhibits, although one was a mess of indeterminate pencil lines, one a draped remnant of dusty pink velvet, a cute button face covered in whipped cream, one or two bald biological inspections. There were tits fashioned out of balloons - the knots served as nipples - and a deodorant stick on a stand with a sign in front of it: '*Ceci n'est pas un prick.*' A joke, he thought. A woman's joke.

He saw Maxine's picture: *Vulvarantula.* Red hot oils on a very large canvas. It was what he got from the *Poppies*, but more explicit, nothing to do with flowers. It had the sensation - more whorls and curves that ran on their own momentum. He could almost feel the wetness and the suction.

'I like yours best,' he said. His lips were very near Maxine's face.

'It's a bit naive,' she said, seriously, but a smile was spreading in the pit of her stomach, 'I still like it.'

She walked around to look at everything else, and left him to it.

She preferred the cunt painting to her other naive one - two pricks crossed like swords, straining foreskins, hairy stems. They'd put it up in the *Macrobiotic Speedline Café*, and had taken it down again at the earliest opportunity. That was where Piers van Damme came in. He was on the circuit, doing studies in spirals. They'd met twice and she'd got obsessed with him - he was so ugly, with a huge head and a crushed nose. She had to have him.

She'd asked him to pose for the picture, and he was too vain to refuse. He stood there in the light, with a hard-on, for quite a while. She wasn't bothered about the rest of him, when working, but it puzzled her that he couldn't keep his eyes off his erection either.

He'd fucked her like someone trying to get the better of someone else in a very complicated intellectual argument. He was a practising Buddhist, and hardly talked, and never seemed pleased or sorry about anything. When she was with him, not having sex, every single depressing thought she'd ever had in her life drifted up in the silence and hung there. It had lasted six weeks, and the last fortnight was touch and go. She wondered if he might show up tonight. She wanted him to see her with someone else.

She preferred her other prick piece - a pâpier maché sculpture of Page Three girls, strategically fraying, with a fat, bulging head, daubed in lube. She hadn't exhibited it yet, but the gallery man in Southwark said he loved it. That was one of his favourites. The crossed pricks were technically competent, but dreadful, she thought, now. Too obvious. Yet then, some of the simplest clichés were true. Robert looked so beautiful in his black jeans and white T-shirt. His proportions were more fluid and less thickset than Piers, more lean and manageable. She longed to get him home and peel the T-shirt off slowly, leave it wrinkled around his chest like a whore, wrap it around his head, her hand on the bulky zip in his jeans, and him there on his back, exposed.

Robert walked around, his eyes roving over the exhibits. New things really did raze down the past. Ten years ago his favourite sex artefacts were at one end *Déjeuner sur l'Herbe* and at the other, *Justine*. Thank God she didn't know him then - *Déjeuner sur l'Herbe* ! The whole exhibition reminded him of times when he didn't entertain any notion of limitations - it was a faint but sure glimmer. Times when he went off to watch short, surrealist films on his own, because they seemed somehow relevant to what he was doing.

He watched Maxine looking at something, arrested in concentration. Nothing she was wearing much concealed what was underneath. There was something thrown together about her and the exhibition that made it all so real, and her seem so accessible.

'Finished?' she said.

In the street she stopped to get her bearings, and they caught each other's eyes.

'What shall we do now?' she said. The street was deserted. 'I'm not far.'

They went to her place, which Robert liked. There was nothing dainty to get in his way. It was a temporary place, but made for intimacies, not display.

Bottles of vodka, tomato juice, Worcester sauce, and a dull silver cocktail shaker Daniel had bought Maxine a few birthdays ago, lay abandoned in a corner. They were on Maxine's bed, legs and arms intertwined, and he grabbed her arse so he could plunge himself in deeper. She threw her arms around his neck, rubbing her tits against his chest. They juddered along, exchanging wet, sweaty kisses. She licked his earlobes and rubbed her cheek across his stubble. He moved his head teasingly over her freckled skin, which tasted of burnt toffee and warm nougat.

She gripped him inside, to keep him where she wanted. The traffic roared outside. Robert's mouth was somewhere around her shoulder. Some frosted nails, an orange wig, some toenail clippings and scraps of fur were still in a box in the room, awaiting Maxine's attention.

6

The Arts Inc office was open plan and in the same building as the Arts Centre it served. The only people who had separate offices were the ones who were never there to use them. Daniel's desk was a long panel, seating five others, with him stuck in the middle. He shuffled papers, re-wrote information, and received memos typed in book quality print, with his name marked in fluorescent pen, summoning him to various meetings. Everyone let out jovial exclamations, sipped a selection of waters and cupped their chins in their hands. Daniel watched while they spoke, nodded keenly, and looked glad or concerned. He had been expecting more talk about books and ideas, but it was mainly incentives, goals and targets. He snapped his folder under his arm at the end, smiled, and relayed the meeting to Priscilla.

'Oh God', 'Oh good', 'I'll write them a note', she said. She had a tight blonde chignon and permanent light tan. He decided she wasn't like Claire. Claire wasn't as lanky, and would never wear so much perfume or gold jewellery. Priscilla was always brushing imaginary crumbs from sponsor's jackets, and was married to an Egyptian businessman. Three times out of five, he couldn't tell whether she was being ironic or not.

A hefty man came in and put a mock-up poster down in front of them.

'It's good,' said the man, '*très* sexy!' He laughed and hovered.

'*Thanks*, David,' Priscilla replied creamily.

He sloped off with his hands in his pockets.

'David Brasted,' she hissed.

'I've never got around to seeing his stuff,' said Daniel.

'A lot of people have that problem,' she sighed. She held up the poster - a woman spread-eagled on a table, with a look of agony on her face, a man standing over her, three decades older.

'Quaite naice though, isn't it?'

'Yes!' said Daniel.

She tapped the actress's cleavage with her pen.

'Date rape. The girl's dying for it, but has a grudge against the man because he's cleverer than she is. She's a screwed up intellectual feminist, who also happens to be a nymphomaniac. She accuses him falsely. It's kind of Stoppardian.' Priscilla screwed up her face. 'Can't help thinking there's a touch of wish-fulfilment in that. I mean Brasted - he's not exactly an oil painting. Wish he'd change his *jumpers* more...'

'Issue play,' said Daniel, thoughtfully.

'If only he'd *alternate* them...What? Yes. So everyone'll take a pitch at it. Good for publicity. We've already got a couple of *Guardian* women up against a right wing philosopher and a man from the *Telegraph* on at lunchtime. Then there's that really subversive DJ - you know? - the one who pretends people are dead when they aren't? Well *he's* doing something! I don't know how I feel about issue plays, though. Do you know how you feel about issue plays?'

'Oh I don't mind them really,' said Daniel, 'I...'

Priscilla picked up the phone. 'Helew?'

He went down a corridor, up some concrete stairs, down a lift, past the back where all the rubbish was kept, past a rehearsal room and janitor's cupboard and into Personnel to drop in Priscilla's expenses.

The woman in charge was leaning over her assistant, Bella, and pulling her hair. The pair were informally known as Hinge & Bracket.

'I can't seem to blow dry it like he did,' said Bella.

'You could do it with rollers...'

'Don't have any. Actually I only go to watch them whipping their combs out of their back pockets. I think that's dead sexy.'

Daniel could tell this remark was for his benefit.

'Oh look Jean, we've got a guest from Creative. You settling down alright?' said Bella.

'Oh yes!' said Daniel.

'You get on with her alright?'

'Oh, fine!'

'I'm sorry but I just don't like Priscilla's type. I pity you.'

'What type's that?'

'Oh you know. Doesn't like women. Still, boys like you can blend in. She's not acting up?'

'No,' said Daniel, perching on Bella's desk, 'but she did tease me in front of everyone for only getting 4 GCSEs the other day. I felt a bit embarrassed.'

'That's rich, she only got five. GCEs, they were then,' said Bella. 'One was Art. Well - you know, nationally, that's not bad. From St. Paul's it's practically mentally retarded.'

They both laughed.

'It's great here. You get to see everyone's CV,' she continued, "why I wanted this job' etc, what illnesses they've been laid off with, or what they said they were…' She added, mysteriously, 'No, I couldn't stand the people you have to deal with.'

'Oh they seem okay,' said Daniel.

'You were very excited about storytelling the other day weren't you? Were you on something?'

'Just high on life!' Daniel cried, tossing his head.

'Right,' said Bella. 'Still, if you want a smoke Friday evenings, come round here. Jean gets it from a friend at the Garden Centre.'

Jean came back and handed Daniel a cheque, looked at Bella sternly, then returned to her desk.

'I don't seem to have got a contract yet,' Daniel whispered.

'Oh we'll get you one of those,' said Bella.

But not now, apparently. Momentarily, she had a look of the snake who sang *Trust In Me* in *The Jungle Book*.

Post-It notes littered his part of the panel like buttercups when he got back.

'Check up on Rosencrantz and Guildernstern will you?' was in Priscilla's handwriting.

Daniel went down a corridor, up some concrete stairs, through to the more stately and public parts of the building. In the Grand Hall, two of the Shakespearean actors were addressing a group of American students.

'I was very glad,' said the fatter one, 'when I heard she was going to be my Miranda, given her stunning bit-part in the TV Amelia.'

'Bit-part - har har - quite! It's difficult,' smarmed the other, 'not to get involved when you're working in such - huh huh - close proximity.'

The students looked at them stonily. Their tutor wore a red suit, and listened with her head cocked on one side.

'Trouble with the wives though...'

They let out well-seasoned laughs. The boys looked perplexed and the girls looked annoyed. The tutor hastily asked them a question about identifying with a role. The actors hesitated, then their voices rolled out like barrels.

'In rep,' said one, 'it's just you, absolutely you. You and your all. You and the words.'

'Yet with the Duke, it's not like one of the Kings.'

'The Duke, yes. Like you now.'

They laughed again.

'Which is again, different from doing the Princes.'

'Or a Count.'

They were the kind of actors who everyone had seen in something, who would never be offered work in Hollywood.

'He's referring to our current production of *Measure for Measure*, by the way. Your third Duke, William?'

'Fourth actually...'

'Better get the adverts in for the punters. You're all coming are you, I presume? Anyone there?'

'We have to come,' said one of the students, agreeably. 'It's on our course!'

The actors' faces were pulled into a thunderous solemnity. The students made them look like cavemen. Everyone clapped politely at the end.

Daniel watched them all troop out. God bless Americans, he thought. God bless their cotton clothes, their amazing teeth and hair, their bionic bodies, their old movies, their pornography, their rendering of salads into something you might actually want to eat, their ability to make shambolic old Europe seem so gloriously dirty, to accept these two rude old bores as noteworthy. He bounced back into the office.

'They alright?' said Priscilla.

'Yeah,' said Daniel, 'they gave them rep tales and smutty anecdotes.'

'Perfect. Tell you what,' she pushed a piece of paper over, 'you could do the Archaic Greek Art meeting for me? The curator can't stand women.'

'Yes!' he said. Do what, he thought.

'You know anything about Greek, huh?'

'Oh definitely,' said Daniel. 'I'll…research it.'

He basked in a feeling of impossible grandeur. Well this was shaping up beautifully. He looked at the notes on his desk. He'd be through by 7.30pm.

He arrived at Maxine's part of town about 8.30pm. There was still the supermarket with cut price posters splashed all over it, a store with a load of rickety planks in the entrance, and a raddled old git sitting on a chair outside the comic shop, with a bottle of whisky by his side and a roll up in his mouth, staring perplexedly into space. He accosted Daniel.

'You for upstairs?'

'Yes.'

'You look like you would be. Tell those bitches the hot water tank's theirs, alright - theirs not mine. That's nothing to do with me - got that?'

'Yeah - thanks,' said Daniel, 'you alright mate?'

'No, it's not alright. Bloody frightening…' the man said. He threw the butt of his roll up near the visitor's shoes. Going up the stairs, Daniel remembered that was Syd. He was surprised he wasn't dead yet.

The door was open so he went in. Inside, it was the same, except the lino in the kitchen had worn away to more concrete, and the threadbare rug in front of a heater had risen into hard arcs at its edges. He suddenly saw a white polystyrene dummy's face with an orange wig on it. It looked gruesomely like Maxine, embalmed.

He followed the noise of a radio - more crackle than pop - and found Lydia in the bath, with her feet on the taps, smoking a joint, with her arms raised upwards.

'Riccy, Riccy, Riccy in here!' she cried.

'Hi,' said Daniel.

She turned round. 'Oh. I thought you were my date. Maxine's at the *Macro*. Won't be long.'

'Oh you still work there?'

'Yes!' She turned on him with a startled pout. 'Why not?'

'Nothing,' he said. 'I mean it's still going is it…I thought there were problems…'

'No,' said Lydia. 'It's, you know, a *project*. We're not just waitresses.'

'No I know,' said Daniel. 'Syd was out downstairs.'

'Oh don't take any notice of him. We don't. Make yourself some tea.'

He washed a couple of chipped cups. There was no milk, but they had half a wrinkled lemon.

Maxine thumped up the stairs, and marched into the bathroom.

'Marcus's going nuts isn't he?' she said. 'Did he say anything to you about wearing black T-shirts?'

'Something to do with new backers…' said Lydia, 'we're being upgraded.'

'Some dickhead wanted to have a long philosophical conversation about why we change the ashtrays like that…'

'Huh. Yeah,' said Lydia.

'…pissed at 3.30pm. Where do they come from?'

Lydia stretched her arm and pointed. 'Look who's here.'

Maxine walked into the kitchen. She and Daniel kissed each other, and nearly missed.

'Oh if you've got tea I'll just…' Maxine wandered into her room.

Lydia sat down at the table in a sky blue kimono, fiddled around in a make-up bag, then started plucking her eyebrows. 'Italy, was that good?' she said.

'Oh yes,' said Daniel.

'I was in Spain for a while, that was good.'

'Are you - uh - still singing?'

'Oh yes,' said Lydia. She cleared her throat:

> Mealies are a lot of fun
>
> Feed your cat
>
> Watch him run
>
> Fit and keen come rain or sun
>
> Meow! Hurrurrr Nnrraoullll!

'Like your purrs,' said Daniel.

'The lyric's not great but I'm telling you I'm definitely using the purrs in something else,' said Lydia. 'I worked on them for days, you know. We borrowed Syd's cat didn't we Maxine?'

There was no answer.

'Advert?' said Daniel.

'Well it's all good practise, you know. The marketing man said they were branching out into a youthful, spry image - as opposed to the sensual sophistication of their other adult cat products.'

Maxine came back. 'So what's this new job then? Got any funding going spare?'

Lydia fixed her eyes on him.

'I don't know,' said Daniel. 'I'm not really dealing with individuals at the moment.'

Maxine smiled. 'Guess not,' she said.

Lydia put the mirror down, licked her finger and ran it along her eyebrows.

'You should meet Paul, my pianist.'

'Oh yes?'

'He's nice. Isn't he nice Maxine?'

'Mmm,' she said. 'Very Brighton.'

'He heals people too.'

'Oh yes?' said Daniel. He felt very formal, wearing a shirt. He thought he ought to stick up for it.

'We've got a play about date rape coming up, at Arts Inc.'

'Yeah,' said Lydia. 'There was something in the paper today. Sounds horrendous.'

'You need the car?' said Maxine.

'Take it.'

They passed a harassed man in a yellow sweatshirt on the stairs. 'That was Riccardo,' said Maxine. 'He takes over when her drummer's got groin-ache.'

She drove swervingly down a dual carriageway and under a flyover until she realised they were going in the wrong direction. She did a scrappy U turn between two bollards and Daniel's hands leapt out and clutched the dashboard. A car hooted behind. Maxine checked her mirror.

'...probably just collecting their video nasties...'

Daniel turned around and saw five faces like lumpy potatoes packed with fury, aimed at them.

They parked at the end of a road, and Maxine led him to a doorway.

'Here it is - the *Romola Brasserie*,' she said. 'No sorry thatza bank.'

They went next door.

They sat down at a table and craned their necks, banging their cigarettes on the table, establishing their right to be there. An hour passed. Daniel had nothing against Robert, but if Maxine mentioned his name one more time he swore he'd smack her face.

'Well this is an improvement,' he said, 'I never did like pubs.'

'Hate 'em. That's another good thing about Robert - he doesn't like pubs, especially old cosy ones.'

Oh God, thought Daniel.

'How often are you seeing him?'

'A lot,' she said.

Twice a week, he thought.

Maxine returned to her assaults on Claire, which had been gathering force throughout the evening.

Something about thinking Claire might try and put Robert off her. Daniel wondered when to introduce Jonathan. If he hadn't done it by 10pm, the moment would be lost. They were playing Noel Coward songs with a plink plonk piano. Mad about the boy, he thought, taking a mouthful of wine, holding it, then swallowing.

'When I was in Rome I looked forward to coming back to Claire's teas,' he said.

'She doesn't do them much now.'

'I never liked Earl Grey,' said Daniel. 'I only started drinking it because it was supposed to be posh.' He coughed awkwardly.

'Reminds you of *mice*.'

'I like cake,' said Daniel. '*You* like cake.'

'I like little tarts with fruit in,' said Maxine. 'I am not over fond of cake. I had a salad at Claire's once,' she continued. 'It had a ball of fluff in it. I thought that summed her up.'

'You never really knew what you'd find in them,' Daniel

added. 'Chorizo sausage. Those funny mushrooms with the webbing...'

'And fish,' said Maxine. 'Fiddle around with bones until you're half mental.'

Three beautiful men in jeans and leather jackets came in. Maxine followed Daniel's gaze.

'Am I keeping you?' she muttered.

Daniel brightened up. 'I rang Claire the other day...'

'Yeah.'

'Got her machine. Just happened to mention Jonathan.'

'Yeah.'

'Got a message back... Good luck with the job blah blah...'

'Yeah.'

'Then she says she thinks I'll find Jonathan much changed.'

'*Changed?*' said Maxine, 'how *changed?* He's always been a complete fucking bastard!'

She sat up straight. 'See that painting over there?'

Daniel strained his eyes.

'It's mine.'

He relaxed, got up, walked over, looked at it, and then came back.

'Great, more subtle...'

'Eh?'

'But somehow bolder...'

'And I've got one in the *Casa Nostra* and the *Macro* have put some in too, and I've got some slides out...' she crossed her legs, 'more *subtle* ones yeah, I suppose they are. What did you last see?'

'Trains,' said Daniel, 'and hats and suspenders. All mixed

up - exploding - with thick paint - collage type things...'

'Yes, but they weren't really objects were they I mean...'

'Um..no,' said Daniel. 'You were doing some project with meat too.'

'Oh that was cancelled,' said Maxine, 'by the regulations. You can't just hang up meat any old place. Amazing isn't it?'

'Yes,' said Daniel.

'No. I'm doing something with toenails - Roccoco thing with toenails, to keep up the Body Art end. Then I'll be through with that. Everyone's doing Body Art now and it just gets boring. Get stuck too much into all that and you're like someone running for a bus and always getting there five minutes late. No so I'm going back to painting, and doing it mainly with the paint, not the drawing. That takes time, but the overall result is much more immediate. I've done a bit of sculpture, but I don't know if it was just because people asked and I was blocked. Branched out with the materials and it's opened things up for the painting. Did you see any sculptures before?'

'No,' said Daniel.

'They'll be in my next exhibition.'

'Oh good,' said Daniel.

'That painting over there's quite old.'

'Oh it's good, I think, very good,' said Daniel, exhausted.

'I don't like it much,' said Maxine.

They seemed to have dispatched the topic of Jonathan.

'I saw some photographs the other day,' said Daniel. 'Someone called Paul Dart?'

'Yeah I know Paul Dart.'

'In Cork Street. Serial killers. They were very blurry, but oddly compelling.'

Maxine stared at him with her chin slightly lifted. She didn't know why he'd gone for this job. It wasn't as if he cared about anything.

'Yeah, well, I haven't seen them. What's Claire's friend like?'

'Priscilla. Quite a laugh.'

'Oh, that's good then. Yeah I think I've seen her at Claire's. She was talking to…Robert…'

Daniel kicked the table.

Maxine went to the toilet and Daniel bought two final drinks. The music changed to Billie Holliday, before she became a tragedienne.

Maxine returned. 'Rothko did stuff for restaurants,' she said, as she sat down. She held up a mirror to apply more lipstick.

> I jumped out of the fryin' pan and right into the fire
> But I lost me a cheatin' man
> And got a no'count liar
> Swap the old one!
> For the new one!
> Now the new one's breakin' my heart!
> I jumped out of the fryin' pan and right into the
> fire…

As the trumpet swooned on with a tone of breezy foreboding, Maxine slugged Daniel such a look from behind the mirror, he could swear she had just asked the barman to play it.

'Rome was great,' he said, into the air.

'Was it?' said Maxine, through stretched lips.

He picked up a menu.

'The *Nachos to Share* don't amount to much,' she said, winding down the lipstick, 'and they're £5.95.'

'There's a chippy near me.'

'That'll do.'

In the car they put on the radio: 'Now here's Steppenwolf - *Born To Be Wild*.'

The car was stuck in a traffic queue. 'I don't know what's wrong with this filter light,' Maxine moaned.

'Yeah - love it!' cried the DJ, as the record finished.

At Daniel's flat once they'd finished their supper they broke into a bottle of duty free brandy and Maxine, now maudlin, worried whether she was getting 'a bit obsessive' about Robert.

'Oh surely not?!' cried Daniel.

They both sat there, thinking of things they'd like to discuss with other people.

'My lodger collected his stuff the other day,' said Daniel, slowly. 'Just came in when I was out and left the keys. I thought we might have a drink or something. I didn't know him that well but...then I thought how sad it was, you know - end of an era.'

'All eras end,' said Maxine, 'you're just disorientated.'

'Are you sure your brakes are alright?'

'Yeah course they are,' said Maxine. ''Night...'

''Bye,' he said.

He poured himself another brandy and picked up a folder

headed *Future Policy Documents for Arts Inc*, but felt too bleary to concentrate. In the middle of the night he woke up abruptly, gasping for sympathy and a cold drink, flayed with guilt.

He got out a pad of Basildon Bond he usually wrote to his mother on:

> *Dear Claire*
> *The new job's great - really enjoying it and settling*
> *in okay (I think!)*
> *Do you want to come and see anything? I could get*
> *tickets.*
> *Will be in touch soon.*
> *Lots of love*
> *Daniel*
> *PS. Are Maxine and Robert an item?*

Because he thought Claire should know.
He added:

> *PPS. Seeing Jonathan myself shortly soon.*

He read over the letter and thought how wonderful it would be if it were all true.

7

Still, Daniel stole off to a library in his spare time, trying to get to grips with Archaic Greek Art. He carried heavy folios from shelves reached by ladders, and turned pages over, reverently, at their edges. The quiet was soft as feathers, religious without the intensity, broken only by a cough or murmur at a distance. The mind's hard work left his body free to dream, and a rosy steam of expectation wrapped round him. It stored hopes for sensations that wouldn't be realised, primed him for imaginary surrenders. Jonathan metamorphosised in the vacuum in a cloud, raining down blessings, an angel in his midst.

Now the day had come, all he was aware of were butterflies fluttering in his stomach.

He found Dolorossa. It seemed more of an evening place than a lunch place. No one attempted to take his order, which was just as well as the cheapest drink was £2.50, and his first pay cheque wasn't due for six weeks. He wondered about his new haircut - whether it fitted the rest of his face. It cost £35. Jonathan was ten minutes late.

A woman in a jumpsuit looked around the tables. She

spotted Daniel and her eyes leapt. It was Deanna with her hair slicked back.

'Oh!'

'Oh!'

'I'm meeting Jonathan.'

'So am I.' He was about to add 'what a coincidence', then realised that it wasn't.

She threw herself down. 'Don't you want to - uh - see him on your own?'

'No! Not...'

'No,' she said. 'No. Oh I see. Oh. Right. Oh *great*!'

A waiter cleared his throat and stood there.

'Drink Daniel?'

'Perrier - um.'

'Two Perriers. No - make that a bottle. Let's go *mad*.'

'Is that all?' murmured the waiter. 'A bottle of Perrier.'

'Here he is,' said Daniel. Jonathan looked more wonderful than ever, like a Greek God, more handsome, more muscular.

'Hi!' said Jonathan. He bent to kiss Deanna, then thought better of it. He touched Daniel's back uncertainly, and looked in another direction. 'I've got a table booked at the back.'

They were handed menus the size of files. A very large sweet trolley crawled past them.

Jonathan ordered a gin and tonic.

'Saucisses frites,' said Daniel, because it was the cheapest.

'Roasted vegetables with the coulis,' said Deanna.

'Fennel,' said the waiter. 'Anything to start?'

'No thanks,' said Deanna. 'This fad for polenta's

completely out of hand. I don't want *that*,' she added, to no one in particular. She turned to Daniel.

'How are you?'

'Oh fine!'

'Work alright?'

'Yes. Just started at Arts Inc.'

'We've just got a new marketing director. PhD from the US. Laurie Colacello. You know what he's got lined up now for ice creams and yoghurts? Nasturtium and Honey, Sharon Fruit & Ginger, Starfruit and Lime, Kumquat. Can you believe it? His bloody pitch is *fucked*. You've got to look at restaurants. What's going through the ceiling? Potato skins, fishcakes, mashed goods. The punter wants comfort food. We've just souped up our Chicken Tikka Masala and it *is* good. I've been there six years and he comes in over my head. Had a meeting yesterday. Said to our director - excuse me, if anyone knows how to market a yoghurt, it's me, and these are going nowhere. No response. We're barking right up the wrong tree thanks to Laurie C, and meanwhile Marks & Spencers walks all over us as usual... Okay - they're like *big*, right? But we could cream off some of their customers in some districts we really could.'

'Mm, tricky,' said Daniel. It was just culture shock. Sooner or later he'd understand what everyone was on about. He offered Jonathan a mystified expression, and got a startled face back.

'He's a total pillock actually - the director, overall. But Laurie C...' she cast a watchful eye over Daniel. 'What a creep. You know he asks my assistant about Nigerian birthing systems just because she's black?'

'Christ!' said Daniel. 'That's not on.'

'And they're sending me out to schools. Well - great, it gets me out of the office. But they wouldn't put me up for it if I was a bloke.'

The waiter fanned himself with the returned menus. Jonathan was undecided. He wanted salmon.

'Filets de Soles Dolorossa,' he said.

The waiter snatched his menu away.

'So - how was Rome?' said Jonathan, looking around for an ashtray.

'Great,' said Daniel, 'but it's good to be back.'

'Huh,' said Deanna. 'Sunny was it?'

'Yes.'

'What do they do, Arts Inc?' said Deanna.

'Looking for sponsors, you know,' said Daniel, warmly, 'lots of that. Promoting arts…generally…Archaic Greek Art we've got, I'm handling that. A production of *Measure for Measure*, starting tonight…'

He looked at Jonathan, who was unwrapping his napkin. 'You could come…' he thought, but didn't say it.

'How are they doing it?' said Deanna. 'AIDS, Nazis?'

'I think it's just uh *contemporary*,' said Daniel.

'Um. Paula dragged me off to *A Midsummer Night's Dream* in Regent's Park last year. She had a thing about the woman doing Helena. It wasn't bad. The lion was funny. Reasonable cheesecake but the buffet was ridiculous.'

'How's Paula?' said Daniel.

'Oh Paula's fine,' said Deanna. They'd split up a month ago

and hadn't spoken since.

'You look very well Deanna,' said Jonathan.

'Thanks.'

The food arrived, decorated in fronds of lollo rosso. They picked out the main course knives and forks in their cutlery, and ate.

'It's been in the microwave,' Deanna muttered to Daniel. 'Would you like some of my rocket leaves?'

Jonathan ordered another gin and tonic.

'How's the City?' said Daniel.

'Brilliant,' said Jonathan, 'long hours - rushed off my feet. Not much time for social life. Eighteen hour days sometimes.'

'Lot of fraud isn't there?' said Deanna. 'Not that I've been following it...'

'No, nor have I,' said Jonathan. 'What car are you driving now?'

'Rotunda 2000. You?'

'Sylph Speedbird 9000.'

Deanna flicked the napkin out of its coronet shape.

'Seen anyone since you've been back?' she asked Daniel.

'Maxine,' he replied. 'She's really obsessed with someone at the moment.'

'Oh well,' said Deanna, pouring more water, 'that makes three of us then.'

'And she's having an exhibition,' Daniel added, hurriedly.

'Yeah I know, I saw her. Espina Gallery.'

'Where's that?' said Jonathan.

'Southwark,' said Deanna. 'Bit off your patch. Or come to think of it, quite near.'

'She's not exactly Damien Hirst is she?' Jonathan snorted.

'You could make the journey,' said Deanna. 'It's not far.'

'Yes.'

'I'll drive you,' she added. 'Will she want someone to help out with the exhibition do you think?'

'Who?' said Daniel.

'Maxine.'

'Oh I shouldn't think so,' said Daniel. 'It won't be very big.'

'Right,' said Deanna. 'You don't know anyone who works in the music business or in housing, by any chance?'

'Not really,' said Daniel.

'Jonathan?'

'Not...personally, I don't think.'

'No,' said Deanna.

'Why?' said Daniel.

'Oh nothing really. My uh niece just dumped herself on me.' She put her sunglasses on. 'Looking for a job.'

'Oh that's nice...'

'Is it?'

'That she could trust you...'

'Suppose so.'

'What's her name?'

'Boo Radley. Seen Claire?'

'Not yet.'

'Jonathan?'

'Not really.'

'I'm doing a book with her - the firm's. It's okay. Feel a bit embarrassed about the obviousness of it all. You know what Claire's like...'

'Yes,' said Daniel.

'They've got that all wrong too. Everything's got to look as if it takes a lot of effort. Everything'd got to look like a bloody flower arrangement, all the frou frous, good taste. Good taste should mean *tastes good* - that's it. But everything's done to impress people. What for? If you don't like them - don't have 'em round! Who's got the time? It just upsets me.'

This was too complicated for Daniel at the moment. 'I can see what you mean,' he said.

Was Jonathan going to look at him, ever? Was he going to address any remark to him? He was studying Deanna with a bitter expression.

'So I'm doing another book of my own, *Under An Hour*: five ingredients maximum, an hour or less preparation time. Took it to Claire. She didn't seem too keen. But she's asked me out Saturday night now, so maybe there's some hope…'

'You could be a TV cook,' said Daniel.

'There's a lot of it about,' said Deanna. 'One thing the last six months has taught me is you have to take care of yourself.' She stabbed a blackened red pepper.

'I don't cook,' said Jonathan, 'what's the point?'

'Well there you are you see,' said Deanna, waving the fork, '*Under An Hour* would be ideal for you.'

'Which would you say out of these three is the healthiest?' said Jonathan.

'Us or the food?' said Deanna.

'The food.'

Deanna studied the plates. 'Well I don't suppose any of it

would kill you would it?'

'I just wanted something to help my skin,' said Jonathan.

'Help your *skin?*'

'Nothing wrong with your skin!' said Daniel, with an affectionate chuckle.

Deanna looked at him sharply, and whimpered, just slightly. She wondered if she looked as helpless as Daniel whenever she met Consuela.

The waiter took the plates, and gave them the menus again. Nobody looked at them.

'*Coffee?*' said the waiter.

'Three,' said Jonathan.

'It was a great Montgomery Clift postcard,' said Daniel, eventually. 'Really cheered me up when I got back.'

Jonathan smiled jerkily.

'Oh - he sent you a Montgomery Clift postcard did he?' said Deanna.

'Yes,' said Jonathan, putting a cautious elbow on the table. 'I did. From *A Place in the Sun.*'

The coffees arrived.

'I can't stand method acting,' said Deanna. 'It slows things down.'

She looked from Daniel to Jonathan, from Jonathan to Daniel. 'You know you can cruise in our stores now?' she said, to Daniel.

'Oh really?'

'Friday nights, I believe.'

Daniel gazed at Jonathan.

'For boys. Well it was just an idea.'

They sipped their coffees. Deanna's thoughts had hooked firmly onto Consuela - her thick black hair, her hips to die for. Daniel stared into space, trying to blank out everything that just hadn't happened, then looked at Jonathan for signs of recognition. There were none. Jonathan thought of what he and Patti had done last night, and longed to be with someone who understood him. He paid the bill with a credit card with a white elephant on it.

'Oh no!' cried Deanna.

'Oh please!' replied Jonathan.

'Thanks,' said Daniel.

'Pleasure,' said Jonathan.

'Lovely lunch,' said Deanna.

'We must do this again,' said Jonathan.

Daniel decided to walk. He stopped at a sandwich shop window, looking at rolls with French and German flags sticking out of them, until he remembered he'd just eaten. He suddenly realised that Maxine's flatmate, Lydia, worked in the music business. Well maybe it didn't matter.

He passed a theatre playing *Not On My Premises You Don't!* and considered his new calling as a chaste bride of art. That didn't matter either. He hadn't come back for Jonathan. He'd come back for new work. He'd come back for *this* - he walked into the office. The poster for David Brasted's play about date rape stared him in the face.

Priscilla was filling her plastic cup with the remains of a wine box. 'Oh dear,' she said. 'Anyone died?'

'Ha!' said Daniel.

She handed him the wine. 'You have it.'

It was half a glass. He drank it.

He flicked through the *Measure for Measure* programme, and fixed on an advert in grey scroll:

> *Love seeketh only itself to please, but how about a financial service that seeks to please you?*

'Do our audiences have loads of money to invest?'

"Course they do!' said Priscilla. 'We've got two ministers coming tonight. Did you get all that crap about ABC1s and incentives out?'

'Yesterday.'

He turned a page, picked up a phone, said 'Oh yeah, just fax it over,' put the phone down.

'It's Blake isn't it? Love seeketh…?'

'Oh probably,' said Priscilla. 'But it sounds like Shakespeare doesn't it? It solves the problem of access. I mean, it's fun trying to remember where all the quotes come from isn't it?

'It is,' he said.

He looked at another ad, one with a huge picture.

> *Gaze upon Frida Kahlo's MY NURSE AND I and what do you get? Force, clarity, authenticity. Precisely the qualities you sense when driving the new Sylph Speedbird 9000…*

'Wasn't Frida Kahlo smashed up in a car accident?'

Priscilla picked up her phone. 'Very clever isn't it?,' she said. 'It's to show you what confidence they have in the product. Michael, how *are* you, little busy now...'

He thought of Jonathan smashed up in his Sylph Speedbird, glad then terrified at the prospect.

'This came in this morning,' said Priscilla. She handed over a flyer headed The PragMATiks, covering a picture of a disembowelled tractor and plough. 'Art exhibition. They've got money from us. We can't do their publicity from here, but you could. Charge them about a hundred quid.'

'Oh thanks. Sure.'

Priscilla rearranged herself, stretched her arms upwards, threw a plastic cup into the bin and smiled.

'You can take an hour or so off if you want. I'm going to have my hair done.'

Daniel called Bella.

The sun was out, but it was still cold. They sat on the grass outside, in their coats. No dope was forthcoming and he didn't like to ask. They split a packet of Rolos. Everything about Bella was so round, he thought. Round brown eyes, round brown hair, enormous tits. She looked like a Rolo. He mentioned The PragMATiks.

'Oh yes, I did an art exhibition a while ago. Just filling in. Body Art in Glasgow.'

'Do you know Maxine Kendrick?' It was a long shot.

'Maxine Kendrick!' Bella cried, 'oh *do* I know her! She was in this Glasgow thing. What a pain! They'd done this tape, for the exhibition - ping pong balls and bogs flushing - it was good, very gentle and eerie. Of course *she* insisted on having a tape of this screeching woman. Said the other tape,' she mimicked a mimsy tone, 'didn't go with the work.' Then she was kicking up a fuss because the paint hadn't dried on her thing. You'd think it was a Rembrandt, not some poxy fanny painting.'

'I suppose it means a lot…'

'Worse thing of all was her behaviour in the pub afterwards…'

'Oh?' said Daniel.

'You know when you go into a pub in Glasgow you go, 'Whit ye lookin a y'auld cunt?' to everyone sitting there…'

'Who told you that?' said Daniel.

'It's just well known.' She adjusted her hair.

If you were a girl, he thought, you could get away with anything.

'Anyway madam comes in, sits down, and talks to the other *artists*! I mean I'd helped to organise it all and she didn't say a *word* to me, didn't buy me a drink. Typical London bourgeois art world prat. Sorry, is she some special friend of yours?'

'Well, I know her.'

'Good luck,' said Bella. 'No I'm really glad to be out of that kind of thing. Jean'll retire in a couple of years and I'll be sitting pretty. Which is just as well because I'm going to plan a pregnancy. You going to the opening tonight?'

'Yes.'

'Yeah, all the flash trash'll be there tonight, all the sponsors, all the critics. I'm going at the weekend, with my hubby.'

'That's nice.'

'Have you got a boyfriend?'

'No,' said Daniel, 'no, no, I haven't.'

He walked back over the grass to the main building, feeling slightly battered, slightly proud, slightly jealous. His teeth were screaming from sugar. He supposed he'd have to start taking Maxine seriously now.

A few hours later the lights went down and he thought he and Priscilla were at the wrong play.

The set was a shopping mall, with plenty of bulging rubbish sacks. Then there was a raised plinth, with steel and leather furniture.

'Of government the properties to unfold…bid come before us Angelo,' said William from the talk, who was wearing a grey suit. Oh I see, alright, Daniel thought. He suddenly saw a shadow of something on the ceiling.

When he looked back, the lights were directed at the shopping mall. Daniel missed most of the following exchanges, riveted by the sight of a bit player slapping his arm energetically in a corner, and waving a giant syringe. A few town worthies in shellsuits came on, carrying boxes on which the word 'Homecare' was discernible. Others pelted each other with chips from MacDonald's cartons. The woman behind Daniel was killing herself laughing. A large old trout in a satin dress came on, gesticulating with a cigarette holder.

There was a performance of a mildly risqué song, finishing off with:

'Phew!'

'Ah me!'

'Ha!'

'Yo!'

The black members of the townspeople's cast launched into a spirited bout of break dancing. There was mild applause. Madame, or was it Mistress Overdone entered again, this time done up as a third rate drag queen. Daniel couldn't hear properly. Then the plinth was lit. 'We have strict statutes and most biting laws…' said the Duke, into his mobile phone. This really didn't make any sense at all.

Daniel squinched his eyes shut tight, trying to just hear the words. Then he tried to remember all the names of the Supremes. He remembered a man he'd sucked off at a place near the via della Stelleta. He wondered what possible next move, if any, he could make on Jonathan.

'Our doubts are traitors and make us lose the good we oft might win…' Lucio's accent, which started off as soft Dublin, had just swerved into harsh Glaswegian. Daniel conjugated several Italian verbs, and thought of what the Italian words were for 'shorts', 'God', 'maiden', 'sin' and 'fall'.

He and Priscilla held their applause until the curtain descended. Daniel unglued himself from his seat. Priscilla sighed. They glided over the carpets, through the electronic doors, and headed towards the hospitality table.

'Well Shakespeare's too dense for most ears now. They have to have something to recognise,' said Priscilla. 'I don't bring Anwar any more. Really no point. Of course you spend all the time wondering what the director's getting at…' She craned her neck to see who was at the table.

'The Germans had *Verfremdungseffekt*...' she added, strapped into her official voice.

Show off, thought Daniel, enjoying himself.

'...And now I suppose we've got it too...Trevor!'

She licked her lips and threw out a smile. 'Leave this to me.'

Daniel wandered around the foyer with a timid expression, moving in a landscape of good timeless cloths, and catching snatches of conversation - Max's Oxbridge entrance, the son with the job in Hong Kong. There was a tremor of discontent at a slow-moving coffee counter. People glared at strangers who dared to seat themselves at their tables. A string quartet scratched away in a corner. The bell went for the second half.

Daniel sat down cautiously. Priscilla joined him breezily and muttered 'We're on for *The Cherry Orchard*!'

He tried to reconstruct the plot from memory. He really should have read the synopsis beforehand.

Isabella came back on, swaggering. He couldn't fail to be interested in an actress who made no impression in an expensive ballgown, but shot into another dimension dressed in a man's suit. He listened now, but he'd lost it. He grasped onto parts, then it fell to pieces. He looked around shiftily at the rest of the audience. Someone was snoring.

He imitated Priscilla's clap, at the end. It was the kind that said, 'I'm going through the motions, but reserving judgment.' There were quite a few of those. There was one 'Thank God that's over, where's my bag?' He couldn't spot or hear a clap that said, 'Congratulations', although, as

— 72 —

applause, it was loud.

Back at the table he poured out drinks, and the sponsors and their partners shook his hand. A white haired critic boomed on about 'riven complexities', and recited a list of productions he'd seen throughout ten years. Daniel smiled to be included in this select group, and they turned their tidily jacketed shoulders towards him. He stepped back and looked, for several minutes, at the foyer's lighting fittings. Lucio came out and greeted the critic warmly, and Daniel suddenly realised why the old man liked it. He saw the next morning's laudatory review in only the finest mist of despair.

Priscilla was laughing triumphantly, came up and said, 'All done, go now, see you tomorrow!' He passed a small notice on the way out:

ART - FOOD FOR THE SOUL
IT SHOWS THE WORTH OF BEING ALIVE

Some kids were hanging around outside. One yelled 'wanker!' as he passed. God knows, he couldn't argue with that.

He took a circuitous route and nipped into a bar he remembered from his first glimpses of London years ago. It had seemed so electric with temptation, then. He'd met lots of new people.

The booths had been ripped out and the old chandeliers had been replaced with beams of frosted glass. The punters looked poorer than they used to be. Many were standing up and facing the back wall. He pushed his way through the crowd and passed seats where they were chatting - 'how do they stick their wigs on, in *Cats?*' - and went to have a look at what everyone else was looking at, so he could have a better look around.

A Mr Universe contest was in progress. The contestants took their places at the front of the stage. They wore high-cut, silver bathing trunks, housing equipment like tubular steel. Daniel's first twinkles of corny desire were pierced by the sound of a microphone backfiring. He nudged his way towards the bar, and thought someone patted his bottom on the way.

'He'll have a Scotch and soda.'

Instant hospitality!

Daniel turned, but saw the request was issued on account of the man's companion, not him. Also that he was in the wrong place to have issued the grope in the first place. He looked around for another likely culprit, and realised it must have been incidental. The man at the bar turned to him, blinked fast, then turned away to talk to someone else.

Fighting views of himself as fanciful and vain, he sat on the seat nearest the door, next to a couple earnestly debating the merits of plain or patterned bathroom tiles.

Mr Universe was chosen and decorated with a sash. The Australian national anthem was played with a ragtime rhythm. He walked out of the place, thoroughly humbled, with the price of the entrance ticket still burning a hole in his wallet, and his untouched packet of condoms jiggling in his breast pocket.

He was stuck near a group of wideboys on the tube,

swatting each other with their programmes from Faust. He got off at the next stop, crossed the platform, and went back into town again.

He approached a venue with a more brutal facade. Yes, no, yes, no - oh go on then, he thought. As he entered there were hot saxophones, and cold sweating walls.

He couldn't quite see the face of the man who approached him, but his body was taut from the strain of self-preservation. In the smack of flesh on flesh, and tongue on tongue, Daniel forgot about the play, Jonathan, the fact that friends were not the same as he'd left them, and that everyone was in the fast lane now, except him. As a spotlight flared on the man briefly, his face seemed older than the rest of him, a face with history in it. He bit the man's neck. It didn't matter. The man had a wrist action that made Daniel's head reel and his knees buckle, gratefully.

He left the bar fit to carry on, and win. He went back on the tube; the crowds were bigger, and they didn't bother him. He surveyed them with a dreamy satisfaction. They don't know, he thought. They don't know about anything.

8

Jonathan's ansafone bleeped.

'Go on then, go on then...*speak!*' he screamed from the bedroom.

'*Jonathan - it's Deanna. Are you there?*'

'Oh GOD!' he said.

'*Look I don't know what's going on but if you want a chaperone call an escort agency, alright? Leave me out of it, okay? That's it. Right. Um...hope you're well. It's just - I'm busy. Bye.*'

Jonathan held his breath. The tape bleeped and wound back.

'Did you hear that? *Did you hear that?*'

Patti shrugged. 'So?'

'You know what she did?'

'What?'

'Had lunch with us and recited what she was going to say at a *meeting*. Where's her fucking sense of decorum?'

Patti was sitting up on the rumpled bed, her chin tucked into her neck, her smudgy deflated nipples staring vacantly into space, like her glazed blue eyes. The champagne cocktail Jonathan had handed her only a moment ago appeared to have already lost its fizz. Her basque, whose ribbons he'd just untied so carefully, lay on the floor like a giant dead insect. She pulled tensely on her cigarette.

Beautiful, he thought. Her pointy nose with its lightly flared nostrils, big Bambi eyes, that silky blonde hair. She was an outrage! He'd act casual. He flung himself on his back, encircling his head with his arm, his body heavy but his eyes twitching fast. Patti didn't do anything, so he sat up again.

'Addicts are fucking unreliable aren't they?' he said. 'Do you think I should give him another ring?'

'You could always go round there,' she said, with feeling.

Those flaccid nipples were driving him mad. He leaned over and pinched one of them, and then pressed it in like a doorbell.

She hit him round the head so hard he didn't realise what had happened until he recovered.

'I told you not to bloody do that...' she said. He opened his eyes, holding his smarting head, and watched her dash to the phone with the sheet around her. She picked up the *Daily Sport* lying by the TV and flicked through it angrily until she got to the back pages. She ran her finger down a column, gave him a little snarl, called the number, and settled down on the floor, with the phone pressed to her ear, and her hand slid between her legs. The sheet was draped around her but he could see her little bum ticking into action.

'Oh that's bloody charming that is!' he said.

He watched her for a while, then occupied himself with a copy of *Butt Sex* from the stash under his bed.

The room was silent apart from their breathy sighs, murmured profanities, and little gusts of over-heated sex organs. Patti came discreetly, with a little 'uh', staggered back to the bed, chucked herself on it and curled up, watching Jonathan with lilting eyes.

He came like a bucking pony into a tissue - she tried not to laugh. He squeezed the tissue, extricated himself from it, tossed it on a side table, then wiped the residue on his ribcage.

'Were you thinking about me?' he said.

'No.'

'That's good. I wasn't thinking about you either.'

He opened his eyes. 'What one did you ring up then?'

'*Make My Pussy Purr.*'

'Oh!' he exclaimed.

It was *Nude Twister*. She didn't think you should tell them everything. In any case she'd been thinking about Christopher Lee towards the end, and…She made a grab for *Butt Sex*. He slapped her away, but she smacked him back.

She studied the pictures, sipping the champagne cocktail. He ran his hand through his hair, and kept sneaking looks at her.

'Oh right…' she said, 'so he gets it up her arse, then whips it out so he can come all over her face. That makes a lot of sense doesn't it?'

'It's surreal,' he said, snatching it back. He sniffed and tucked the magazine under the bed again. Some of the papers came apart as he did this, but he swore and kept stuffing them under the bed anyway.

'Why do men like coming all over girl's faces?' said Patti. 'Is it like custard pies?' She giggled and threw her head back and kicked his legs. 'Y'know - *infantile?*'

'Gerroff,' he said, pushing her.

She laughed.

'I don't know do I? Charles comes all over Ginny's face, apparently. And her tits too.'

'Oh sure,' said Patti. 'Were you there, then?'

'No he told me.'

'Well I'd better ask him then,' said Patti. 'He's revolting.'

'I quite agree!' said Jonathan. He considered telling her about the Polaroids, then thought no, maybe not.

Much to Jonathan's surprise, Charles and Ginny had gone away for a weekend in Paris recently. She was all very dapper and trim in her linen suit, with her going away vanity case, or whatever it was, and looking as if butter wouldn't melt in her mouth, hanging around their desks on Friday evening. Charles treated her with a sickening gallantry in front of them all. He didn't understand women at all sometimes.

Patti skipped over to the glass table, arranged two lines of coke and snorted them daintily through a straw. She dabbed her nose. All very nifty, he thought. It was something, looking pretty even doing that.

'That's it for tonight, Jonathan. You'll have to take it away from me now.'

'Do what the fuck you like!' he replied.

She fell over him. 'Aren't you having any?'

'No,' said Jonathan. He picked up his watch from the side table, looked at it, then threw it back again.

'I don't like you doing smack Jonathan. Suki's friend nearly DIED!'

'He opened a boutique in Ibiza didn't he?' said Jonathan. '*Wanker.*'

She turned on the TV '...don't do it with your foot, you'll make it all greasy...', flicked through the channels, turned the sound down, put Millie Jackson on loud, '...not so bloody loud...' he said, went to the bathroom and locked the door.

Now where's she gone, he thought. Maybe to 'direct the faucet at her clit', as every woman he read of in every novel he looked at seemed to do at some point. He didn't care. He was glad she'd gone because he wanted to pick his nose.

Come to think of it, he didn't know what a 'faucet' was anyway. Probably the thing you did your hair with, except he thought that was 'the shower attachment'.

He couldn't be dealing with Millie Jackson's chuckly voice going:

> Go out and git some
> Get it out'cha system

on and on. In the circumstances he wasn't in the mood for her rap about logs either. Black men obviously had a lot to cope with. They had his full sympathy. He changed the CD to Dinah Washington doing *Mad About The Boy*, lay back on the bed again, threw his prick from side to side, and thought about the other day. Daniel and him could have had a really good lunch if that lipstick lezzie hadn't turned up.

'Oh, thinking about himself for a change,' thought Patti, hearing the music change. She lit a joint and examined her roots in the mirror. She had only been in London about four months when she went back home for the weekend, and her mother had taken one look at her and said if you had too much sex too early on, it spoiled things for when you were married. Well she should know.

She heard the doorbell go, muttered 'Thank Christ', and examined her gums. She smeared some KY jelly on her eyebrows, sat on the toilet and picked up the copy of *Sexual Perversions in History* she'd stolen from the bookshop near work. It didn't do much for her - too many accessories - and read as if it was hastily translated from the Hungarian.

She danced back into the main room. Jonathan had a face pack on.

'...for my spots...'

'What spots silly?' she said.

She knocked out the CD.

'Oh don't turn it off...' he whined.

She put on NWA very loud.

'Oh not that...' he said, '...*please*...'

She danced to the fridge and got out a box of sushi.

'Greedy guts, you've not long had dinner...' he said.

'I'm hungry now tho' and heh heh your mask has cracked!'

He touched the mask with his fingers and it started to flake.

She polished off the sushi, dancing around.

'You'll have to get that mask off somehow...'

'Yeah...You gonna get it off?'

She pulled his arm. 'If you like. I'll run the bath. You want oils?'

'No…yes…alright. But not Y'lang Y'lang oil…' he yelled as she went out. 'That's got a funny smell to it.'

They got in the bath.

'Piss on my face,' he said.

'Aw Jonathan we already did that once!'

She dripped over him, nearer, picking off some of the loose bits in the mask.

'Well drink two peppered vodkas…then piss on my face.'

He was already cheering up.

'*Peppered?* It won't make any…'

'Whatever. Get on with it.'

She brought the drinks into the bathroom, and sipped them slowly, watching him moisten his lips, his cock floating and hardening in the water. She sipped the drinks faster, knocked them back, burped and giggled.

'Get on with it…' he said.

She drank all the drink, got into the bath.

'We'll have to wait a bit,' she said, draping herself over him, 'but not long.'

'Yeah,' he said, stroking her hair, kissing her mouth, pulling her on top of him. She trickled some water over him, just to get things going.

'Alright…' she said.

She threw a knee over his face, watching his lovely waiting face, with its eyes closed and its lips slightly parted. She curved her back so her hair flopped forward, so she could watch, and then relaxed in her pits so that piss ran out thickly, in a warm stream. She moved her hips round and round, covering the circumference of his face, which was smiling now, and clean - the skin was showing - then further and further round and round and in and in until she reached a still centre, like a spirograph. The steam rose quietly, and the mask had turned to soft clay and run off his face and dissolved in the bath water. She watched him with a head full of glitter, seeing she had hidden talents yet.

He ducked himself under and came up again and pulled her right on top of him and ate her very thoroughly and then carried her into the main room - oh it was so romantic! like Lancelot and Guinivere! - and fucked her all she wanted, after that.

'Have my spots gone?' he said.

'You didn't have spots Jonathan!' she laughed.

He got up and fiddled with his wraps.

She fell back on the bed, knocking back the last of the champagne cocktail.

'I'm taking this in the kitchen…'

'Night night then,' she said. 'You-are-an-arsehole.' She made her fingers into a gun, pointed at him and went 'Pcchhh!'

'It's the best fucking painkiller in the world,' he said, going into the kitchen. Which was true.

'What pain…' she muttered. 'We're seeing my cousins tomorrow night,' she called, 'don't do that in front of them will you?'

'No,' he slammed the door.

Jesus, she thought.

She went into the bathroom and swished the steel shower claw around the bath. She sniffed. Her eyes felt all funny now. She took a temazepam and knocked it back with tap water. ''Nother drink', she thought. She bumped into Jonathan coming out of the kitchen, and sorted through his Gaggia gadgets in the sink.

Couldn't deal with that. She ran herself a glass of water and put it by the bed.

9

In the middle of the next morning, Jonathan got a sense that someone was onto him. His machine suddenly started selling shares without him telling it to. He watched helpless as the green, eye-ache columns appeared on-screen and started to empty themselves - chom chom chom. They rose up again, slipped down again, then settled, to nothing. He broke into a sweat, and pushed a few buttons which did the bleep back at him that meant 'Don't interfere now' and 'We can't do that now, we're doing something else - okay, dickhead?' The blasted machine did what it liked. He pushed a load of buttons at random, but it didn't act on them, just bleeped long and low in protest, before returning to its own, more decisive, business.

He stared at his Flexifone at the side, expecting it to burst into flames. It rang at a decorous interval from the computer's burst of activity - he thought it was the usual space of time it took to ring. He counted the seconds - and there was a robotic voice offering a confirmation. '*Okay - $30,000 - check?*' Jonathan just listened. '*Okay - $30,000 - check?*' it insisted. It said it again, in exactly the same tone.

'Yep,' said Jonathan, and the line went dead.

He looked around and no one had noticed, no one was involved. They were all intent on negotiations that het up and calmed down when he looked up at them again, massaging their brows between bouts, preoccupied with their own thoughts, or troubles. This was normal. This was okay. This was how it always was. Charles was standing up and swaying with a hand in his pocket, holding the phone with his shoulder. He was talking in his fake bass voice and looking very serious. So this latest panic was no mischief caused by Charles, either. Everything was okay. Charles had his hand in his pocket, rubbing it up and down. What do you look like, Jonathan thought. You fucking gross hippo.

He flew down the corridor and saw Patti and stood close, blocking her weightless, agitated stride, and whispered into her face.

'My fucking computer's started selling shares without…'

'Well it does doesn't it? It always does that. It's the facility…'

'What facility. Explain it…'

'You know what facility. For Chrissakes Jonathan…' She looked around furtively. 'That smack's going to your head.' She swept down the corridor, clearing her throat.

He didn't mention it to Anthony at lunch. Anthony took him to a restaurant he wouldn't dream of entering, normally. A long hallway like the kind of school he'd never attended - you couldn't see the end of it - and everything in long-winded French. God, thought Jonathan, life's so complicated anyway - they want to make it worse. Why put the simplest thing in long-winded French, with that thin, elongated typescript you had to squint over to read it? The cutlery and plates made a terrible noise, the waiters sneaked up on you, and Anthony didn't eat or say much.

'Oh yes, Anthony,' Jonathan said eagerly.

He watched Anthony's grey, baggy eyes that looked even older, and his loose jointed fingers fumbling with the china cup half full of espresso with the scum on top. Anthony sipped at it, without stirring it or anything. Anthony talked about the Medicis and Florence, but in such a quiet, slow voice, Jonathan had to concentrate very hard to hear it. He felt a fire igniting in his head.

Anthony wrote a cheque for the lunch - very old-fashioned really, very olde worlde, Jonathan thought, with a short laugh - a piece of paper waiting for your instructions to be written on it with your own pen. Your own little account slip at the side, just to remind you. Then Anthony wrote a separate cheque to Jonathan, and Jonathan shook his head.

'Oh no Anthony. That's perfectly alright Anthony...'

'I promised...' said Anthony, softly.

Jonathan folded up the cheque and wondered if he would ever do anything with it.

He took Anthony to see his new car - the Sylph Speedbird 9000 - which he'd brought up and parked in an all day car park. Anthony looked at it, slightly rounded at the shoulders. Jonathan had got a silver blue car in deference to what he thought Anthony would like. Anthony looked at it, but didn't say much. Anthony couldn't drive, of course. Not his fault. He never had to.

'It has a Frida Kahlo picture in the ad…' Jonathan said, to Anthony, 'the Sylph Speedbird.'

Anthony gave his blink that meant 'how unspeakable', though it was difficult to tell whether it was adverts, as such, or Frida, particularly, causing this offence. Jonathan looked around the empty car park, thinking this was the place, in films and on TV, where people were often murdered.

On the way back he went through a square with a sculpture in the middle - a crocodile made out of shiny pieces of blue and green glass. He stared at it, trying to get something out of it. Trying to think what it meant, how it could help.

He went back to the office and glanced at the other slugs, and made a killing, at least until 7pm. It often worked like that. It usually worked so long as you didn't waste too much time thinking *how*.

The evening approached. Anything urgent seemed less pressing as the daylight dwindled. It was a glowing spring night. He walked back to his car and adjusted his Walkman around his shoulder.

'*Conosciama questa sistema monetaria,*' it said.

When he had been practising his Italian in recent weeks, he had got to the stage where he could relay the contents of Signor Falucci's living room in sentences, and answered the questions before the tape had finished asking them. He was just getting adept at composing his own sentences. He had forgotten all of this in the past 72 hours. All he could call to mind were a series of short greetings. He supposed this would do for Patti's Italian cousins.

He got into his car and went up to town changing from first to second gear and back again, at a snail's pace, hanging onto, then barely touching the steering wheel which was like a fat black coiled serpent under his hands. He reached a square in W1, and crawled round and round and round it before finding a parking space.

He felt he deserved something special after his day, and slipped into a bookshop to browse around, hoping to fall accidentally on a photographer Daniel had mentioned quirkily in his letters.

A few of the photographer's works lay at the back, wrapped in crinkly cellophane. Jonathan stroked his finger along their titles:

ONE ON ONE
PARADISE REGAINED
UNTITLED III
ABWEGIGE LEIDENSCHAFT.

He picked out *Abwegige Leidenschaft* and supposed the contents would justify the price.

There was scarcely anyone at the bar when he arrived and the Italian barman served reluctantly. Jonathan said *'per favore'* and *'grazie'* when he ordered, but the barman also appeared to be deaf. *'Avete appetito?'* he asked himself, cheerfully, and *'Benvenuti in Inghilterra'* - that was about it.

The bar was slicked in otter's hide black, and decorated with chrome tubes and mirrors. There were spiral staircases that led nowhere, and cages with nothing in them hanging on the sides. Jonathan looked up at the ceiling and it was a kind of Sistine Chapel, Fragonard kind of effect. Or maybe

Chagall. One of the barman's colleagues disappeared, and returned with a couple of monkeys on leashes. He led them to the cages, locked them in, and the monkeys jammed their faces into the iron bars and beat their heads with their hairy hands. Jonathan stared, hypnotised, then planted himself on a pneumatic leather seat.

As others came in he noticed their pony tails, stretch jeans and pingy lycra clothes. He felt like a shoebox in his suit, but it was a five hundred quid suit - he bought it in a sale - so he ordered an *acqua minerale* and thought he should worry. He realised that Patti was about an hour late, which meant she should arrive quite soon.

He shut his eyes and allowed the chat around him to subside into an agreeable blur. After a while he heard Patti's drawl at a distance, stood to attention, and went to the bar. She was accompanied by two blondes with impenetrable features, peasant outfits and olive skin. Jonathan pawed his way through the crowd and the cousins spun around their bar stools to face him.

'*Buona sera*,' he exclaimed, '*Come state?*'

'He Italian?'

'No. You are. *Voi lo siete*,' said Jonathan. 'I'm English. *Sono inglese*.'

The cousins looked at him, then bustled off to the toilet together.

Patti turned to the barman and addressed him in rapid Spanish. He laughed with her. He handed her a salt-frosted glass which she peered into, then knocked back. Then he gave her another one and she knocked back that too. She licked her lips and regarded the crowd.

'How do you like our Kenyan cowgirls?' she said, to no one in particular. 'Aren't you drinking anything?' she added, to Jonathan.

'I'm not thirsty,' he lied. 'I thought you said they were Italian.'

'*Father's* Italian. They live in Kenya. 'Kenyan cowgirls, geddit?' She was already restless. 'Where's Suki?' She sighed to herself. 'Got a phonecard?'

Jonathan searched through his pockets and handed her one. She adjourned to the payphone to yell at it for fifteen minutes. When he next looked in the direction of the Ladies he saw Patti's cousins being chatted up by Italians.

He watched the monkeys, who were now in distress, and attracting a fascinated crowd.

The cousins sidled up and he ordered more drinks. They sipped their fizz and stared at him.

'Are you a friend of Patti's?'

'Yes, I work in the City.' His eyes shifted.

Patti returned and slammed her clutch bag onto the bar. 'Fucking old cow - she's still at home!'

'Had she forgotten?' asked Jonathan, hopefully.

Patti paused. 'No. Aren't you hot in that suit?'

Jonathan took his jacket off.

'What's wrong with those monkeys?'

'Don't like it, I suppose.'

The blondes looked at the monkeys with great interest.

'We'll have to keep them in hand tonight,' said Patti. 'They've just finished their exams.'

'What, the monkeys or the girls?' said Jonathan.

No one laughed.

The cousins introduced the Italians to Patti, who threw her head back, above such capers, and went on to address them in Italian. It was all very quick and Jonathan couldn't register anything that corresponded to the formulas he'd learned. Patti looked Jonathan up and down.

'Can you see Suki anywhere?'

'I'll have a look around.'

He hovered at the door and thought he might nip into the Gents and have a quick look at his book. It would only take a few minutes and when he returned the Italians might have gone again.

The Gents was cool and aired and had three cubicles, with thick wooden doors that touched the ground. Perfect, he thought. His groin tingled.

He stuffed himself in a cubicle and sat on the toilet. He unzipped his flies, careful to do so quietly. He extracted his cock and gave it a few strokes, shutting his eyes to relish the sensations. He removed the wrapped book from his briefcase, and sliced his fingernails into the cellophane. He flicked through the plates to find suitable images, finally regarding the pictures one by one. They were studies of fruit and vegetables, interspersed with bizarre little portraits of celebrities he'd half heard of.

His cock dangled between his legs.

He eased it back beneath his underpants.

He put the book aside, pulled his cock out again, and examined it idly - was that a new mole?

He screwed his eyes shut, and held onto his prick, rubbing and stroking faster and faster: stinging arseholes, a hairy arm round his neck, glistening steel poles, a stretch limo with tinted windows…It slipped out of his hand, he grabbed it again, it started to thicken and dribble - ah, ah, ah, ahhh.

Trade outside was becoming more boisterous. The swing doors flew open and thudded back more quickly. He left the cubicle and was confronted with a large sign 'NOW WASH YOUR HANDS'. So he did. He walked out, with a noncommittal expression, greeted with smoke and braying perfumes.

Suki leaned next to Patti at the bar. She regarded her with a sly smile.

'Where have you *been*?' cried Patti. 'Suki's been *waiting*!'

'Drinks?' said Jonathan.

He ordered champagne.

The monkeys had been removed from their cages. In their place were two muscular men in electric blue shorts with black string vests, who danced with a tired implacability. Patti's two cousins stood at the side, heads bent together, noses wrinkled with glee. One of them climbed up the spiral staircase, swaying on the bannister and tottering on her heels, and joined one of the men in the cages. He turned in one movement, and danced at her. She weaved her arms and flung open her mouth. Jonathan turned to Patti and Suki. The girls stared indifferently at the spectacle.

'Monkeys got too messy,' said Patti. 'Just an idea that didn't quite work out s'pose.'

Jonathan swallowed a mouthful of champagne.

'It's revolting,' he said.

'It's not as bad as what you do,' she said, 'piss artist.' She regretted it, instantly. Their little secrets.

Suki looked away with a knowing smile.

'Shall we move on?' said Jonathan.

'Yeah where?'

'The Incognito?' he suggested. He'd read somewhere it was ambiguous.

'Where's *that*?' Suki screwed up her face.

'Froggit's,' said Patti. 'What about Froggit's?'

Suki spluttered into her drink.

'Froggit's,' said Patti to Jonathan. 'We'll go to Froggit's.'

They found his car and the cousins admired it.

'It's a Sylph Speedbird,' he said.

'Is it new?' asked Suki.

Jonathan turned the CD on full blast and opened all the windows and sped and braked hard. Suki and the cousins sat in the back and Patti settled complacently in the front. Every now and again she touched Jonathan's thigh whenever she turned to address a remark to the back. This, thought, Jonathan, will be a night to remember. They moved out of the centre and he pressed the accelerator.

'Any of you hungry?' He called to the back. The wind stroked his hair and the music lifted his spirits. This was the kind of life he thought he could only dream of.

The girls were busy rustling something, but he couldn't tell whether it was make-up, sweets or drugs.

Jonathan pulled up jaggardly at the side of a road beside a lonely sign for a trattoria.

The restaurant looked as if it was about to close but Patti and Suki mooed engagingly at the waiter. The girls settled down to thick, bent pizzas, while Jonathan insisted on having grilled chicken. Patti apologised on Jonathan's behalf, and reversed his choice of wine as punishment. Jonathan picked a fight with her about 'fancying antipasto' in the middle, and Patti tossed pistachios into her slackened jaw saying 'oh whhy, Jonathan, whhyyy?' The girls finished off with flaming Sambucas. Jonathan sulkily stirred a portion of vanilla ice cream.

'Can't drink, driving,' he said to one of the cousins.

'Oh.'

He asked them about their exams.

'Oh *Jonathan*,' cried Patti, 'don't be so fucking *boring*!'

'Let's-go-to-Froggit's-Let's-go-to-Froggit's!' Suki banged her spoon on the table.

'Ooh are we going to a nightclub?' said one of the cousins.

'Yeah-ess,' went Patti, and rolled her eyes.

Driving through and out of town again, Jonathan's nerves began to jangle. He was lost and while a map was lying on Patti's lap, she hardly ever looked at it. Whenever he turned to her to ask for a direction she fudged it or issued an instruction too late. His driving became more erratic. Wailing police sirens flashed behind him. He pulled into the kerb and jerked to a halt.

'If you've got anything on you you'd better throw it out of the window.'

'What?'

'If we throw it out of the window,' said Suki, 'they'll see us.'

'Eh?' said the other cousin, who had been asleep.

'What's he on about?'

'Who?'

'Jonathan.'

'I'm serious!!' Jonathan screamed.

'It's the Police.'

'Eh,' said the cousin.

'Ah,' said the other one.

'Shut the fuck up,' said Jonathan.

He pressed a button to open a window. Two thick chested cops sauntered to his side. Keep cool, keep clam, Jonathan thought, then he changed tack.

'Good evening!' he cried.

The cops stared at him. He looked in the mirror. The girls' eyes were like saucers. He looked back at the cops. They were wearing guns.

The police checked his documents, asked him where he was going, checked his documents again, asked them all to get out, let them stand on the street for a while, then told them to get back in the car again. They remarked to Jonathan that he must be having trouble, handling that lot all at once.

'Not at all,' he replied.

Patti and Suki laughed.

Keep calm and cool, Jonathan thought. Just like these bastards to resent his car.

The Police took some final details.

'Nice car,' said one. 'Runs on a turbo does it?'

'Eh?' said Jonathan.

'Runs on a turbo?'

Jonathan shrugged. 'I dunno.'

The girls sighed and groaned in the back.

One of the policeman exchanged a glance with the other.

'Yes!' said Jonathan. 'Actually it does.'

Suki stifled a laugh. Patti folded her arms.

'You obviously…' said one of the policemen, glancing at his partner.

Jonathan's heart went whoomph, then whoomph again.

'…haven't been shown how to fold your documents into the wallet properly.'

He performed this action very carefully and Jonathan watched him with rigid eyes.

The other policeman told Jonathan one of his tail lights was out and that he should get it fixed.

Fucking computer, Jonathan thought. It should signal automatically if something was wrong. Or maybe he hadn't noticed. He considered telling the policemen this.

The policemen suggested that he drove carefully, said goodnight to the girls, and strolled back to their vehicle. They slammed their doors and drove off at high speed.

They didn't even book him, they didn't even breathalyse him. Patti was disappointed. He could tell.

He drove cautiously, conscious of every action.

Patti issued crisp directions.

Jonathan parked at a distance from the club, but when they found it the streets were empty.

'I'll bring the car round.'

'It doesn't *matter*,' said Patti.

He went off to get it, anyway.

When he arrived the girls had vanished. The doorman waved him in. He found them huddled together at the back, beside gold statues vomiting water. A spray of lights danced mauve and red on the floor. The girls sloshed champagne into glasses.

'Jonathan! Jonathan! Look, he's arrived,' cried Suki. She handed him a glass and pushed it into his face. He picked it from her and put it on a table.

'Oh you wanna dance, youwannadance, youwannadance. Pat-tee he wants tadance...'

Patti didn't take any notice.

Suki led Jonathan onto the dance floor. They were playing tired versions of 80s hits. Suki held Jonathan's hands loosely in hers and swayed back and forth mouthing and chugging.

After three songs, Jonathan had had enough.

He disappeared to the Gents and threw water over his face. He arched over the basin and tried to throw up. Nothing happened.

The girls had disappeared except for one of the cousins who sat alone in an overheated booth. Jonathan sat beside her and picked up a menu. It recommended a cocktail which came in a bucket and included Grand Marnier, Cointreau, Bitters, and two bottles of Dom Perignon, for £225. It looked quite old. He hid it under the table.

'What exams have you just done?' he asked aggressively.

'Fashion Design Part 1,' said the cousin.

He thought he ought to dance and got up and sat down. His arms and legs felt like they had splints attached. He wanted to go home and read Daniel's letters. He knew exactly where they were in his flat. Daniel was his oldest friend. He had known him three years. He went back to the table where the others were sitting, once he realised the cousin had left the booth.

Patti and Suki were being rolled in the arms of middle aged men who looked like crooks or journalists. They were regaling the girls with sundry details of some dodgy deal they'd just pulled off.

A gong sounded, and the lights went off. Two video machines relayed images of a couple with tangerine buffed skins humping energetically. Echoes of failure shuddered round Jonathan's frame. Patti flopped off the lap of one of the men. When she was more zizzed up she had thought he might be a bit like an experience she once had in Marseilles, but studying his reaction to the videos, realised he would probably turn out horribly avuncular. She pretended to crash out. Jonathan averted his eyes to the ground, stroking drops of moisture from his untouched drink.

At the bar they were offering barbecued shark steaks. The goods were advertised in a cascade of pink lights. One of the cousins gripped Jonathan's jacket and said she was going to be sick, now. He followed her into the Ladies and held her head over the basin, noticing the other cousin in a corner. Her arms were wrapped around her, her eyes were staring at something that only existed in her head.

'Oh no bloody pantomimes now,' he shouted at her. But she didn't change.

'Go back now,' he said to the other one. 'Just go back now.

You alright now?'

'Uh huh,' said the cousin, shuffling out.

Jonathan approached the remaining cousin, still staring. He snapped his fingers in front of her face, then pulled her hair like a church bell. She looked at him, clutched her scalp and giggled very slowly.

He pressed himself against her, putting his whole weight on her.

'Yet it's very funny,' he said, 'it's very very funny.'

He rubbed his hands over her breasts, almost flat, baby breasts, but tender. Her skin was almost translucent. She put vague hands up to cover herself, but he pushed them away.

Her top wasn't much. The material looked cheap but felt like silk. He undid the tiny buttons. The girl bit her lip, then struggled. Jonathan shoved his hand between her legs. She elbowed him and his hand gripped her throat. She shook her head, hard and tight.

'Oh don't panic, he said, softly, 'don't *panic*. Mustn't *panic*. Didn't anyone ever tell you that?'

On a sofa by the dance floor, Patti stirred and discovered the other men had gone, leaving a crumpled £20 note. Suki was sitting at the bar, chatting up one of the barmen.

The cousin was in a crumpled heap on the floor of the toilets. Jonathan stared at her, disgusted. He couldn't do anything. He hadn't done anything. He stepped back. He couldn't understand, he just couldn't *stand*, anyone being so careless of themselves, when they looked like that, a bit like he used to. So careless.

He left the toilets and walked past the cousin who had just thrown up. He grabbed her.

'Your sister…' he said, 'or whoever she is…' he jerked his thumb in the direction of the Ladies, 'doesn't seem too hot.'

'Shit,' she replied. She passed out. Jonathan carried her out to the car, past the doorman.

'Bit excited,' he said.

'Uh huh.'

He chucked her in the back of the car, and went back to pay the bill.

'We're off now, alright?' he yelled at Patti.

'Jonathan,' she said, yawning, 'no need to get so *nasty*.'

The unconscious cousin lay in the back of the car, Jonathan and Patti sat in the front.

'Are they fucking coming or what?' he said, revving the engine, drumming his fingers on the steering wheel.

'Oh my God,' said Patti.

Suki and the other cousin got in. Jonathan tore off. The other cousin was crying.

'What is it?' said Suki.

The other cousin kept crying.

'What happened?' Suki said to Jonathan.

'Nothing,' said Jonathan. He put his finger to his head. 'She's out of her fuckin' *face*.'

Suki caught Jonathan's eyes in the front mirror. He didn't alter them. She kept looking and her face fell as she turned back to the cousin. She looked at Patti, who wasn't paying attention, still. Nobody spoke. As Jonathan drove them back into town, the unconscious cousin woke up, moaned and banged her head hard on the ceiling. Suki yelled to find the button to open the window, too late. The cousin retched all over the floor. They all moaned.

Jonathan wasn't stopping. He wondered why they had to stay in Chelsea in the first place. It wasn't near anything.

He and Patti drove back through the City. She gently put Dinah Washington on the CD. 'I don't even like Suki - she's only my friend!' she said, at last.

He didn't listen, but put his foot down and broke two red lights. Patti screamed.

'*What are you trying to do fucking kill us?*'

That's better, Jonathan thought.

Dinah Washington was singing *Makin' Whoopee*. Patti, recovering, remembered how she liked Michelle Pfeiffer doing this one.

She looked at Jonathan. 'You could maybe take the car in a garage and they'd clean it up or something?' She knew he wouldn't. Too much pride. He was a Leo the Lion.

They arrived back at Jonathan's, and he went straight to his stash. Oh my angel, oh my baby…

Later, Patti curled up beside him, nudging her bottom on his thigh. In the middle of the night he turned over and squeezed her tits like he was wringing out a hand wash. She pushed his hands away and thought she'd sleep on the floor, thinking he was definitely on his way out. Some people you couldn't help. She unstuck herself from his moist chest and thought bye bye baby, bye bye.

10

It was 5pm and Deanna had done her part of the meeting an hour ago. They were talking about barcodes and their do-it-yourself foods.

'There are too many bits and pieces,' she said, 'the checkout staff can't stand them.'

It went quiet. The others hesitated deferentially.

'Yeah,' said Laurie, 'too many items. At the checkout. For the girls. Too much.' He looked at Deanna, and licked the top of his pen.

Everyone agreed.

She smiled back at him gaily. Nothing got done without his agreement now. She fantasised about *Under An Hour*. Claire had asked her out - something might work.

'Alright Deanna?' said Laurie.

'Integrated packages, yeah.' She cast her vote and left.

Now Deanna stood behind a counter under a banner - Love Food - in one of the main stores. It was a special promotion for the account-holding crowd, who were piling in, pushing and shoving. She wore a little black dress, and her feet were squeezed into a pair of high heels. Deanna's badge - 'May I Help You?' - hung uncertainly from her lapel.

Miranda was supposed to be doing tonight, but Deanna had an urgent meeting with the Housing Office tomorrow, so they'd done a swap. It was no hassle. She'd do anything to get out of the house to avoid Boo. It was all Paula's fault. If it hadn't been for Paula, she wouldn't even have been in Mabel's that night.

She surveyed the counter - Laurie's palette, in the style of Lucrezia Borgia. Plump heart-shaped pizzas were attended by delicate scrolls of Parma ham. Pushy steaks reclined on beds of watercress, wearing facetious hats of garlic butter. Cumberland sausages and huge plates of tomatoes stood alone, with boorish implications. A bowl of gazpacho held cucumber slices set in gelatine. Fake ice cubes floated in jugs of Sangria. The crowning glory was a silver platter on which a mound of dough, glycerine and face cream masqueraded as *Chicken à la Champagne*. White ultimate couple food. She'd failed *that* test. And they'd already moved it three times to get it away from the lights.

Deanna bounced a fish-slice in her hand, and tried to keep track of which food was real and which was not.

'Are you serving this, or what?'

Deanna smiled tightly as she shovelled slices of pizza onto paper plates. She ladled out Sangria into plastic cups, carefully avoiding the fake ice. A giggly couple stole off in the corner with a sausage each.

The thing with Paula had hit her nine-month ceiling, so she shouldn't have been surprised it went dead when she wasn't looking. There had been prickly remarks that had proved them unsympathetic to each other's work, so it was difficult to talk. Deanna had snogged Consuela at a party, and Paula hadn't regarded it as a joke. That dried up the sex. Their last session had ended up in the middle of nowhere.

A trial separation had only allowed space for minor annoyances to swell into major grievances. Deanna now knew that Paula wasn't the love of her life, but she didn't want to end up on her own again.

She had felt amongst friends as soon as she'd hit the bar, even though she didn't know anyone there. Even though the bartender, in a tough little vest, had smacked her change on the counter without looking at her.

Paula was late and wearing a brown suede jacket that touched Deanna's heart in its utter Paula-ness, and also irritated her to the point of insensibility. Paula saw Deanna and gave her the same defensive look she'd given her last time. She'd got more drinks and they'd sat there, not saying anything for ten minutes. Deanna couldn't even see Paula's face on a pillow now. She wanted to rip her shirt off and slap her.

'Headmaster sent a memo round today. 'Well done staff and all in 4B for dealing so well with the armed raid'.'

'Were you there?'

'No. But one of our twelve-year-olds nearly got shot.'

'Well it's not my fault!'

'I didn't say it was.'

They'd looked at each other. Nothing. Deanna remembered Paula taking her most intimate pulse, and couldn't imagine her doing that again.

'They're sending me into schools now,' said Deanna. 'Packages arrived today…'

'Whaaat?' Paula had said, and screwed up her face. Truly, she didn't look good like that.

'You can't.'

'I'm sorry?'

'Jesus - what'll they do next? I suppose in the future there won't be teachers at all, just different public relations people doing sales pitches.'

'I can do a talk on nutrition as well as anyone else!'

'It's not that, it's the principle. Where are you going?'

'Derby, first of all. Well they might find it interesting and…'

'But you're only going to flog them yoghurts, aren't you?'

'Not necessarily. They're just presents actually,' said Deanna. 'They can't get addicted to them. We might be doing organic vegetables soon too…'

'At a price,' said Paula. She'd looked at Deanna. 'Your head's still full of señoritas isn't it?'

'No,' said Deanna.

'Hopeless,' said Paula. She got up. 'Just because I earn less than you doesn't mean my time's not precious.'

With that, she had left.

'I never said anything like that,' Deanna had said, to the table. 'I never ever mentioned that once! What's the *matter* with her?'

She switched from Beck's to double whiskies immediately. Some half hoarse woman was moaning about dreams of Hollywood. There was a gale of laughter and someone dropped a glass. Some skinny blonde who had been batting around all evening came and sat down.

'Whew it's hot isn't it?' she said.

'Do you want a drink?'

'Oh yes whatever you're having. Whisky? Thanks a lot.'

Deanna got them. 'I've just been dumped.'

'No! Terrible taste if you don't mind me saying...'

'Excuse me?'

'Wanting to dump you. Tch!'

'Yeah, amazing. I mean I suppose it was heading that way anyway...'

'Yeah...'

'But it's just a bit of a shock.'

'Yeah...'

'She disapproved of my job for godsakes. Can you believe it?'

'Really? What's it you do exactly?'

'I work in food...'

'God, that's pretty interesting isn't it?'

'It's quite interesting yes. I sort out the new lines, market research...'

'Mmm. I bet you cook up a lot of tasty dishes!'

'Oh well, y'know...sometimes. Yeah. Thanks.'

'You need someone who appreciates you.'

'Yeah! I do! She never did!' Deanna stared into her drink. 'She could make me come like no one else...'

'Ahhh! Well I 'spect someone else could probably do that...'

'...before we stopped doing it, before this crush thing...'

'Crush thing...'

'and okay, maybe I was too tired sometimes, but so was she! Some things just aren't viable on weekdays!'

'No? Oh dear.'

'God the prospects aren't bright are they? I don't know about this other woman. We snogged but...' She surveyed the rest of the crowd with mounting dismay. 'I'm going to be celibate for the rest of my life!'

'I'm not with anyone.'

'Oh? You're not? You're on your own?'

'That's right!'

'Just dropped in did you?'

'Yeah.'

'It's like that poem 'I loved them they didn't want me something'.' Deanna drained her glass, pulled herself up with the help of the chair and got another round.

'Boo Radley,' said Boo, when Deanna returned. 'After Boo Radley in *To Kill A Mockingbird*. Have you read it?'

'No,' said Deanna. 'Thought they were a pop group.'

'Like my tattoo?' said Boo, and bared her arm. 'Just had it done. They threw in the T-shirt too!'

Boo pulled at her T-shirt. It had 'MAYBE' written on it in red. Deanna draped her fingers over Boo's snake tattoo. 'Yeah, yeah, thaz really cute...goesh all the way round doesn't it?'

She looked at her idly then took her hand away.

'Are you thinking about that woman again?' said Boo.

'A bit...no, we weren't compatible except doing it sometimes and yes everything...both of them...and...' Her voice was a quaver. 'I'm a caring and passionate person and deserve better than someone making me feel shit all the time just because I earn more I never had a go at her about that I never did. She never fuggin appreciated me God. No one's ever loved me really. Not for what I am. They just liked the look of my car. I didn't even do much with Consuela and...'

'What's that?'

'Eh?'

'The car.'

'It's a Rotunda 2000. Yellow one.'

'I've always fancied a ride in one of those. You need someone to look after you.'

'Yeah.,' said Deanna.

'Shall we go back to your place then?'

'Yeah,' said Deanna, 'yeah, that's a good idea, yeah.'

As far as she could remember, it had been a session marked more by enthusiasm than finesse. Boo had a lean, athletic frame, wrestled a lot, and had a couple of surprising skills. Towards the end, with an aching jaw, Deanna thought she might have been faking it, but couldn't care less. She was out for the count anyway. Zonk.

She liked being nudged awake by someone who didn't have a litany of complaints against her already. It was the air of finality with which Boo put on a neglected dressing gown and went to make coffee that made her anxious. Suddenly Boo looked a stone lighter and very pink. Quite unlike anyone she usually met. Younger.

'How old did you say you were?'

'I didn't. Eighteen. I liked last night. You were very

passionate! Arabic or Colombian?'

'I was drunk,' said Deanna. 'Sorry.'

'No you weren't. Don't you remember? I said 'you alright to drive?' You said you'd got a really fast metabolism. You took a wrong turning at the Ring Road, I think, but you were back on course in a jiffy. You're a good driver aren't you? I like that.'

'Thanks,' said Deanna. 'Can I give you a lift anywhere, now?'

'No not really,' said Boo. 'I don't really live anywhere at the moment.'

Boo put two cups down. Deanna stared at them.

'You've done your place up nicely haven't you? Sort of Mediterranean feel.'

'Work?' said Deanna, faintly. 'Do you have *any work?*'

'Not yet. But I've only been here…'

'How long?'

'A day and a half. But you know - early days. I'm a very good swimmer. 'Cept I was thinking more the music business.'

'Music business,' said Deanna.

'You don't know anyone?'

'Not offhand. What are you living on?'

'My mum's Abbey National book.'

'Oh, fantastic!'

'…down to the last £200 now. She hated me anyway. Chucked me out. My dad didn't mind so much. You know. He likes things to be a bit different. But he went to Australia…'

Deanna left Boo with a Yellow Pages opened firmly under Record Companies. It was the kind of effort that had worked for her, once, about fifteen years ago. It failed this time.

Boo stayed on. She tidied the flat from top to bottom, and put everything away where Deanna couldn't find it. She rejuvenated the house plants, washed the carpets and curtains, and organised her books and CDs in alphabetical order. She asked Deanna if she was alright every half hour, and kept offering her a shiatsu massage. If she wasn't out by the end of the week, Deanna had decided to kill herself.

Two men, recently swilled in beer, approached the counter where Deanna continued to serve.

'Bit skimpy with your portions aren't you love?'

'Maybe you'd like to try some of this?' she heaved *Chicken à la Champagne* onto a plate.

They ate it then spat it out.

'So sorry, that's not for eating. I forgot.'

She threw their plates into the bin and sent her badge in after it. They swayed out.

Boo wasn't in when she got home. Good, she thought. She checked her answering machine. There was no message from Consuela, and none from Paula. The gym was open for another hour. She put on all the clothes, felt springy and corsetted, and strode up and down the living room, smoking, for half an hour, wondering if she should call the hospitals.

Boo arrived at 10pm, having painstakingly bought three carrier bags full of ingredients for a Malaysian meal. She occupied the kitchen, with a lot of clashing of pots and metal instruments and good natured swearing. Deanna wandered in and out, asking if she could help, and being shushed out. My kitchen, she thought, *my bloody kitchen.*

She turned on the TV and saw an LA awards ceremony, where everyone looked as if they'd been cooked up in a lab. She watched a few seconds of Whitney Houston accepting an award, and praising her Heavenly Father, and zapped her off again.

She went back into the kitchen, and took out a pack of tortilla chips. They ate about midnight, when their hunger had worn off.

'Is it okay?' said Boo.

'Lovely,' said Deanna. 'How much do I owe you for the food?'

'£43.70 I'm afraid,' said Boo. 'I know I've got to go.'

Halfway through the night Deanna thought she heard the bedroom door open. Boo crept under the sheets, stuck a butt plug up her rear and held a vial of poppers under her nose.

'Stoppit!' cried Deanna. She felt dizzy, recovered, pushed Boo off, pulled the plug out - it popped like a cork - and fell into a foetal position. She cupped her hand between her legs and kept it there.

'Look you....Christ - ow - get a manicure for Godsake!'

'Okay,' said Boo, 'error of judgment, fair enough. I was just trying out different things to see what you'd like. I mean it wouldn't be my kind of thing but y'know, whatever rings your bell. Interesting little device isn't it? Do you use it a lot? I'd be happy to have a go with your turquoise appliance!'

Deanna sat up, attempting dignity. 'Those things were for *me and Paula*! What were you doing rooting around in my drawers anyway?'

'You were happy enough for me to root around *you*...'

'That's different.'

'How? Tell me - do you think you should get sex toys made by women for women, or don't you have any preference either way?'

Deanna grabbed her by the shoulders and shook her. 'Look, shut up, just shut up - I couldn't give a toss - it's three o'clock in the fucking morning. I didn't invite you here. I want you *out*, alright? Soon...'

Boo stood at the door. 'You only like having sex when you're drunk,' she muttered, nobly, and shut the door.

'*How do you know?*' Deanna screamed. '*We only did it once!*'

She went to the bathroom for a sleeping pill and heard Boo snuffling in the front room. She stalled, then went and sat beside her, and rubbed her shoulder. This didn't have much effect so she poured a drink.

'I didn't mean it,' she said. 'Well I did. But not like that. I shouldn't have shouted.'

Boo's face was red and drenched. She looked about ten.

'Margie Dean said all you London dykes were really cold and hard,' she sobbed. 'Stuck up fashion victims the lot she called you!'

'Who?' said Deanna.

'Margie Dean, friend in Southampton.'

'You could go back there, maybe?' She said quietly. 'To Margie's?'

Boo started yowling again. 'No room!'

'You don't just meet someone, have a shag and move in

with them!' Deanna shouted. 'Ever! That's not how it works!'

Boo dried her eyes shiftily. 'How does it work then?' She turned to look at her. A very firm look. Deanna didn't know. It hadn't happened. 'You date longer,' she said, 'I suppose.'

She got up.

'Can't you do or say anything without fetching a drink first?' said Boo.

'No,' said Deanna, 'not at the moment I can't, no.'

'Is that something to do with me being here?'

'Not entirely, no. Night night.'

She left the room.

Deanna sat on a wooden bench in a building with peeling paint. She sighed irritably, and kept looking at her watch. A man next to her, with his slightly balding head thrown between his legs, studied her violently.

There was a woman playing around with her kids, high on chemicals or no sleep. A drunk down and out was shambling about, and everyone was staring at something else.

Her name was called on the tannoy.

The office had grey cupboards like school lockers. The woman was about her age. Her bright red polo neck and hoop earrings were brazening it out against her pale face.

'I have this friend who needs housing fast…'

'Oh yes,' she said, 'why can't she come in then?'

'She's looking for a job.'

'I see,' said the woman.

Deanna sat down.

'Previous address?'

'I don't know,' said Deanna. 'Southampton. Does it matter?'

The woman looked up, looked her up and down, then looked out of the cloudy window.

'Pregnant, psychiatric problems, any, uh, features like that then?'

Well, give her a chance, Deanna thought.

'She's 18 and homeless!'

'You just said that.'

'She's a bit underweight…'

'Underweight, I see…'

'She's a lesbian!' Deanna added, remembering.

'Well I hardly think that constitutes psychiatric problems does it?' The woman ripped off a sheet of paper, threw it away, and twisted her mouth.

'No,' said Deanna. 'I…never mind.'

The woman blinked.

'Well what's she supposed to do?'

The woman ripped off another piece of paper, and pushed it over.

'I'm not voting Labour again,' said Deanna. 'What's the point?'

'Write down her details,' the woman said, 'she'll have to come in herself.'

Deanna wrote, and moved to the door.

'Excuse me…' said the woman, '*Boo Radley*? Is this some kind of joke?'

'Oh,' said Deanna, getting out her pen again. 'She's named

after Boo Radley...'

The woman nodded.

'I can't actually remember her real surname...'

'So,' said the woman, '*Boo Radley wants accommodation*. I'll remember that...' She pressed her buzzer and said, 'Paul Furness, please... This isn't an easy job, you know. I wouldn't mind the odd wind-up but this isn't even funny is it?'

When Deanna got back to the office, Miranda had a tasting session in full swing.

'I wouldn't have thought bread with sun dried tomatoes was intrinsically funny would you? I think this lot must have slightly boring lives.' She called out, indicating with her finger. 'Just mark your answers in the boxes. Extra comments on the extra page. Take your time.'

She stretched her ebony fingers. 'You know I'm having second thoughts about these acrylic nails. Have you seen the state of Michael Jackson's face?'

Some of the testers were giggling at the lemon meringue pie.

'I knew that fluting was a mistake,' said Deanna.

'Appointment go alright?'

'Bit of a waste of time...' Deanna looked at the floor, then into Miranda's face and Miranda flashed back 'cancer scare'.

'Just family business,' said Deanna, 'nothing much. Nothing serious.'

Miranda leaned up against the table and held her clipboard to her chest. ''Nother little scene with Raymond last night. Made up alright though,' she smiled broadly. She called out 'Yes. That's right. Dry, cakey, chunky, gluey, fishy.

Just tick your boxes.' Her voice dropped. 'How's Paula?'

'Oh Paula's fine.'

Deanna supposed she could keep that up for another month.

When she got home Boo was on the sofa pretending to read a biography of Agnes de Mille. Deanna played her messages back.

'Hello. Sue Riddle, Housing Office. Look someone's rung in offering a caravan in their back garden. I can't do it from here, but it might suit your *friend*.'

There was a name and a number. 'Tell her to come in. If she can prove she's in moral danger, she gets a few more points on the housing list. 'Bye.'

Deanna went into the front room, beckoned Boo, played the message back, gave her a notepad and pen, and handed her the receiver. She shut her eyes and counted to sixty. Boo came back.

'They said I could go round now.'

'Fine,' said Deanna. ' Go and see Sue Riddle too.'

'Is she nice?'

'Laugh a minute. Your moral danger stuff's nothing to do with me.'

'No, unfortunately.'

Boo packed her stuff and stood there.

''Bye,' said Deanna. 'If they want a deposit...give me a ring.'

Boo left. 'See you,' she said, to herself.

Deanna put some music on and her feet up. Thank God for Claire. Her release from all this. She might get a book.

Claire's life didn't have anything to do with messy sex, housing, office politics or worrying about your love life. A divine relic - Claire reminded her of an old style haute bohemian, before sex had taken too much of a hold and frizzled its edges with anarchy. She had a constant air of disenchantment, which at this point, suggested to Deanna a mature approach to life.

Claire came back from shopping very early to get changed, three times, she couldn't decide. She sprayed a vial of perfume behind her ears and knees, put on tights with a mink sheen, and changed her dress again. Anthony was away. She hummed a waltz, put on more perfume, added a scarf, sighed, and decided on reflection not to take the car.

It was so long since she had been out alone like this. She was very alert. Everyone looked so pretty on the tube. Girls with elaborate make-up and hair shook fluffy stoles, and chatted with a man in a makeshift dinner jacket, with no arms, just a billowing shirt. Someone carried a red rose in a cellophane box. There were hats, shiny skirts, bare midriffs, clean faces, more perfume and aftershave, and a blonde with such an exuberant mass of curly hair Claire wanted to bury her face in it.

The pavement was still wet from a summer storm, and gold sheets of light shone on the windows of the restaurant. Inside, intricate ironwork tables and chairs glittered under chandelier light. Claire looked around at the young people, at the emerald walls, at the lights, and listened to the music; *Manon* by Massenet, she thought. She inhaled an atmosphere of smoke and wine flavoured food. Couples leaned together with softened intimacy, and whispered. Claire's eyes sparkled.

Deanna was at the door. She wore a witty toque, and a redder rosebud mouth than she wore in the week. Claire lingered over her greeting kiss. Deanna didn't quite know what to make of it.

She watched Claire, looking like she'd never seen her before, with that perfectly formed summer dress and tinkling jewellery on her neck and wrists, her pale ivory skin and her eyes more animated than she'd ever seen them. Was this the show she put on for her emaciated husband? What a waste.

Deanna learned in time that Paula was a bore, yet her book proposal was just fascinating. The summer rosé bubbles hit her head. She was tickled pink. It was a gift, like a frilly box of luxury chocolates on a spare Bank Holiday. They stirred the brandy into the coffee, around midnight - they were the last people in the restaurant. Deanna asked Claire if she wanted to go home with her, as if it was a sudden impulse. She saw, in Claire's face, that two low down pressure points had just been found, and were slowly releasing honey.

II

Claire's marbly body was chaste and sensitive, and Deanna felt like the bridegroom on the first night of a honeymoon, enjoying the feast of tremulous flesh at leisure, not doing anything that might scare Claire, yet. Claire responded in quiet echoes of what Deanna was doing. After Boo's stridency this was very touching. Afterwards, Claire's long white arms were pressed against her face. Deanna pulled away and kissed her - once for luck, and once more for courage.

Claire was all wild embraces in the kitchen the next morning. They sat down in front of two yoghurt pots, into which a smaller pot of muesli was tipped, and mixed. Claire's face and hands shot up with more alarm and delight. Deanna didn't know if she could take that much alarm and delight, yet noticed that women, seen in that particular morning light, always did look ten years younger.

'One of your things?' said Claire. And Deanna realised that Claire was incapable of being humbled by anything.

'Not one of my things,' said Deanna, and kissed her again to stop her saying anything else like that.

'Couldn't you, though - make this yourself?' said Claire, just nipping the spoon at its edge with a skittish air.

'Most people couldn't be bothered...' Deanna looked at the phone and played back the flashing light they'd ignored last night. She did, after all, have another life. She thought she'd better get back to it, now.

'Hi, s'me. Settled in the caravan. It's not that bad. The owners are nice - Christians.' (Long pause).

'I've got a motorcycle messenger's job too. Just mornings. Three a week. If I fell off me bike I'd get disability allowance.' (Clearing of throat).

'Only kidding. Anyhow, I'm thinking of setting up my own business now - 'Manicures for Sex'. I put a notice up in Mabel's. Only two replies so far and the second one didn't show. Still, early days yet eh? I averted most of the set-up costs by nicking the manicure stuff from the chemist's - DUH, just another joke ho ho. Still, just thought I'd let you know and see how you are. I'll send you the address. 'Bye then.

Oh Boo, thought Deanna.

'Who on earth's that?' cried Claire.

'Oh, just my niece.'

Claire was examining her hands reproachfully, and Deanna suddenly felt bored and trapped. You can go now, she thought.

Claire had a simpering 'Well I expect you'll deal with that' air, and looked up again. These were servile tics that could rapidly get demanding. Claire talked about everything as if she owned it. Deanna saw how this could be extended to include her. She thinks she's in Nirvana now, Deanna thought. She'll blame me once she discovers she isn't. Boo looked good, at this distance, and it was nice to be able to take some things for granted.

She drove Claire all the way back home, still feeling responsible. Claire reminisced about the past, and times they'd met before, working out how it had all led up to this - mm - hadn't it? She didn't mention Deanna's book, and Deanna now remembered it hadn't been mentioned in any practical sense last night. They'd talked about her company's book, only that. But I didn't do it for that, not that only, she reassured herself.

She was cowed when they arrived at Claire's house. She forgot that people had houses as big as this, in town. She hadn't been in many - only Claire's. The rest were hired for work parties, business addresses. She couldn't quite believe anyone still lived like this, with ancient furniture, floors and ornaments, all polished and preserved by unknown and silent hands. She imagined what Paula would think. Imagining Paula's outrage gave her a quick glimmer of pleasure and triumph, but she was suddenly conscious of whether she was doing everything right or not, in Claire's terms.

When Claire offered her tea - would she ring for it, maybe? - Deanna said she had to be moving along. She kissed Claire hard on the mouth for goodbye, though, because she still liked the way Claire looked at her when she did that.

She drove steadily round and out of the manicured streets around Claire's, lolloping over the speed bumps. This would be great if she ever needed an ambulance, she thought, although she didn't suppose Claire ever would. She went through a weekend-clear centre of town, and put on a Prince tape to hike her back into her old life, before last night, which was where she wanted to be, now.

Well, this is it, she thought. Claire reminded her of herself in her teens. Now she'd become the woman she wanted to be seduced by, she wanted someone who would turn out less improbable. Claire couldn't be thinking it would continue. She was married, for godsakes.

She arrived home and had a bath. She got out some work papers - 'Classic Dishes for the new middle class. Quick 'n' easy as servants were in the olde days.' She couldn't stand much more of this. She went to her computer and ran three more *Under An Hour* synopses off and sent them out. At the post box, she noticed that her street had just got its first car phone user. She stared. Would this mean she'd soon have to put iron grilles on her windows, like Claire? It wasn't an encouraging thought.

She went back into the kitchen and considered chucking out all of Boo's barely used Malaysian spices. She picked up a couple and put them down again. She wondered what to do, now she had some leisure. She looked around the flat. Even Boo's most conscientious ministrations couldn't disguise the cracks in the walls, the cobwebs flourishing in ceiling corners, the sink collecting grime…and God, it was small.

The doorbell rang. Not Boo, she thought. It was Consuela. She was wearing jeans and a blue T-shirt. Her black hair was scooped into a chignon and fastened with a large red comb.

Deanna had been haunted with the memory of her curves, and the heaviness of her breasts. She'd forgotten how thick and glossy Consuela's hair felt.

'Just passing,' she said.

No you weren't, Deanna thought.

She watched Consuela take off her jacket, throw it onto a chair, light a cigarette, walk into the kitchen, return with a saucer, fling herself on the sofa and place her feet with cool deliberation on the coffee table. She was wearing new boots. Deanna knew this as Consuela looked at the boots, then at Deanna, then back at the boots with a haughty aspect.

'Nice surprise,' said Deanna, deadpan. 'Coffee? Drink?'

'Anything,' said Consuela. 'Or we could go out...'

She picked up the leaflet for the olde worlde dinners.

'This yours?'

'It's the new boss's.'

'Still having a hard time?'

'A bit. It's not worth talking about...'

'Let's go out, then,' said Consuela, 'now.'

'A park?' said Deanna.

'A park.' Consuela's eyes lit up. She might have been imagining it. Deanna changed into her best casual clothes.

Was this just luck, or what? She couldn't quite believe it. She fastened her attention onto anything in front of them - a supermarket trolley parked in the middle of the pavement, a woman in a sari shuffling along with wriggling children, and at the tube station, two black kids hurling themselves up the down escalator, pausing for breath, then charging up it again.

'So much energy!' said Consuela.

She was wearing a dusky perfume and Deanna was becoming entranced at the smell and intrigued at its motivation. She couldn't think of anything to say.

The park was approached by pink ceremonial roads, suitable for taxis and other exclusive vehicles. Horses and carriages had travelled on the thoroughfares, buses and coaches were still unimaginable. The roads were thinly populated with weekending families and lone strollers. No one to disturb them. The paths and lakes were so evenly spread, and the trees so intimately clustered together: they hung over and trailed in the waters so dreamily, as if they had heaved such a deep rooted sigh, no recovery were possible or desirable. The breeze from the lake calmed the park's inhabitants. Consuela's perfume drifted across, softened in the new expansive air. The sky was wider and more brightly exposed than visible from the busy streets. It highlighted the pleased, wafting edges of trees and threw clear outlines on the frosted cones and pinnacles of ancient buildings that lay beyond them. Its breadth and generosity of spirit swept aside Deanna's last misgivings.

'I wasn't expecting you to call or anything,' she said.

Consuela looked surprised. 'I always meant to.'

Deanna was becoming drunk on fresh air.

They crossed the bridge and leaned over the railings, capturing the panorama of trailing trees, the wide blue sky, the sharp frosted pinnacles. Some soft-coated swans floated on the lake. The breeze comforted their faces and emptied their minds.

Deanna took her jacket off.

'Are you hot?' said Consuela.

'Mmm.'

They made their way into an isolated copse, passing a fountain gushing at its centre, straight and arrowy at its tips, which tingled them with faint excess spray. They walked over the bare ground in the shade of the bushes and Deanna threw her jacket down.

Consuela pulled her into her arms, and unleashed her tongue in Deanna's mouth. They tumbled under a tree and found quick routes through hastily unbuttoned clothes. This was it, Deanna thought, straight to the heart and nothing in between. She did everything slower and harder than she had done with anyone since she could remember. The only sign of their activity was the faintest rustling of the bushes and two abandoned bags beside the tree. They drifted into sleep, with sweetened hands and lips, under the trees, behind the bushes, away from the crowds, all under the bald gaze of Buckingham Palace.

When Deanna was still shifting between waking and sleeping, her head was tucked into Consuela's neck. She breathed in her skin, stroked her waist, and pressed her pubis into Consuela's thighs. The sound of approaching voices and a ray of sunlight snapped her eyes open, and she realised they were in the open air, dishevelled.

'Christ!' She sat up, and ran her fingers through her hair. Consuela yawned and rolled on her back. Her breasts and tufts of black underarm hair exposed.

'Huh!' she said. 'Your Queen lives there. Hello…'

She stirred lazily.

'We've got to move,' Deanna rasped.

'I have to do my boots,' said Consuela, 'they'll take the longest. Shall I put them on first or last? First. First, I think. Wait.'

They quietly got back into their clothes, which were lightly brushed with grass clippings. They tidied up, kissed, separated, and appeared from behind the copse.

'Later, then?' said Deanna, as they reached the main road. She ran her knuckle over what she could feel of Consuela's spine, under her jacket. Consuela moistened her lips, and looked away.

'Later,' she said, and grinned hugely. 'Call me.'

Consuela slung her bag over her shoulder, put her hands in her pockets and was off, slouching, in the other direction. Deanna watched her from the back.

On the way to the tube she dodged through Sunday shoppers, armed with impatience and carrier bags, all having completed necessary outings, and now grown self righteous at the prospect of trains and buses. She felt dazed. She could still taste Consuela on her tongue. Her perfume had been absorbed into her skin.

By the tube she was arrested by a large screen punching out a list of slogans:

ABSENCE MAKES THE HEART GROW HARDER
ARDOUR IS THE BETTER PART OF VALOUR
HORSES WITHOUT HOOVES RUN FASTER

She stepped into the tube, vaguely recalling that in the old USSR they got long-winded chunks of Lenin. Another slogan flashed in her head from the past - 'Let's kick racism out of town.' Was that the USSR? Was that Lenin? She couldn't remember now.

Later that evening she dozed and woke up. She played Chrissie Hynde doing *I Go To Sleep*. What a voice. It had all happened now. She lay back and remembered the afternoon, feeling light headed and silly. She drank half a glass of wine lying on the floor, got into the car, and went round to Consuela's.

Her street was quiet and the lamps were half out. She didn't want to wake up the rest of Consuela's house. She picked up a small stone and lobbed it at Consuela's window, in a slow motion arc. It missed. She did it again. Consuela appeared at the window, still wearing the same clothes. She leaned out and flashed a smile in the dark. Oh goody, thought Deanna. She had come a long way, in all senses, from the girl who had the job as recipe checker on *Recettes de Volaille Choisies de ma Vieille Tante Paysanne*.

12

Claire slid her bureau drawer shut. No - she mustn't - but oh how much she wanted to! Inside it were four postcards picturing great women of the past, addressed to Deanna, with messages. They had seemed so apt and playful when she wrote them, now she wasn't so sure. She didn't know what to do. It was the first time this had happened to her.

She wanted to call Deanna at work, but had no reasonable excuse, and work conversations could be so fraught. Anthony was horrid when called at work. Claire had booked up a lunch with Maxine, now she had something to tell her. Dear little scruff. She probably didn't get to eat anything decent much.

Jadine, Claire's assistant, had gone AWOL. Claire hadn't noticed at first. She buzzed her for the third time in a morning, and she didn't come or answer. Claire walked briskly into Jadine's office, which was vacated. This is it, she thought, this is really final. She felt braced and excited at the idea of firing someone.

She spent an age searching for Jadine's home number, intermittently preparing a ferocious speech, which moved from actual firing to obscure threats, as Claire realised that firing her would prove rather a nuisance. Someone who sounded suspiciously like Jadine answered the phone, and said her name was Sheryl. 'She left, didn't she, Jadine?' she said, and hung up. Claire dropped the receiver back onto the phone, and sweetly confronted Frank in the accounts department.

'I had no idea,' she said. 'These girls are so erratic now.'

'She seemed all set,' he replied. 'She was doing accountancy exams anyway, wasn't she?'

'Was she? I had no idea.'

'Yes she was,' he said.

It appeared that a month's pay was statutory, as far as he was concerned. Something she'd get blamed for. Ghastly man, she thought. She made a mental note to complain of Frank's inefficiency at the next directors' meeting.

She put an advert in her local paper, to save money, and received no suitable responses. She phoned an agency where the woman laughed at the salary offered, and said she would get back to her, but didn't. She put an ad in the Media *Guardian* and interviewed two bright girls who talked and talked about French philosophers and the feminine aesthetic, but had yet to obtain the appropriate computer experience. She felt desperate. Keying in copy to the computer herself had already cost her over a hundred pounds' worth of lunchtime massages.

Following a tense discussion with the director, Michael, who accused her of being difficult and was obviously having personal problems, he and Frank agreed that Claire could have a temp, two days a week. You could change them if you didn't like them, she supposed.

The agency provided a hulking Australian girl, who Claire regarded in quite a different light to how she would have, had they met even a month ago. She was rather strapping. Very. Great tan too. Very well travelled and highly intelligent. She clocked in at 9am, did all the work properly, and signed off very decidedly at 5.30pm.

Their lunchtimes were quite serene. Amanda sat in her office, eating a powerful Bhel Poori and reading a Sarah Paretsky. Claire, meanwhile, comforted only by a wholegrain sandwich filled with lots of lettuce, galloped through the Lavender Menace titles, which she read behind an Aga saga: '*Grace ran her fingers along the fine whalebone in her mistress's bodice, she bent over the dressing table and...*'

It was too thrilling. She couldn't wait for the next time with Deanna. She had known, instinctively, oh so long ago, that her thing with Paula would never work out.

She borrowed Amanda's copy of *Time Out*, with an eye to future outings.

Clit Club at Fanny's:

Shake your funky stuff. Blind Date for dykes. Cash prizes

Yahoo! at the Central:

KD, Nanci and more! Strict Western dress code. Free bar snacks and pool table.

It was difficult to see herself fitting in at any of these events. There was a poetry reading - that was more like it - but it was in a pub. No matter. Maybe they'd just have dinner again - *Les Hors d'Oeuvres*, maybe. Starters! Just like

Claire herself. She called Buckinghamshire and got them to send cleaners into the cottage. She would whisk Deanna off there some time next month.

Amanda, once settled, got cheeky.

'Do people actually read these books?'

'Why yes, of course,' Claire replied, hurt.

Claire was disappointed to see her collected by a tall blond man in the week. But still - Claire did not have to measure herself by her. Amanda was not part of the master race.

Claire tried to work from home inasmuch as this was possible, and Anthony was away, which made it even better. Anne was back, wearing a tracksuit and pony tail, and seemed in reasonable spirits as she set to Claire's housework.

They had cut into Anne's legs. Claire was of course aware that operations like this took place all the time. But she had never been in hospital herself, considered having a knife cutting into her, being paralysed under an anaesthetic, being told to stay in your bed and not move, or having a plastic band with your name on it tied to your wrist. Anne had just related all this, her vivid account seeming to propel the furious whirl of the floor polisher. And it excited Claire's own morbid turn of mind to previously unimagined heights.

Anne was only ten years older than Claire, and Claire wondered how long it would take before they started wanting to refashion her own body in this manner. She suspected that once it started, it never stopped. She suspected that once they started, they never got it right.

Anne worked on, casting occasional looks at Claire, who was lying on the sofa checking her papers. Claire rose occasionally to change the record - Rossini it sounded like - and gaze into space with a soppy expression on her face. She kept breaking into smiles, throwing her head back and fluttering her eyelashes. Whatever it was, Anne thought, it was nothing to do with what she was meant to be working on. People rarely got excited in that sort of way about gardening.

Anne had been employed as a supply teacher, a shop manager, an aerobics instructor, and in her time had been a mean professional shoplifter, but had fallen into cleaning because it was less stressful and more regular. It satisfied her curiosity. Recently, she had started up a sideline to supplement her income: tipping off tabloid journalists about imminent scandals. She thought she had a real tasty one on this lot, but didn't know whether she could make it stick yet. She started rubbing her legs. Claire looked up with cautious sympathy. Anne groaned lightly. Claire took off her glasses.

'Would you like to sit down for a bit Mrs Brasted?'

Anne sat down and heaved a sigh.

'Are you sure you're fully recovered from that dreadful operation?'

'Oh yes,' said Anne. 'You blank out all the details really. It was the wait that did it. Two bloody years. The nurses eat your food.'

Claire sighed. 'Brandy?'

'Oh thanks. They have television in the wards, but they only put on all the rubbish.'

'Really?'

'You don't feel like variety shows when you're not well.'

'No,' Claire replaced the decanter. Oh what the hell, she

thought. She was bored to tears with trawling through *English Country Gardens*. She poured herself one too.

'Silly boys squealing at glove puppets...'

'Yes.'

'Panels of bald men with beards, staring at boards of numbers and letters. Australians carrying on. The accent's very wearing after a while. Bungee jumping. Thanks a lot.'

'Chin chin,' said Claire.

'You want something with lots of violence really. Puts it all in perspective.'

'That's an interesting thought,' said Claire, considering it. 'Mrs. Brasted, really you should have said something about your legs earlier. We could have given you a loan or...'

'I don't believe in that.'

Claire wondered if Anne was a member of some fanatical religious sect.

Anne gestured to Claire's work. 'You should watch that...'

'Watch what?'

'Working from home. That's what they want everyone to do. They can pay their own heating and lighting and keep their own computers, and buy their own paper, and pay the telephone bill...'

'Who's they?' said Claire, with an airy smile.

'The employers.'

People like me, Claire thought.

'I'm not sure if that's true Mrs Brasted.'

'Right,' said Anne. 'I'm just going to have a wee, then when I come back, I'll let you in on a secret.'

'Alright,' said Claire, watching her go out of the room. She picked up the gardening manuscript again, and put it down.

Anne returned, filled her glass and poured some into Claire's.

'I'm a member of the Revolutionary Communist Party,' she said. 'It's supposed to be a secret, but what's the point of having secrets if you can't share them?'

'Yes,' said Claire.

'I wouldn't tell anyone else,' Anne continued, 'but I thought I might as well tell you. I see you support the liberals.'

Claire looked at her glass of brandy, got up, and sat in Anthony's chair, her hand resting lightly on one of its arms. Double the insurance, she thought. Do it tomorrow.

During the course of the next hour, she learned that Anne also had three sons. Two were philosophy students. The other one was a playwright.

'We've fallen out over factional differences,' said Anne, of the youngest two, 'so I kicked them out. There's only so much quantity of unwashed male you can take in your house at any one time in any case.'

'Oh quite, I'm sure,' said Claire.

'You don't have any kids do you Claire?'

'No, no, I don't.'

'He didn't want any did he - your husband?'

'No, he didn't,' said Claire.

'Spends a lot of time on his own doesn't he, your husband?'

'He works a lot yes,' said Claire. 'I suppose,' she speculated, 'you'd prefer your sons did that than say, working in a bank…' she giggled, 'or something like that?'

'If they worked in a bank,' said Anne, 'they might be able to afford a washing machine between them by now.'

'They don't…?' said Claire.

'They haven't got one,' said Anne. 'They come round and do it themselves, but fill up my kitchen every week. David's no better either, but he does his own washing now, or gets it done for him.'

'David…' said Claire. 'David Brasted's your *son?*'

She might have seen something of his once, but couldn't remember.

'There was an article about him in one of the Sunday supplements last week,' said Claire. 'He was described as an 'ex punk rocker'.'

'Well,' said Anne, 'I don't know about that…' She poured out more brandy, and rearranged herself more comfortably. 'He tried to be their manager for a fortnight. Then he came home one morning, turned round to me and said 'I was fucked up the arse last night mother'.'

'Goodness,' said Claire.

'It was pre-AIDS days, Claire. I wasn't bothered. He might have done himself a mischief, but nothing serious.'

Claire nodded. David Brasted - gay too! She couldn't wait to tell Priscilla. He didn't look the type.

'Do you see his plays?' said Claire.

'I offered my frank opinion on his earlier work,' said Anne, 'and we stopped being invited.'

'That's a shame,' said Claire. 'His work's awfully well received.'

'That's as may be,' said Anne, 'but personally, superimposing the Tolpuddle martyrs over a picture of the contemporary urban homeless was completely wrong-headed to my mind. This latest one about rape just sounds ridiculous. David's not a woman. What would he know about it?'

Claire looked at the clock. She was quite out of her depth.

'I'll do the upstairs now shall I?' said Anne.

'Please.'

'That's six hours you owe me now.'

'Yes,' said Claire.

'Like Rossini don't you?'

'What? Oh yes,' said Claire.

'*Il Trovatore*'s my favourite - Verdi. Very loud, very moving.'

Oh enough, Claire thought. That's quite enough of that. She and Deanna would live here, sack Anne, and get a sweet little French au pair - the sort that could do perfect mayonnaise and soufflés, and be discriminating on your behalf.

Anne dragged the floor polisher up the stairs. Nothing yet, but she thought she'd warmed Claire up.

Claire returned to her work. Jane Brown and Meredith Bell had little appeal, at the moment. She wondered if they were gay too. She set to the manuscripts with more ardour. She glanced at Deanna's proposal for *Under An Hour*, in between. She held it admiringly. But she couldn't see anything like it catching on. And in any case, Claire had decided she wanted to be loved for herself.

13

Seated at a table at Chen's, regarding its paper tablecloths, the spare decorations, and the mainly Chinese diners with infinite patience and kindness, Claire felt infused with an almost Buddhist sense of high spirituality. She thought any moment she'd take off.

Maxine appeared. Her hair was frizzed out to almost twice its usual dimensions. She looked at one of the waiters, but he only saw her hair and gave her a funny look back. This kind of thing always seemed to happen when she was with Claire.

'Your hair!' Claire exclaimed.

'Extensions,' said Maxine. 'To ensnare a man in my hair,' she added, without much conviction. 'You look nice too.'

She'd never seen Claire in a suit. It looked like it was wearing her. She looked well, apart from that. Uncannily so. Claire wanted duck, Maxine vegetables.

'Is that all? You look a little peaky.'

'It's alright,' said Maxine, 'been working a lot.'

She asked for a Tiger Beer, but the waiter didn't hear, so she had to ask twice.

'Just a mineral water for me please...' Claire smiled at the waiter. 'I mustn't drink and I can't stay long. I have a massage at 2.15pm.'

He really wanted to know that, Maxine thought.

'I've got an exhibition. Solo this time. You must come.'

'Oh yes,' said Claire, 'Deanna told me.'

'Oh,' said Maxine, 'oh.'

'And what have you got for us? More vulvas?'

'There was only ever one. No, more abstract stuff now. More collagey. And a bit of sculpture. Fun sculpture. Found objects. Opening things out a bit. How's your job?' she added, finding herself up a blind alley.

'Oh thriving.'

'Doing any art books?' Maxine said.

'They're not cost effective,' said Claire.

'You ought to do something on Tiggy.'

'Tiggy?'

'She only goes by her first name. She does sculptures in sweets. They're very popular.'

'Yes,' said Claire. Any more special pleading like that and she'd be forced to get quite sharp.

'Have you seen Jonathan?' said Claire.

'No,' said Maxine. 'You know he sent me hate mail? Well, a hate poem.'

'*Hate poem?*' Claire laughed. 'And why on earth would he hate *you*?!'

'I don't know,' said Maxine. 'Really don't know.' She regarded Claire very steadily. 'But it was a long time ago.'

Claire just smiled to herself. 'He writes poetry, Jonathan,' she said. 'Interesting.'

'I expect he got that urge off you,' said Maxine.

Claire rearranged her napkin. 'But you're still living at…'

'Yeah…'

'And working there?'

'Yeah…'

'That must be awfully inconvenient.'

'No it's a big room. The light's not bad. It's crowded now because I'm recovering all the old stuff. But the *Macro* takes some of it and…'

'Who?'

'The *Macro*.'

'Is that a gallery?'

'No, a restaurant.'

'Oh, a restaurant.'

'Where I work…'

'Waitressing…'

'Part-time,' said Maxine. 'It's a *project*.'

Claire watched Maxine, and looked away again.

'And how's Robert? I understand that turned out alright?'

Maxine chased a mushroom with her fork and it flew off the plate.

'Whoops,' said Claire. 'Leave it,' she added.

Daniel, thought Maxine. Fags *will* talk.

'Yeah,' she said. 'We might work together.'

Robert, thought Claire. Poor lamb to the slaughter.

'I trust he's satisfactory in other respects?'

'Satisfactory,' said Maxine. 'Yeah I guess he is. Julius bought one of my paintings. *Motorway*. For his restaurant. '

'Can't he take any at the Portia?'

'Have you seen the stuff he stocks? It's all watercolours. I can't do that.'

'Can't or won't?'

'Just don't,' said Maxine, 'just don't.'

Claire raised her eyebrows.

God this food's bland, Maxine thought, showering it in soy sauce and stirring it in. Claire looked at the gesture, but not at Maxine.

'So who's coming to this exhibition?'

'Everyone, you know,' said Maxine. 'Dealers, some press maybe, Deanna said she'd come.'

'Have you *seen* Deanna?'

'Not lately.'

'I did. Last week,' said Claire. 'We compared favourite painters. She likes Monet.'

Maxine smacked her tobacco tin down and made herself a roll up. 'Colour gets a bit sickly on them at times. You know they'd be nice colours to do your bathroom in or something. Some of the landscapes I like. *Gare St. Lazare*'s the best. I suppose there's something in all that atmospherics. I wouldn't have thought it was Deanna's type of thing.'

Claire threw her head back and went 'hah'! Maxine jerked. What was wrong with her?

'I'd prefer Rodchenko, given half a choice.'

'Lychees?' said Claire.

'Lychees would be nice.'

Claire ordered them. 'They're curious aren't they?'

'Yes,' said Maxine, 'like the tips of pricks, except sweet instead of salt.'

'You think?' said Claire. 'I think they're really more like a woman.'

Maxine froze, and watched Claire, who said it again, the words accompanied by glittering eyes.

'I think,' said Maxine, crunching a lychee on her back teeth, 'they're more like the tips of pricks.'

Claire shrugged.

'Deanna and I had dinner at *Les Quatre Chats*.'

'Never heard of that,' said Maxine, quietly.

'It was really rather wonderful. Anthony was away. I stayed, you know, with Deanna. I somehow always knew…'

Claire cracked the final lychee open, then broke into a wistful smile, knocking back the juice from the shell, savouring it, and wiping her hands and mouth.

'Shall we get the bill?'

'Yeah,' said Maxine. The world had gone mad and she'd been left out. She reached for her purse.

'No. No. I'll get it…' said Claire.

'No,' said Maxine.

She picked up the bill, laid it down again and handed Claire a couple of coins and two scuffed £5 notes. Claire smoothed their wrinkles down with the edge of her hand, and gave them back to her.

'So?' said Claire. 'Where is it again. Your exhibition?'

'The Espina. It's…'

'Oh I think I know. Do they have a tube out there?'

'Yes. Tube, then ten minutes walk.'

'Oh I'll take the car. It'll just take hours otherwise.'

The receipt arrived.

'And we'd better leave a tip too hadn't we?' Claire opened her plain leather wallet.

Maxine plopped her coins onto the plate, trying to forget that the waiters here probably earned more than she did.

'Fine!' said Claire. She smiled with her lips but not her eyes. 'You're alright are you?'

'Yeah,' said Maxine. 'I'm fine. Thriving.'

They kissed each other on both cheeks.

Early evening Claire went to *Claudine et Paulette Vont En Bicyclette*. It had no plot and very little happened, so Claire could let it wash over her as she considered herself. The film wasn't good, but the tableaux were pretty. A book of photographs culled from special moments in French films was still a pet project she hoped to launch. Memories of Deanna swum in her thoughts. She felt exquisitely poised, just waiting.

14

It was raining - warm summer rain - but Maxine walked to the furthest tube. She wished it would rain more so it would fit her mood. Her canvas shoes were soaking wet and her hair extensions were dampening and beginning to smell of wet dog from the rain. She might chop them off later. They weren't a good idea. They already itched.

She went through the shop, avoiding Syd's gaze because he was sober for a change and she owed him back rent. The truant boys downstairs were sniggering over the comics and he was watching them, expecting theft.

'You make up your mind if you want 'em or not. This isn't a bloody library,' he snarled, pulling his beard. 'I haven't got all day…' Except he had, of course.

Upstairs, Lydia's clothes hung over the bath. Clothes took so long to dry in this place that by the time they'd dried they barely looked as if they had been done, and felt like cardboard.

Maxine sat in front of the canvas that looked good when she went out, but now she was back with it, didn't make much sense. It looked like she'd barely started. It looked dead. She squinted at the canvas and some shapes crawled out of it, but she didn't dare touch it.

She picked up her sketchbook with the preliminary drawings and tried to get a hold of what she first intended. She picked up a crayon to try something out on paper, then tried to see if she could do something fluffy and soft with the crayon, just to see if she could do it - and then thought, what are you doing, stupid?

Her head was still jammed with clutter from the lunch. And what was Deanna thinking of? Throwing over the Spanish one for a wispy thing like Claire? What was Claire going to do? Salary them all? She flung open the window and looked down on the street, at the pathetic little supermarket that stocked nothing edible, at people half limp with exhaustion at the bus stop. She shivered and wrapped her arms around herself. It was either too hot or too damp, here.

It was through Claire that Maxine had met Julius and got one day a week at his gallery, just sitting there. It was okay. In quiet times she could do her sketches, and have her own thoughts, uninterrupted. It was £40 cash. It was an expensive environment, in Kensington, and something about even being there tickled her. She had bagels for lunch, and the dash of metropolitan expense pleased her. She wrapped up paintings she couldn't stand, and smiled quite happily at the punters. They bought jolly scenes of very jolly crocks and tablecloths, washed out maidens in broderie anglaise staring wistfully out of windows, country scenes as comforting as a good shag-pile, royal occasions penned with a jocular angularity, and yachts. So what?

Her paintings, Maxine always thought, weren't made to be hung on the walls of a living room. If this is what people liked for that, she didn't have too much argument with it. But seeing Claire made her loathe the paintings and her function there all over again.

There was loathing for the Anthonys with their wavering eyelids, who couldn't stand a whiff of a woman unless they were jolly nice, like the woman who did their washing at school, or a pleasant niece of an old friend who could be tickled under the chin. She held Claire almost entirely responsible for this state of affairs.

Julius, Claire's friend, was different. He had a smile full of sunshine and wine and mischief, and held his gold fountain pen over the business triple decker cheque book, and circled it and settled it down, making it £500. *Motorway* for his restaurant, to show he knew the difference, or at least appreciated the effort.

She'd made mistakes and she'd wasted time. Five years doing group shows that were supposed to show someone something, but which ran at a loss, and were attended by only the most pale iconoclasts. *Fuck Art*. Except no one really felt like that, not about their own stuff. 'We are defined by what we're not.' That was too rigid too. Endless meetings, where everyone slagged everyone else off, and pretended it was all about issues. *Pandemonium I: Exercises in Organised Chaos*. That had been an especially tough one. Where were they now - old associates? Sitting in warehouses, clutching crystals and trying to make their minds go blank. Thinking of concepts, executing them, then spending the next two weeks meditating.

There was work from that period that she'd enjoyed at the time. *Love's Just A Urinary Tract Infection* - a sculpture. But she'd felt cagey about it ever since complaining about anything sexual having gone out of fashion. The only thing that mattered now was getting the work done, and selling it. She had a few hours left that week, before she got back to doing work that paid upfront.

She began to remember what she originally intended, and picked up a stick of charcoal, carefully. Yet Lydia had just come in and was practising scales, and every time she hit a flat, Maxine's arm jerked. She put the charcoal down and leaned back in the chair. Hell, truly, was other people.

She got out the box with her found objects in it and slapped the fur scraps, frosted fingernails and toe nail clippings onto her table. She wound the fur round her hands and then flattened the pieces out, and let them settle into their natural curves. She varnished the underside so the curves would be set, then laid out the nails and started painting them blood red, the false nails, and the real thing.

Something was happening.

She jammed the nails into the fur, so the fur bushed up in shock. She arranged the false nails, very carefully, so they looked like those of a long hand, in the centre. The other real nail scraps would be scattered around the circumference, once she'd sewn the fur scraps together. She was pleased with the centrepiece, as she pressed the final thumbnail in, and the fur stuck out.

She returned to the canvas, remembering now. She was

back with it. Lydia was singing in phrases. Maxine felt at home, she felt alright again, she wondered why she ever cared what anyone else thought. She'd come home, and home wasn't a scruffy flat, but a place of privacy and acceptance where she produced something she could be proud of. She didn't need her sketchbooks any more. She mixed up the paints, midnight blues, which were her favourite colours at the moment. She smeared the paint over the canvas with her fingers, shaping it, and having no hesitation in front of the barely covered space. She felt her concentration thicken inside and explode into live material, connecting her with other impulses and taking her places she thought she'd never go, with nothing so self-defeating as a slow plod through an idea. If it didn't exist in life, you only had to create it.

She'd said that to Robert the other night.

There was a new exuberance in the movements of her arms, her hands and back, and every part of her that painted. The prospect of her exhibition helped, having Claire to kick against spurred her on, and it was something to do with Robert. She remembered their evenings together, whispering and giggling, and finding restaurants with alcoves or long tablecloths so they could feel each other up while they were eating.

In post coital twilight dazes, she lay in Robert's arms, and rubbed herself against him in the night, like a bear scratching itself against a tree. And the pictures glowed so vividly, and were there when she woke up. She didn't need to pause and think now. It was all there.

Around teatime, once Lydia had gone to work, some idiot

hillbilly music that Syd liked to play drifted up and it made her smile. His grey cat - Cyril - sat on the table watching her, and for once she didn't shoo him out. By the middle of the evening she was starving. All she'd got at home was a vat of potato soup whipped up two days ago on an economy drive. She'd fudged the recipe by improvising too freely. It was too thick, like paste, and while she'd been eating it stoically for the last couple of days, tonight she deserved decent food. She'd go to the *Macro* and have the leftovers. She phoned Robert to tell him where she'd be. She passed the bathroom mirror on her way out and pulled at the hair extensions and decided she liked them just the way they were.

Robert had just trimmed the commissioned building to the spare specifications permitted by the reduced budget. It was now the kind of building that no one would notice or care about, even if they used it. He was doing a lunchtime meeting in a restaurant, dressed for the occasion, opening out the plans before the clients: is that okay, is that alright, his expression and workmanlike leather jacket begged of them. Their plump cheeks inflated with interest. He took them through the revised details, hiking up his engineering skills, being quite expressive with his wrists and fingers in a restrained sort of way. They didn't want an artist, not on this one - such terrible reputations.

His eyes lit on Maxine's *Motorway* painting in the corner. It was what he'd got from what she'd shown him at home, but ten times stronger. The restaurant was designed like the inside of a spin drier, but it was kind to paintings, showing them off. A slick, varnished grey with murky blurs of yellow light, *Motorway* was painted with juggernaut energy and brushstrokes. Tyre marks and pieces of metal were worked into its thick surface. It was a surprisingly forceful picture to be found here, and he was obscurely proud of her for pulling it off. He could still feel her burnished hair in his mouth and her arms wrapped round his neck and her breasts in his face.

And it didn't disappoint him now that he was paid for his capacity to have ideas at work, though not to execute them. This was just a job. He'd set his sights on other things. Projects of his own, maybe.

Going back to Maxine's late at night, he'd kiss her under her ear and slip his hand around her waist. At least she produced something every day. Something on canvas that she talked through in words he hadn't used for years, but recognised. Bizarre and ordinary objects transformed into something with different dimensions that surprised him.

They went to galleries and she got something out of Wendy Chapman or Bruegel that was immediate and not analytical. They were usually through in an hour, departing with a few ideas, and sometimes a handful of postcards. These were things to be used, not admired in passivity. He'd revered art for too long, having thought it was nothing to do with him.

The clients were finished with the plans. He took one last look at *Motorway*. He liked the fact that Maxine lived in a rough part of town and had connections in Kensington. It made her seem like she'd made deliberate choices.

His senior partners were in the Dordogne for a month, so he could make some time for himself in the afternoon. He stopped off at a building site to confer with a foreman. He barely needed to be there; the foreman had overseen so many buildings like this before. Robert checked the schedules and ticked them off, pretending to concentrate. Outside the site, a mural was painted on the hoarding, hoping to arouse public interest. New employees were depicted alongside the builders, their gaping smiles hewn in some old school Weimar style, lately debased, with all the fine tone and love of humanity of a seaside postcard with the humour and smut extracted.

He went to the riverside over a bridge, dodging past a pink bus blushingly advertising Thai holidays, and a lemon and maroon Kentish bus trundling off in the direction of the City. Flatpack buildings were peppered about. Sneeze too hard and they'd all fall down. Staccato rhythms, but no melody, no songs. Like a giant toytown. It was awesome.

He saw the Canary Wharf tower at a distance, the blue light ticking at the top. That at least said something, it made some kind of statement, for better or worse. A high tech blue glass edifice had steps down the side, fit for King Kong to walk up. It stood next to a slender Wild West building, with arcades with 'To Let' worked neatly into their surfaces. In the background was a lonely square building, a relic of a more severe age: made of concrete, with slit-eyed windows, it was redolent of paper clips, box files and jobs that an uncle might have put up with, but you never wanted. There was some sense in this. A Welfare building - a place to get away from, like you needed parents who didn't understand you.

He went to a place he'd been involved in - a shopping

emporium. The concept was based on the Albert Hall, originally. The Guggenheim museum had also been mentioned. It didn't look like that now it was finished. Chocolate brown curved walls held a great glass dome rising above garage-sized shops in a perfect curve, that no one visited. Some of them had closed. Stalls were scattered around, selling Victorian potatoes, Mexican crafts, Bonsard bags and sweets in baskets. But no one was buying anything.

The British, at heart, were more Mediterranean in their outlook than most of their holiday fantasies. The sun came out in London and suddenly everyone was in a good mood, getting their kit off. They spilled onto outside tables at bars and coffee shops at the first opportunity. Their devotion to outside street markets - in all weathers - bordered on the devout. So they built them this. An empty and foreboding echo chamber. No wonder no one visited. He was glad he wasn't personally liable for this. He'd done the dome. The dome was good, except it was completely out of place. He didn't know why he wasn't building himself when so many clueless people were involved in it.

He sat at an ornate brown table in a deserted café, drinking a watery cup of cappuccino and planning his next day's work. He wanted to do something else.

He visited his company's Georgian housing development. He had been asked to check it out. It looked like a model, so clean and unused. The air inside felt like it had been especially doctored. And while the development was built in Georgian style, its dimensions were minuscule.

He introduced himself to an estate agent, who was sitting

in one of the lounges with a bored expression. He sat behind a pinched desk in a tight suit with a huge stack of untouched, glossy brochures. The estate agent sniffed discreetly, every gesture bitten off and held in self defence, except it was all for nothing, as no one wanted to see the show flat.

Robert spent two hours checking the ventilating system. It passed, just. He was bored senseless.

Back at the office, he went through the correspondence and saw that the plans for Falklands House had been changed to Dunkirk House. The budget had shrunk. Same old story. There was a message from Maxine.

Maxine went down the mossy steps by the river and arrived at the *Macro* late. Its shy location was designed to make visitors feel they had embarked on an adventure. It was run in a way that made some feel like it was a home from home. Others were struck by the curiously intimate house style of the *Macro*'s staff.

It was full, and the bustle, and the cool sea-shell smells of it, and the trance music lifted and comforted Maxine's spirits. It felt like her place, still, with her loud and rancorous paintings on the walls. She watched the customers looking at her paintings, and smiled a secret smile to herself. Robert was there and Marcus, dressed from head to foot in white, was already showing him the scrapbook where he kept magazine cuttings and pictures as inspiration for food. They'd used it when discussing new designs, Marcus always liked to show people that.

He'd already given Robert a series of dishes as samplers, in smoky blue saucers. They were trying to do something different, at least they were trying.

'If someone wants to come in and just have a bowl of soup, that's okay.' Marcus' emphatic tones drifted over from the table. 'If they want the full works, that's okay too. If I don't like the look of them, I don't encourage them back. You get a sense off people, you know whether they're alright or not.'

Robert smiled, having been declared alright, having to deal with the un-alright much of the time. He flipped through the scrapbook. The pictures were the kind of things he liked. Maxine headed for the kitchen, filling up a regular Japanese couple's glasses on the way, with the bottle at the table.

'Thank you…' they said.

She fetched them another bottle, slipping them a flyer for her exhibition, then she went into the kitchen.

Janet, Marcus' wife, knew a lot about life, and her permanently wan expression testified to it. She stood by the cooker, tossing over vegetables in a wok. She was counting down the seconds.

She banged the wok down, gave it a final shake, lifted out a courgette with a fork and bit it delicately.

'Ung,' she said. 'This look alright?'

'Alright,' said Maxine.

'What have you got in mind here?' She gestured with the fork to Marcus and Robert.

'Marcus could get him to do the new building.'

'He's into that is he?'

'Yeah.'

They served up the food and sat at Marcus' table.

'A lot of people,' Marcus enthused, 'especially round here, have the idea that if you eat out or try anything different then it's going to be expensive and everyone'll be nasty to you. Not here. We have various schemes - three courses really cheap - Free Food for the Kiddies. Well that's alright 'cause kids don't eat much - just push it around the plate and chuck it about... There's a lot wrong,' he continued, 'there's a lot wrong. Like how many times do they need to remix that *Rhythm Is A Dancer* song? How many versions of *Don't Go Breaking My Heart* do you really need? Call me a traditionalist, but I preferred Kiki Dee on that one.'

'Yeah,' said Robert.

'I mean,' Marcus gazed at the ceiling, 'Björk! Yeah - why not? Why does everything have to be like everything else? And why does everyone like David Bartlett films for Chrissakes? He's not one of your faves is he?'

'No,' said Robert, 'except *Rodiregious*.'

'Yeah that was alright,' said Marcus, 'the fights were good.'

'Marcus...' said Janet.

'Yes. *What?*'

'You were going to do the sauces for tomorrow...'

Marcus looked up, feigning startlement. 'Oh this is business, dear, new building.'

'The parsnip fritters don't work either.'

'What do you mean don't work?'

'They don't stick together.'

'I shredded them correctly this morning Janet.'

'New building, right,' Janet looked at Robert and folded her arms. 'It's nice for him to have a friend. I'll get on with the sauces then shall I?'

'If you could make a start lovey...'

'Cos it's funny - I thought we'd agreed I knock off early tonight...'

She went back into the kitchen, tugging her fair hair back into place, collecting some plates on the way. She didn't bother to rearrange her face to look friendly. Robert kind of admired her for that.

'Can't believe it,' said Marcus, more to himself.

'So,' he said to Maxine, 'we've discussed your designs, haven't we?'

'Yeah,' said Robert.

'Oh good,' said Maxine.

'And you know it's as well to remember, we're not too puritanical here. Like we're not strictly macrobiotic are we, Maxine?'

'No,' said Maxine. 'Well basically no one would eat it.'

'And there's no point having a restaurant with food no one wants to eat,' said Marcus, 'that's just wasting it. Got to go easy on bulgar wheat.' He pulled a chewy face. 'And remember that fiasco with the spinach juice?'

'No one ever finished a glass,' said Maxine, 'not once.'

'No, not too puritanical,' said Marcus. 'I mean, if you want to stuff chocolates and watch porn videos all the time I'd say go ahead, it'll only come out some other way,' he added, ominously. 'It's newish, but not faddish. It's just something we've made up for them, out of *love*. That's not to say we always get it right, but people want something that looks as if it means it. Something sincere. That's us.'

Maxine got up to join Lydia at the counter. She was pulling apart mint leaves and laying them on the desserts.

'Alright?' said Maxine.

'Rehearsals went okay. The new guitarist's got a thing about colostomy bag jokes. Did an advert yesterday. She sang *'Don't forget your Bassett's lozenges!'* It didn't even rhyme. It makes the Mealies one look positively intellectual in an Edith Sitwellish sort of way. The hot water tank's burst…'

She looked at Maxine.

'Syd's been shot, Riccardo was run over, Janet's leg fell off lunchtime.'

'Uhuh,' Maxine said, watching Robert and thinking how much she liked the way he scribbled drawings on serviettes.

'Nature calls, I see,' said Lydia, tossing mint sticks in the bin.

Marcus stood and surveyed his place, pride glowing behind his eyes. He manoeuvred round the tables, trusting everything was alright with every customer. He walked past Lydia.

'About time,' he said.

'Up yours,' she replied.

'You shouldn't stand there,' Marcus said to Maxine. 'You aren't wearing a black T-shirt.'

Maxine took two dessert plates of strawberries covered with peppermint cream over to Robert's table. He showed her his scribbled drawings. A real round building, with a tree in the middle. No 90 degree angles. He was going to do it - get it right this time.

'With models,' he said, 'not the computer.'

'Sounds alright,' she said, and slipped her spare hand between his legs. They'd go to his place tonight. Lydia could deal with the hot water tank. She didn't have the time.

The peppermint was so harsh, it caught in their throats.

'Well?' said Marcus.

'That's enough of that,' said Maxine, wincing and putting her spoon down. 'It's really upsetting me. Ruins the fruit.'

Marcus picked the plates up. 'Still, you've got to try things out, haven't you?'

'Right,' Robert said.

Later, at Robert's place, he and Maxine watched a video by a Japanese director with scenes of atrocious violence. Suddenly the world didn't seem like such a bad place. Robert's toes curled and unfurled and he stretched back his arms and Maxine crawled all over him. Mmm, she thought, he tasted so good. He watched the film, not really taking much notice, thinking of his old notebooks which he rifled through and could draw treasure out of, which could be used, now. Flesh and blood was coming back. The body and the spirit were coming back, Marcus said. Maxine and the gallery man, Tim, talked about this too. All the time he was hardening under the material against her cheek.

'I love you,' he said.

She ran her tongue over his nipples, into the saltiness in his groin. I love you, I love you, I love you, she thought, gulping his hardening prick in her mouth, gobbling as it thickened and he splashed her face and throat.

15

Jonathan watched his screen, gripping and massaging the panels on his desk. He shut his eyes as if in prayer - oh c'mon you bitch. A cigarette shook between his lips. Do it for me. The columns started moving. Aw fuck, fuck, fuck, he thought. His pelvis tensed and stirred. He fingered his belt. Then there was an answer. A cheer shot up in his chest and a shudder went through him. That was it, that was it. Better than expected. Rely on the instincts. Always worked. He ground his cigarette out, gritted his teeth, smiled, screwed up a piece of paper, aimed it at Charles, gave him the finger and kicked his chair. It was the only way to end a week. Charles looked back at him, puzzled. It didn't look so good from where he was sitting.

At home, Jonathan's car was in its parking space, as normal, except 'SCUM' was spray painted on it. He wasn't surprised. Patti's cousins had called around recently.

'Let us in,' they demanded, in not very well disguised voices.

'Fuck off and die,' Jonathan had said.

The caretaker of the block spotted him, came out and

shook his head. 'Didn't see a thing,' he said.

'Local yobs,' said Jonathan. 'It's either one thing or another, isn't it, round here? I'll get it fixed.'

He got into the car, and turned on the ignition. The car heated up like an aircraft, he could feel the suspension. He played with the switches. They seemed adequate. Inside it still smelled faintly of sick, despite his most strenuous efforts with the car vacuum and a bucket full of washing up liquid. He got out of the car. The concealed headlights stood up stubbornly, while the windows failed to slide down. He supposed Patti's cousins had done something to it. He drove it steadily to a garage, and left it there. His orphan, his most prized possession. See you soon, he whispered.

He sat on a table by the window in his flat, wafted onto the blissed-out plane where no one and nothing could reach him. There was a click in the lock, Patti came in and marched up to him.

'We've got to talk.'

Not now, he thought. Oh not now.

'What the fuck did you think you were doing?'

'Mmm?' His eyes lulled.

'With Karina? My cousin?'

Oh not now, not now, he thought. She was looking at a lamp, and pulled it out of its socket. Oh don't do that, he thought. The lamp whizzed past his head and smashed on the wall behind him. Don't smash my furniture, he thought.

'Karina. What did you do with Karina?'

Oh that was her name, he thought. He couldn't remember. It was nothing. Just a bad night. Best to forget it. He'd forgotten it now.

Patti was smoking very hard, and striding up and down.

'What did you do? Why did you do it? Why? Tell me.'

He didn't answer.

'Or didn't you?' she added, hopefully.

She had mixed feelings about Karina's accusations. Her cousin couldn't give a coherent account of what had happened, except it had been 'very scary'. Suki had seized the moment - 'Oh Patti, he's a complete psycho, really' - which made Jonathan sound more interesting than he actually was. There was no physical evidence that Jonathan had attacked her. And in any case, Karina was talking about the man Patti was shagging. A gnawing thought in the back of her head said Karina was lying.

'Tell me what you did.'

Jonathan shut his eyes again. 'I wanted...' he said, 'I wanted her to feel like I feel sometimes...'

'Feel *what*?' Patti yelled. 'You don't *feel* anything.'

He opened his eyes and her face was pulled into the most drastic of expressions.

'Do you?'

She looked like some old crone with unaccountably silky blonde hair. He laughed, quietly to himself. She belted him round the head. He hardly felt it. Patti looked at him, just sitting there. She was pissed off and confused, all round. She cast one last distressed look at the smashed lamp. Two doors slammed and she was gone. Good, Jonathan thought. Good riddance.

'I didn't do anything,' said Jonathan, to the empty room. 'I didn't do anything at all…'

Strange portents, though. Strange. He wondered if he was being followed, or watched. His sense of it had grown. The silence was so tense the crackle bit his ears. He wondered if, at work, they were waiting for him to make the big mistake. A man that passed him in the hall that day looked like a man he'd seen somewhere else. Someone was out to get him, and it wasn't Patti's cousins. Not only them.

He went to a drawer and got out a gun he'd obtained from Buzz Snag - he really wondered, wondered a lot, if that was his real name sometimes. At the time the gun had seemed like another wondrous perk to his astonishing newfound power and mobility. Now it seemed like a ridiculous acquisition. He didn't want to throw it out though. He ran his hand over the cold steel, knocked out the carriage. There were two bullets left, real ones, death pellets. He held the gun against his face, and looked at one of his clocks. Three pyramids, piled on top of each other, turned in contra-motion, slowly. The time was told by looking at the numbers lined up on the side with a faint charcoal mark. It always took five seconds, at least, for him to work it out. It irritated him. He pointed the gun at the clock, squinting. This was silly. This was wasting time. He put the gun away, put his jacket on, and went out, careful not to turn his back on anything.

He rode two stops on the train, looking at the bare, brick flats outside surrounded by rubble, and spare trees that looked as if they had just been planted, with wire cages wrapped around them.

He got out at a wasteland. He had to keep referring to his map to remember the streets. He couldn't recall any of the landmarks. They looked just the same as everywhere else around here. He was drawn by clanking sounds of life, and found the street. It had the right name on it. The metallic intestines of cars laid agape, and there was a man, in blue overalls, leaning over one of them.

The man turned around.

'Sylph Speedbird,' said Jonathan, 'if it's ready.'

'Ah yes,' said the man, wiping his hands. 'We've done the re-spray.' His voice sounded incredibly loud. He gave Jonathan a full explanation of what had been done, but every other word ended in 'ator' or 'ation', and Jonathan couldn't keep track. He didn't know these words.

'There's been a lot of trouble with the Speedbird,' said the man. He looked at Jonathan, for a response, and got none. 'Talk of taking them off the market. Computers can't handle the input. Clutch is alabaster. Very weak for town driving…'

'Oh yes,' said Jonathan.

'They're changing them on the new model.'

'As an improvement,' said Jonathan, 'on the general roadworthiness?'

'And to stop the mechanics getting lung cancer,' the man added.

He drove the car away. It drove stiffly. He could still smell the vomit. He stopped off at a petrol station and bought some lavender car deodorant, and a couple of car magazines. The deodorant's smell was only slightly less foul than the one it had been brought in to overpower. He coughed.

The light on his ansafone was still when he returned. The flat had an odd chill about it. Things had been left as they were when he went out. He could die in this place and no one would know. He wrapped up the remains of his smashed lamp in a newspaper, and swept up the smaller remains with a dustpan and brush. He was stuck with hung boredom. He looked around the flat. Its objects were self sufficient and standoffish. They offered him no means of amusement. Except perhaps *Abwegige Leidenshaft*, on the bookshelf.

He looked at it on the floor, on all fours. He looked at it on the sofa, sitting upright. He sat at his table, slightly bent over, and looked at it. He stood it on the table. It fell down. He held it and ran his fingers over the pictures, but his wrist began to ache with holding it in one hand. He couldn't read it. He couldn't look at it. He wondered who had designed such a useless object.

He wondered what to do. His colleagues often went away for the weekend. He could maybe visit home. He owed them a visit. A scenic drive, food, his old room. He called his mother and she answered on the third ring.

'Coming down okay?'

'Whatever you like, dear,' she said.

'Fine.'

'What time will you be arriving?'

'Mid afternoon,' he said. He hung up.

He drove at a leisurely pace, in case something else was wrong with the car. There was little traffic once he got on the A roads. He was charmed by the sight of a donkey in a field. The countryside: just what he needed.

He stopped off at a pub halfway. It was surrounded by stony gravel. Three thick-framed men in work clothes stood at the bar, talking to the barmaid, who looked like a squirrel.

He asked for a water. All they had was tonic. A wearied murmur seemed to pass around the men. Jonathan sat at a small table by the window. The men kept casting glances at him. He wished he had a bunch of flowers to make the purpose of his journey obvious. The tonic tasted like tin, but he sipped it until it was finished. He wished he was wearing more inconspicuous clothes, but he didn't have any. His legs didn't quite fit under the table.

Back in the car he searched for a tape. He was finding the silence deafening. His Dusty Springfield was missing, and he had a yen for her doing *Stay Awhile* or *24 Hours from Tulsa*. Dusty Springfield was the only one he liked. The bastard at the garage must've stolen it. He didn't look the type. He hoped he bloody well enjoyed it.

The roads were slow and cluttered with vehicles with less power than his. He fumed and depression overwhelmed him. Its movement was slow but irrevocable. Fields looked pointless, and there was nothing now but closed mock Tudor pubs and boorish warehouses, and superstores like grotesque, enlarged Wendy houses.

He pulled in at the first town and followed signs directing him to a 1,000 capacity car park. Nearly everyone had gone home. He parked and went into the shopping centre.

It rose to three tiers, all thickly arcaded, with long glass corridors with fountains at the end with amplified splashes resonating. There were the same chains of stores found everywhere else, and Jonathan felt comforted. He spotted a suburban branch of a central department store, and went in, relieved at the wealth on display.

He bought his mother the most expensive bottle of perfume, with the least sexy packaging. He searched for something for his father, but it was all too particular and unlikely. A bell went off and a smiley woman's voice announced the closure of the centre. She issued a reminder about Wednesday's late shopping, and next Saturday's fashion show on the theme of Gentry Clothing. Jonathan picked around and eventually settled on a Handi-sized pocket radio for dad.

The water from the fountains hushed around him and he twirled a rack of postcards. A mirror caught him, his reflection distorted. He bought Marilyn Monroe in tulle. Passers-by stared at him, sitting alone by the fountain. He wondered if they saw the distortions too. He buried his head over the postcard, shielding the top of his head with his palm.

> *Dear Daniel,*
> *Just enjoying a quiet weekend away from it all.*
> *Hope to see you soon.*
> *Love Jonathan.*

He got out the car magazines and stared at their print. There was no information about how anything worked, just tabulated details about assorted models. It was assumed everyone already knew the rest. He left the magazines on a table, looked in the mirror, and turned away from its glare.

He posted the card in a slit in the wall, painted yellow. Presumably, it was real, and the postcard would get there.

Since receiving their son's unexpected phone call, Jonathan's parents had been making preparations.

His mother had changed the bedclothes in his room, substituting new sheets and a guest bedspread. She had washed the good glasses, cleaned the bathroom, tidied the living room and cooked some food.

Jonathan's father had mowed the lawn.

There was some uncertainty about the evening. Jonathan's father thought they should eat in. His mother thought they ought to eat out. She wasn't sure what he liked, these days, she said. A restaurant would be best. They didn't know what had brought him down so suddenly. He rarely returned their phone calls. Jonathan's father said it might be some upset with a girl. Jonathan's mother doubted this.

Jonathan arrived and the house looked smaller, and they seemed older and more frail. It made him feel vulnerable. He could see his father had been persuaded into his best trousers.

They gave him some tea, and he produced his presents. They said he shouldn't have spent so much money. He told them about his car, and they told him about his cousin's new baby. He told them how much money he'd earned recently - *Want any of it?* he wanted to shout - and they told him about a recent coach trip to an Abbey. He wasn't sure why he'd come down, now. He went into his old bedroom, where his absence was replaced by a large soft toy on the furry bedspread. The selection of his old schoolbooks in the bookcase recalled bleaker times: *New Maths IV*, *French Revision II*, *1984*, *Cider with Rosie*. Times when he was resigned to a local job, and normality.

He went over to the bookcase to study them closer, then came across a pile of old magazines, neatly stacked, blatant to the view, that he'd bought secretly in his teens, by post.

He flicked through them, totally shamed. His mother knew then; he thought he'd thrown them out. He looked through the grainy black and white prints of nude adolescent boys, and stories of startling crudeness, related with gusto. He bought them to make some sense of everything. Now, they stared back at him, and accused.

He held his steering wheel and shook. His mother sniffed in the car and said what was the air freshener - was it lavender or what, it was very strong.

'Someone was sick in here the other week,' he said.

'Was she ill?'

'Ill, drunk,' he said. His voice cracked. He was driving thirty thousand quid's worth of car, and felt about six.

'It's a very overpowering smell,' said his mother.

'Very sharp,' added his father.

'They do a nice Fern,' continued his mother. 'Did you *choose* the lavender?'

'Yes I *did*,' said Jonathan.

'It's a bit strong,' said his father.

'I don't mind it,' said Jonathan.

His mother asked if they could open a window. Jonathan

pressed the button to roll the lot down, in panic.

'Oh watch that,' said his mother, 'you'll give your father a nasty shock!'

They arrived at a restaurant that Jonathan could tell was a wild guess at what he might like. He squirmed at his mother thanking the waiters for the slightest attention, and his father asking them to explain the contents and likely outcome of each dish, one by one. No one minded. The rules had changed, and he didn't know what they were any more. Jonathan was the odd one out.

His mother enquired about the girl who had been sick in the car. Was it the redhead they met, once?

'No, that's Maxine,' he said. 'She's a painter. Patti,' he added, simplifying matters, 'is…my girlfriend. Her dad works at Sotheby's.'

His mother looked out of the window.

'Is she doing well, Maxine?' said his dad.

'Not especially,' said Jonathan, 'but she's got an exhibition.'

'She needs a gimmick,' his dad declared. 'There was that one who had the fish in the tank. I paint a bit myself,' he continued, 'painted the hall!'

His mother nodded and laughed. Jonathan suddenly felt oddly protective, of himself, of Maxine. She was the only person at the time - at any time - he thought he might trust with his parents.

He offered to pay at the end, but they refused. He insisted and produced a credit card. His father said he should watch it with those - 'neither a borrower nor a lender be'. His mother said his suit seemed an expensive one, for weekends.

"Hyes,' said Jonathan. 'It is in a way, yes.'

He had trouble sleeping that night. The bed at his flat was more comfortable. On Sunday morning he stacked the magazines in his car boot before they got up. His mother produced lunch.

It was homemade quiche and coleslaw. A bit bland, Jonathan thought, abruptly. It could do with a bit of pepper. He told his mother this.

'We've got pepper!'

His father produced a cruet.

'Pepper's black,' said Jonathan. 'Proper pepper.'

He returned on the motorway, blank and quietly startled. He had known for a long time that he wasn't interested in their lives, he couldn't believe they were equally indifferent to his, and that they distrusted him as much as he once distrusted them. Home was not sweet. Home didn't exist.

He pulled off into a service area - a bright white Palazzo on tarmac, and thought immediately of Claire - Claire was really more of a mother to him. He looked around the Palazzo. He supposed the establishment was mocking the old palaces, the real Palazzos, a notion which affronted and delighted him.

He went to the shop. It was a newsagents, mainly, stocking Top Twenty tapes and CDs, maps, and a selection of soft porn. A girl eating a wafer biscuit in a maroon cap looked at him drearily.

'Henry VIII Banqueting Hall's on your right, Brancuzi Café straight ahead,' she said.

There was very little food left on the café counters - a few ham and cheese rolls, perspiring from neglect, with small salads, wrapped in cellophane. There were meatballs and disgruntled looking carrots on hot plates, and a note about Stilton soup with croûtons chalked on a board. He had that. He sat by the window. It had started to drizzle.

The croûtons left spongy deposits on his teeth and the soup tasted of liquid porcelain with a hint of something else. But this was better, he thought. This was better. This was more like it. He felt more like his old self. His bit into his crusty granary roll and a grain as hard as a pebble chipped off a piece of tooth. He picked the bit from out of his mouth, and dropped it on the plate.

He returned to the shop, which had a new assistant. He found a Bach CD, and bought it.

He played it, back on the motorway, and a diamond grid of discernment shimmered over his head, reminding him of his current status. But they only gave you tastes of different bits and once he settled with one drift, it changed to something else. He pulled onto the hard shoulder, flicked his emergency lights on, and tugged the CD out of the machine.

'Can't you just settle?' he said.

He looked up at the blue signs that heralded a split in the motorway. Memories were charging up hard and fast. He could go straight back to London, or he could take a detour. He roared off from the hard shoulder, and took the Buckinghamshire road.

The Bach tape was back on and seemed to be snarling at him, then mocking him, then whispering under its breath, insidiously, blaming him. He thought he heard police sirens.

He thought he saw Charles streaming past him in the fast lane. He thought of his parents. He could have been warmer. But it's what they wanted. They wanted him to change. They didn't want him as he was either. He didn't belong, somehow.

He remembered coming up to town to see Uncle Anthony and Auntie Claire, as a boy, choosing presents he knew even then Auntie Claire would leave in a drawer, or give away, the same as his parents would leave or give away the presents he had just bought for them. Uncle Anthony had taken him to see Santa Claus at Christmas. 'Go with Uncle Anthony,' said his mother, smiling politely, reminding him about 'please' and 'thank you', and not scratching in public, or kicking his legs when he sat down. Jonathan would ask if Auntie Claire was coming. She didn't, not at all. She was rarely in the house and never there when Uncle Anthony took him to their cottage, which was a secret. Just their secret.

He preferred being with his mummy, yet visiting Uncle Anthony was a treat. 'You mustn't be shy dear...' They wanted him brought out of himself. Uncle Anthony was educated. They thought he was strange, their son, when he cried a lot. He cried a *lot*. And it was so comforting to get back to his mummy, put his arms around her neck, be held in the comforting smell of vanilla talcum powder, and her bun with its hairgrips nestling in it, and her air of always knowing best. There was one thing, though, she didn't know about Jonathan. Uncle Anthony had spotted the difference in him, and excavated it. He didn't want quiches and coleslaw at home, or Italian food he could have got in the supermarket. He wanted food like they used to have, food that would remind him of a time when he was innocent.

Uncle Anthony was the first person to buy him real Italian food, in a restaurant with wooden chairs and red darkness, and candles - even at lunchtime! And the waiters made a fuss of him, especially at Christmas, and helped him with his knives and forks, carefully indicating the ones to use, while Uncle Anthony looked away. He'd never had chicken with such a sharp tang to it.

They were different from his parents, Anthony and Claire. When he first visited their house he looked at it, and at Claire, with wonder and longing. Claire was taller and of a different shape to most of the women he'd met until then. Taller than teachers. She had kept her chin level with Anthony's, and only glanced at him occasionally.

He remembered wandering around their house one day, while everyone else was in the garden. It was huge. Uncle Anthony and Auntie Claire had lots of bedrooms, and bathrooms with baths with little feet on them. There were high ceilings. They ate cheese with blue veins in it, that tasted nice, they drank rich red liquids, ate big fat birds. He wanted some of this. He wanted some of this on his own terms.

In the house, that day, the curtains were closed on the biggest room, and a huge box of chocolates lay on the table, covered in faded green brocade, with a bow. He went over to look at them, maybe take a couple. He knocked them onto the floor, and they all spilled out. Claire came in. She was very light-footed, wearing a dress of blue fabric with flowers on it, and a straw hat. She wasn't cross, or anything. She picked up a couple of chocolates off the floor and put them in her mouth. He didn't know you were allowed to eat chocolates off the floor. He put one in his mouth too, slowly, watching her.

'What's that one?' she said.

'A caramel.'

She ate another one.

'Have another caramel…' She remembered what he'd just said. They didn't do that, at home.

'Take some home,' she whispered. 'We can't eat all of them here.' She got a lace handkerchief, tied its corners and made a little linen bag for him, a Dick Whittington bag. 'Our secret.' Which was maybe when he got the idea, first of all, that secrets were good things to have. Then she took his hand. 'Let's go and see what the others are doing.' Her hands were softer, much softer, than Anthony's, later.

'How old are you?' he asked.

'Twenty seven - ancient!'

'How old's Uncle Anthony?'

'Thirty eight - practically dead!'

It was nice, being treated like an adult. Claire and Anthony never described him as 'he', or discussed him as if he wasn't there. They talked directly to him. That was different. Yet he hadn't seen too much of Auntie Claire, after that.

The drizzle was hard now, and he was off the main road, twisting around narrow country lanes with his headlights on. Jonathan remembered this route by heart. He wasn't surprised. He arrived at the cottage. It was like a great big doll's house. He let himself in. He had his own keys. Anthony was so careless, so sure of his trust, that he never asked for them back.

It had hardly changed. There were comfortable chairs, wood in the grate in the fireplace, tiny diagonal windows, and on top of the fireplace the clock he had watched, so intently, hoping that his time with Anthony there would soon be up. And yet these shared secrets, there was something precious about them, so private. He wanted to destroy them.

He knocked the clock off the mantelpiece, and went into the kitchen. A pair of garden shears lay by the door. Such comforting, Home Counties shears. He picked them up, went back to the clock, and smashed it to smithereens. He raised the shears to strike elsewhere, but something inside stopped him. The loud tick of the clock had stopped. And what was there had nothing to do with it. He couldn't destroy anything else, because he was implicated. He double locked the door quietly behind him, and squeezed the keys tight in his hands. Maybe later, maybe later, he'd do more. But not yet.

He got lost on the way back, pursued by memories. The roads were wet and he skidded into a bank on the road. He stood on the pavement, arms and legs gripped tight, and looked ashen-faced at his skewered car, half heaped on the bank, wheels locked at right angles, its monitors flashing red and green blips, by the side of a terrace of houses where everyone seemed out or asleep. He climbed back into the car, grabbed the steering wheel, then massaged it with his palms and fingers. He buried his face in its frame, and bit his lips hard, so hard he cracked the skin.

'Ssh, ssh,' he said to himself, 'ssh.'

He wiped the blood away, the same colour of blood as he'd shed for Anthony. Two dull red smears dried on his hand. He dabbed his lip with his tongue, the blood was familiar and comforting.

A porch light lit and a family stumbled out of one of the houses opposite, and the mother and children climbed into the back seats of their Range Rover. The man moved to the boot, and put suitcases in. He stared at Jonathan's car, then stonily at Jonathan. He moved into the driver's seat, slammed the door, and they disappeared in a stately cloud of dust.

'Oww!' Jonathan uttered a small cry.

They had gone. Where were they going? On holiday? Jonathan had never gone on holiday as an adult. He couldn't think of anyone to go with.

He bit his nails. He pressed some buttons on his monitor. Nothing changed. The blips and the lights were making him twitch and shiver. He punched the buttons with his fists. The blips continued. He punched them again. Hot tears splashed his steering wheel, and he gripped it.

'You bastards' - it whistled through his teeth - 'you bastards - you fucking bastards, you ruined me.' His knuckles glowed white.

He punched the buttons again and everything cut dead. He could hear music and talk and plates and barbecue hisses, and Anthony's official voice, and private one, but the voices were all in his head.

'Ssh,' he said, 'ssh, ssh.'

He turned on the engine and it screeched and made him jump. He turned it off again, turned it on, and it hummed. It wasn't right, it was croaking, as if something was caught in the exhaust. A rat? A withered hand? Rags with petrol, to blow him up? Please, he thought. It was humming properly now.

He drove away, back into London, his eyes fixed and unblinking, occupying a space where everything was silent, a space filled with empty static, where he couldn't hear anything. He could only see, and only feel, what had happened in the past.

His first long trousers, Anthony's gnarled hands, and his sickly, crooked smile, and his words soothing him about their secrets being precious.

He arrived in London. This was better, London was better. The traffic lights, even, were like jewels here - ruby, amber, emerald - glistening with such promise of moneyed delights, and speed and being able to go anywhere, or do anything, to get your own back. It was worth it. He darted his head at the other traffic. A taxi panted amorously at his side. A bus crept out in front of him, its light ticking a courteous warning. And that was the worst thing, the longing and recoil, especially with Anthony. Even now the thing he hated was also something he loved. Whenever he required a quick and brutal orgasm, he knew whereabouts in his mind to go.

Look Jonathan… his mummy said. A London bus, a red London bus… And he and Uncle Anthony went to the store at Christmas, crunching their heels in the snow. Is Auntie

Claire coming this time? he said. She never did. Auntie Claire can't have children, said his mother. Poor Auntie Claire. Does Uncle Anthony love Auntie Claire? asked Jonathan. Well of course! said his mummy. Like daddy loves you? said Jonathan, insistent. Of course dear! Naturally! Is Auntie Claire Uncle Anthony's *wife*? Yes, said his mother, wearily this time. How many more times? she said. She told him not to keep on and on about it.

So he didn't.

He was confused with the roads now. He got muddled, and as he charged around a roundabout for the third time a monstrous roar escaped his lips. An Indian family overtook quickly and the man in the driving seat regarded him with alarm. Jonathan got off the roundabout, passed a sign for a place called Good Memories House, then laughed so much he cried. He blinked very fast, pulled over, breathed deeply, then drove off again.

He arrived home. He walked past the caretaker's window and peered in. He was sitting there with his young wife, and her two kids. They were all watching TV with trays on their laps. What was it, the food? Sausages? Mashed potatoes? Chops? He couldn't quite see, but his mouth watered. Definitely mashed potatoes. He would buy some potatoes one day and learn how to make mashed potatoes, with butter and pepper, thin brown pepper, like his mummy, his real mummy, used to make for him, to remind himself of what he'd once been like.

He went up to his flat. There was a card. He turned it over. It was from Maxine. Oh. But still…

Dear Jonathan
Please come to my exhibition.
It's Sunday fortnight.
Here's a map.
Love, Maxine x

He could go. He didn't know why she was being so nice at the moment. He hadn't been nice to her - it served her right. But he could go. Once, he'd seen Maxine as an escape, and it might be like that again. He remembered going to her place once, so long ago, to her grotty place that doubled as a studio. He'd met a girl there who looked like a ghost, and she said hullo and shut herself in her room and started wailing. That's what she did for a living. Just like he felt practically all the time. They were the only grown up people he'd met met who didn't act differently from how they felt.

And Maxine had given him an orange. He liked that. Sitting on the floor and eating an orange with her. It was sweet and juicy. He'd felt that such a scruffy place should have horrible things in it, but the orange was nice. The orange was good. Maxine had shown him her paintings, talked about them a bit, and didn't seem bothered about his game plans or what he did. And he felt such a coruscating envy for those two girls whose only demands of each other were that they be themselves, who didn't seem to worry what anyone else thought. He knew he could never be like that.

Then things got funny. They'd gone to an off licence to get drinks. They'd fixed some cocktails. Jonathan said Anthony had fixed him cocktails when he was younger.

'Cocktails?' said Maxine. '*Anthony? Cocktails?* Come off it!'

'And opium,' said Jonathan, 'when I was young, pretty young. No one at school did opium!'

He realised his bravado was shrill, here, and regretted saying anything. He didn't like the subject being brought up with her, now he'd said it. Maxine didn't want to know how the other half lived. Just wasn't interested. He didn't like the way she said '*Anthony*' like that, as if it didn't mean anything. She looked as if she didn't believe him, hadn't got it. A sly, hungry look, her red mouth shining and ugly. He wondered why so many girls, now, wanted to look like Myra Hindley. He remembered the times he'd thought Anthony might kill him. Then he remembered that Maxine was related to Claire, vaguely, and concluded that they were all in league against him. He hated himself for even thinking of trusting her, and realised now he could trust no one. If he'd told Daniel the whole truth, he'd thought, Daniel might have been jealous. Jonathan was sometimes jealous of himself, then and now. Anthony had told him he was among the chosen. They had a secret pact.

'Well we haven't got opium here,' Maxine had said, with a thin edge of contempt. And he realised that in his greed and longing, it had all been his fault. He said she was a stupid shit, and enjoyed leaving her startled there, still holding a pathetic cocktail shaker, with her cool affectations all limp and battered.

It was his first act of defiance. He thought he could do anything after that.

But then he saw Maxine again and nothing had been proved. She was so nasty about his job in the City, as if he was inadequate; as if he didn't know what to do with himself. He sent her his poem and she didn't get back to him. He supposed she was insulted, but he'd only wanted a response.

Tears sprung on his cheeks and he flicked them off, and looked at her postcard. There were no tricks in it, now. He traced the picture of the gaudy flowers, then her signature with his finger. He cried and cried and couldn't stop, crying for his past, and for his future. He picked up the phone, dialled Daniel's number, but couldn't speak after the bleep.

Later, Daniel came home from a long meeting with The PragMATiks, pressed the button for his messages and got the sound of a receiver being replaced defeatedly. He wondered, but then thought, no, don't even think about it. Jonathan was a lost cause.

16

Claire stood by her window at home and opened the personally addressed card, hurriedly. It was a Monet. Her heart leapt. She opened the card. It looked like a long message.

> Dear Claire,
> Miranda will be taking over the book while I'm doing Outreach for schools. Please get in touch with her, whenever.
> Best wishes,
> Deanna

She turned it over in the hope that there was another message. She read it again and went cold. She closed her eyes to shut out the pain. A door had been slammed on her dreams that was final as a coffin. She read the card again. Nothing. Deanna had given her something to hope for and care about. Claire had never sought out anyone like that before. She knew this was about It, as much as it was about Deanna. Yet a new life had briefly fanned out in front of her.

All over, all done, finished. She was stuck with herself, maybe for ever.

Her cottage had been smashed, just enough to make it clear that the intention was malicious. That was a premonition of this. There would be no bucolic weekends there now. She didn't know who had done it, who could hate her that much. She thought of Jadine, then dismissed the notion as ridiculous. Anthony had thought it was just kids. When she said it appeared to be more personal than that, he said she was imagining things. She had been imagining a lot of things, lately, it seemed. Anne was there, polishing the china, and regarding Claire intently. Claire went to the bowl of flowers, started toying with them, then crushed one of the hyacinths in her fist. She walked away, humming to herself, but had no pitch and made a terrible noise, like a rabbit caught in a trap, on its last gasps.

Oh here we go, thought Anne. Go on, crack up, spill the beans.

'Would you like some music?' she said.

Claire nodded.

Anne put on *Orpheus and Eurydice*. Its mandarin strains only seemed to confirm Claire in her sense of ancientness. Anthony came in.

'Won't the salmon go *off* if it's left in the sunlight?' he said, and went out again.

She hated him.

They were having people around tonight. Claire couldn't think of anything she'd enjoy less. Anne stared at the door Anthony had just gone through, thinking that her own

— 183 —

husband would never talk to her like that. Claire and she exchanged the kind of look that office girls, Claire had recently observed, swapped with each other daily.

'Still upset about your cottage?' said Anne.

'Yes. I suppose.'

'Funny business that.'

'Yes it was.'

'Any idea who did it?'

'No.'

Anne shook her head.

Claire went to Anthony's study to see how she'd fare in the event of change, although it was belated. Change to what, exactly? The crusted papers with their fraying pink ribbons, ornate calligraphic lettering and formal pronouncements, held tight so many lies and evasions. They meant nothing to her.

She wanted to know if she would miss Anthony? What if she wanted to check the spelling of *chiaroscuro* in a hurry?

In the middle of their civilised marriage, there was a huge absence. He had always shut her out, and made it seem like this was alright, this was what was expected, this was how everyone else acted. She knew they didn't - not from the start, not from the first, not forever. She found herself voluntarily retreating, keeping out of his way, because this was clearly what he wanted. To make room for what? She'd pretended it was work, although she often doubted this. She wondered if Anthony saw other people - this, too, seemed unlikely. Did he visit prostitutes? She retreated, in the face of his unfathomable silence; a life that, even though he was her husband, she knew hardly anything about. She hardly knew anything about it at all.

She replaced the legal papers, then her eyes focussed on a thick oak box she hadn't noticed before. It was the kind of box that usually held family memorabilia and wedding photographs. The box creaked as she opened it. Now the only sound in the house. Respectability's hinges creaked, and all the grot came tumbling out. Later, she half wished she hadn't touched it.

There were small black notebooks, written in Anthony's spindly hand, but with slightly more pressure behind it, an unexpected pressure. It was over ten years old, meticulously dated, and was all about Jonathan, nothing else. Jonathan's pearly tears, his shivering limbs, his sweet plebeian reluctance. 'My Ganymede', 'my Frigid Prince'; Jonathan's grace and delicacy, Jonathan's quiet perfection. It was written in a tone of hideous gentility that belied the absolute degree of force employed. She was not imagining this. It was all there, in black and white, in Anthony's hand, the hand in which he had signed his will and wedding certificate.

There were some old photographs of Jonathan, taken when they first knew him. In a couple of them, she and Jonathan's mother featured: spliced straight down the middle, with sawn off smiles, caught unaware of what was going on, what lay beyond the picture being taken. There were a few of Jonathan alone. One with his hands over his eyes, in an effort to keep the sun out of his face, his legs apart, standing as if they might crack or wrench. There was one of Jonathan in his school uniform, one of Jonathan in shorts, sitting on a rock, at a place she didn't recognise at all. She looked at the pictures and shuddered, remembered how Jonathan's fringe, at that age, would not stay down no matter what was done with it. She remembered that when he first stayed for the weekend, the fringe had a particularly raw and decisive edge.

She shut the box and left it on the floor. This was what Anthony called love, and it was much more than he had ever felt for her. Yet it made some kind of terrible sense, this sick love. She had been its unwitting accomplice.

She went back to their papers. Jonathan was due to come into a lot of money, as much as her. Anthony referred to him as his lost son. The papers dropped out of Claire's hand. Anthony's lost son.

At dinner she made one slight alteration to her usual fare. Something from *Under An Hour*; great big aubergines, exuberantly stuffed. They got some funny looks. They caused some slight disquiet - how sensitised Claire had become to these senseless nuances - and yet they tasted alright. Someone said that Claire seemed quiet. She said she was just exhausted.

She looked around the table and the company she used to feel part of. It was lucky this lot were born into a fortunate class as their inbred, overbred characteristics could hardly be trusted to get them very far otherwise. Braying voices, lantern-jawed faces, no love, liking or interest in anything they didn't manage or own. A life measured out in how much fowl they could stuff down their gullets, and how many pronouncements they could make on matters they knew nothing about.

A woman called Pamela was possessed of a tweedy masculinity and had a face like a horse.

'My daughter, you know, the lawyer, says they have children to get them into council accommodation. Melanie says she can't understand them!'

Thin laughter passed around the table. And Claire thought there was no better way for a woman to endear herself to a man than criticising other women, with an oily enthusiasm that could only be attained by those too plain, dull and toadying to have ever really counted as full members of the female sex.

A grey-haired columnist was pontificating on ordinary people. They couldn't be doing with all this rot. Five minute divorces, single parent families, condom adverts all over the shop.

'You'll never interest them in this fine art of yours Anthony!'

Anthony smiled. He didn't care. It wasn't made for them in the first place. Claire wondered if Anthony had smiled like that at Jonathan, in that supercilious way, to convince him. She wondered what her fine guests would think of Anthony's secret activities and predilections.

He had always believed in beauty and truth and fine ideals and decorum. When she first met him he had been incomparable: so much better than anyone else; wise about everything that seemed to matter; not trivial or belligerent like other men she'd known. He had been patrician and hated everything vulgar. She was to become his angel.

She would rise to his standards and shed the more unwieldy parts of herself in the ascendance. He drew out the threads of her curiosity and stretched them so far she was blinded by their distance. He must have done the same for Jonathan, once. He did all that to Jonathan too.

Anthony went to his study to fetch a monograph to show to one of the guests. He would see the box now, disturbed. Claire held her breath. He came back and sat next to one of the men, throwing the most impartial glance in Claire's direction. And she saw, all of a sudden, that he really did expect her to keep quiet about all this. She saw that he didn't expect her to be very surprised at all.

Anthony went straight to bed after the guests left, leaving Claire to the clearing up. She dumped the plates into the sink, put on *Orpheus and Eurydice* again, stared at the head of salmon, its eyes hardened and damp, and watched the oil on the plates and bowls form into tight, glistening bubbles.

She and Anthony had led a life of unwavering dignity. Anthony's interest in her soon waned, as if the effort of keeping up with his discriminations was too high a task for a mere mortal, his graceful shadow. The vowels in her French went flat and her vocabulary was found lamentable. Her ear for music was awry, her taste in opera coarse. She gave up reading French novels and took up cookbooks instead. Anthony demolished her in the most elliptical ways. It was no effort for him, none at all. It required only the slightest turn in a facial expression, or the definition with which he occasionally uttered the word 'Claire' or 'my wife', in public. Every insult Anthony had put her way made her bones tighter, her legs lock closer together and her social gaiety more forced. As she attempted to shape her mind to his, she re-fashioned her body and reflexes too. She turned herself into an eggshell, which preserved and protected him. An eggshell was the sum of what Deanna had got.

When he had first shown an interest in Jonathan she had been pleased. Anthony rarely showed any interest in anything that wasn't an artefact. She had thought his interest was honest, and the real horror was not that Anthony was evil, but that the apparent licence he allowed himself was so extreme.

The music played on. Quiet, still, velvety chords and the soft modulations behind the soprano's voice arced into something quite beyond in its longing, and Claire was stillborn in her own orbit. Her marriage lay slaughtered on the ground while the harsh light of reality rose behind it. The music came from another world, surrounded by mountains and mist. It made suffering seem beautiful. It had no right to do that. There were two ways of approaching middle age, she supposed: 'This is it' or 'This is it!' She wanted to follow the second course, but had no idea how to do so, not yet.

It was getting light outside. Claire had finished off a bottle of brandy while lying on her couch. When she woke in the morning Anthony had laid a locket and one perfect white lily beside her bed. She snapped the chain of the small locket, then crushed the lily and threw it out. Downstairs, the china Anne had polished yesterday was pristine behind the cabinets. She smashed the figures against the wall. Anne came in to find Claire surrounded by cracked china, with a flushed and tearful face.

Dear oh dear, she thought. The penny's dropped.

'Overtime?' she said.

Claire raked her hand through her hair. 'Overtime. Yes. Overtime for now. Can you see to it?'

'Oh yes,' said Anne.

17

Daniel wore a suit and tie to meet the curators of *Archaic Greek Art*. He'd prepared four pages of suggested marketing strategies, a shoal of diagrams and a list of bullet points. He had practised his speech until it had attained the taut and secure rhythms of a tune in his head. He'd conferred with Priscilla throughout, and she'd approved. He felt like a TV pundit.

The meeting was held in an oak-filled room and all the other men had grey or white hair. It soon became clear that no one expected him to know anything about the art. The main curator contributed a speech that sounded very learned, and had no connection with Daniel's own researches, or anything he'd ever thought about before. He felt stupid for having spent so much time on it, assuming that expertise could be got so quickly, although - somehow or other - Priscilla seemed to manage it.

He read his presentation with the right smiles and pauses, but it felt like someone else's face and voice. He was conscious of the attendant men swapping amused, then exasperated glances. His diagrams were shunted around the table. He laid his papers down, and was faced with a panel of expressionless faces, laced with just a slight hint of lechery. What a tedious bunch of old queens you are, he thought.

The main curator grasped his hands together and leaned forward, patiently.

'Most interesting,' he said, 'but we already have our own arrangements.'

'We have produced our own 'pack',' said another.

'Own *packs*,' said Daniel, accepting one and smiling. He tapped it on the table. 'Well maybe this helped us establish our goals more clearly. Yes. Thank you.'

His chair scraped noisily as he got up. Looking at the current exhibits in the museum space, he realised he would never, unprompted, have anything to say about any of it. '1042', 'King Alfred's reign', 'the Battle of the Boyne', and a couple of dusty helmets. He moved among men who seemed retrieved from dustcarts, and mothers clutching kids with plummy little voices, determined to bang some culture into their tiny heads if it killed them. They pointed at mumbled obscurities, engraved in stone - observe, little children, the wisdom of the ancients. There was a cloak dated '1234', some bits of cankered jewellery, moth-eaten dressage of war, nothing that fuelled curiosity. The curators reminded him of Anthony, with his arcane air and heavy brow. Jonathan sprung to mind. Daniel's studies had been energised by feverish readings of Catullus on the tube:

'I hate and I love. And if you ask me how, I do not know. I only feel it…torn in two.'

> *'Cancel the expectations of friendship - cancel the kindnesses deemed to accrue there, kindness is barren, friendship breeds nothing, only the weight of past deeds growing oppressive…'*

He remembered the quotes off by heart. They had little to do with the job in hand. He had received a postcard from Jonathan. Warington Bracket. Maybe some expensive new watering hole that Daniel had never heard of, that Jonathan had visited with someone else. He had put it in the toilet at home and sworn to do nothing else about it.

'Their own packs?' exclaimed Priscilla. 'Oh well. We're the face of the future, whether they like it or not. Let me see?'

Daniel handed over the example.

'Bit strained isn't it?' She pulled it apart. 'It's not very interactive either. Nothing for the kiddies to tweak, twiddle or pull.'

He glanced at the up-dated poster for David Brasted's play:

BIMBO OR BITCH?
COME ALONG AND DECIDE FOR YOURSELF!

'You have to go on what's been published,' said Priscilla, through a cigarette. 'We're a national debating platform.'

She laughed.

'Anyway,' she stubbed the cigarette out and shook her pen in her customary way, 'I've had a great idea - *Shakespeare in Tuscany* - an eight day package. For the subscription crowd. They can have wild boar on a spit, maybe in tents. It's no sillier than those Dracula packages people used to go on is it?'

Daniel's mind was trying to work, but it was just whirring in motion.

'Then maybe we could have a similar thing in Greece. *Greek Drama in Greece!* It could work. You know all those Greek myths are used in a lot of people's therapy now?'

Daniel wished he'd thought of that, but doubted if the curators would have appreciated the connection.

'PragMATiks show tonight,' he said, keenly.

'Super duper,' said Priscilla, uninterested.

He spotted Bella in the corridor.

'Oh no,' she held her hand up, 'very busy at the moment. Jean's just gone to the doctor's with her heart. Shame really isn't it?'

All he wanted to do was ask if there was any news of his contract.

There was a man sitting at Maxine's kitchen table later on. That was a nice surprise. The back of his neck was so finely shaved and honed, Daniel wanted to collapse and run his tongue all over it. The man turned around and the prospect was enchanting. Hardly a disappointment. A face long and poignant as a Modigliani, an irresistible sadness lurking under his soft brown eyes. The man stood up. He was very tall and lean. Daniel felt an attack of goodwill coming on.

'It seems to be my lot in life,' said the man, 'to hang around waiting for Lydia to show up. Paul.'

'Daniel,' he said, quickly.

Paul opened the fridge. 'Well I suppose we could help ourselves to this.' He brought out two beers and opened them.

Maxine and Lydia hadn't done him justice. Girls never knew, Daniel thought.

'Why isn't she here then?' he frowned theatrically. 'Are either of them sick or anything?'

'I think,' said Paul, 'the jury's still out on that one. Cheers.'

'I've been in a museum all day,' said Daniel, sitting down, 'that was pretty dull.'

'Oh?' said Paul. 'Really. Museum eh? Interesting. Do you play badminton?'

Maxine came in to find Daniel and Paul looking like two cats who had just been interrupted in a fight, and now wished to disclaim any responsibility for it. She looked at the beers.

'Make yourself at home,' she said. 'Are we going to this thing of yours or what?'

'I'm looking forward to your exhibition,' said Paul, looking at Daniel sweetly.

'Good,' said Maxine, 'we'll see you there then.'

'What would you be if you were a song?' said Daniel, the minute they got out. He was keeping his thoughts on Paul to himself.

'Don't know,' said Maxine, '*Edelweiss*, probably, wouldn't you say?' She turned a fierce face on him. 'You'd be *Tulips from Amsterdam*.'

Arriving at the gallery, Maxine saw the neat trays of white wine and a choice of two waters, and recognised the show as one with the holy air and tolerant ethics of something that had got both commercial and government funding. Daniel's voice dropped to a hush as he handed over their invitations, and introduced himself. Oh, she thought. He really does know people here after all.

Their footfalls echoed softly on the polished floor. Maxine left Daniel to look around on her own. The exhibits were splayed with light emitting from tiny halogen lamps, wedged into the ceiling.

A stack of straw tied with masking tape stood next to a stained teacup on a plinth. A huge white canvas held a solitary blade of grass. In a corner was a heap of strewn wastepaper. She wondered if they would change it around for different viewings. It had a calm charm she admired and resented because it wasn't part of her repertoire. She looked around and wondered if what she spent her days working on was hopelessly outdated.

Daniel joined her and they silently regarded a cheese grater filled with moulded cheese, and a collection of faded objects drawn from a dead person's house.

'Mmm,' Maxine said, 'like the chest of drawers.'

Daniel sipped some water and twirled around to survey the rest of the room. His foot was planted with mock casualness on a platform. His eyes returned to the objects in front of them.

'I like it,' he said.

'Why?'

'It's like Mayakovsky.'

'What's that like?'

'Full of peace and hope.'

Words failed them. Why doesn't she say something

intelligent, Daniel thought. Maxine stared ahead mournfully.

Daniel never usually talked like that. Maxine wondered how he really rated her stuff, and blotted it out.

'What did you do for this?' she asked.

'The posters, the copy on the flyers.'

'Oh good,' she said, 'good.'

He knew she hadn't looked at them.

He went to talk to the artists, gratefully. He'd developed a real liking for them. Their words were gentle, their skin smooth as eggs. They talked with him as if his opinions mattered.

Maxine exchanged a thin-lipped smile with someone she saw around a lot, but couldn't place. Daniel watched her from a distance and wished he'd brought someone else along, someone who would just be interested. Maxine looked at the exhibits again, assuring herself this time that the only problem was that it wasn't her kind of thing. It might look different in six months. She knew now why she didn't go and see more. If it wasn't on your current wavelength, it just got in the way. She looked across at Daniel, chattering brightly. He's so bloody charming, she thought. And she knew, at this moment, they weren't quite friends any more.

She stood in front of a mangled piece of iron from a tractor, and a heap of compost dotted with fluorescent vegetables. Daniel returned with a woman with a serene air and a tuft of blonde hair. Maxine turned, apparently woken out of a trance.

'Judith Bowen,' he said, 'Maxine Kendrick.'

One of the artists.

They shook hands, limply. Maxine pointedly didn't say anything. This, thought Daniel, was a match made in heaven. He wished Maxine would stop looking at him as if he'd set her up.

'Maxine's got an exhibition coming up soon,' he said.

'Oh where?' said Judith.

'Espina,' said Maxine.

'Espina,' said Judith, nodding, aware that it was a smaller venue.

She turned to Daniel again. 'This,' she said, addressing the compost, 'was a collaboration with my lover Piers van Damme.'

Maxine was very still. She looked at Judith more thoroughly. She was glad for them really.

'I worked with him once,' she said. She slowly got a postcard out of her bag and handed it over. 'Mine.'

Daniel noted that Maxine's self-marketing was crude but neat. There was something about this which both touched and annoyed him.

He returned to the drinks table, sighed, yawned, and opened another bottle with a harsh stroke. It must be very good, what a life, he thought, to be doing what you want to do all the time, to know what you want to do all the time. The people he was working with now, they all had something in common. So light-hearted and adorable on the surface, but with a deadly seriousness in their core, about what they did and its importance. He found it funny when he didn't find it bizarre.

He and Maxine walked up the road.

'Seen Jonathan?' she said, trying to reclaim him.

'No,' said Daniel. 'Robert alright? Claire didn't try and interfere?'

'No,' said Maxine. Oh don't take the piss, she thought, not now, not here.

She wondered if he knew about Jonathan and Anthony, what Jonathan had told her all that time ago, which at the time she'd written off as exaggeration and lies. Now she wasn't so sure.

He'd called around out of the blue, answering a casual open invitation she hadn't expected him to take her up on. He seemed to like being there, until Anthony was mentioned, and she suddenly realised why he always seemed so persecuted. He'd reacted hatefully to her, as if it was her he hated, even though the evidence against Anthony came tumbling out of his mouth, evidence that was dressed in an almost slavish admiration.

Maxine wondered if it was true, now. She wondered if Daniel knew, then decided he probably didn't. She kept it inside her, a difficult secret.

And yet - Jonathan and Daniel had each got a slice of the Claire and Anthony cake, and had settled with it. She wondered what Daniel had to do for his treat of a job. Probably not much. She'd got nothing. She felt proud and alone and dejected.

There was a furniture shop with a garish display that she and Daniel would normally have made jokes about. Neither was in the mood. They stopped at the end of the street, ready to travel in opposite directions.

'So - Sunday week then?' said Daniel.

'Yep,' said Maxine. 'It was nice, you know, but I'm a bit preoccupied at the moment.'

'Yeah,' said Daniel, 'yeah.'

She stood at the bus stop and nothing happened. The crowd and traffic were getting thinner. She walked to the nearest phone box, pressed her head against the pane of glass, and called Robert to get him to come round.

The cut of Robert's jacket, the bottle of wine pressed to his chest and his obvious delight in seeing her cheered her up. Her face was so pale, he thought. It was almost blue. He touched it and kissed her.

'You're cold.'

'I've been working in a cold room all day,' she said, in a voice that sounded as if it was coming out of a well. She had already decided not to mention The PragMATiks, not at all. Not important.

'When we do the restaurant,' she said, 'people can serve themselves, get a little bit of everything, not someone else's idea of what a meal is. It's easier.'

She didn't want to be a waitress any more.

'Marcus said something about that,' he said, 'today.'

'You saw him?'

'Yes.'

Their project.

'Round walls?' she said. 'My designs?'

'Yes. They're wonderful.'

They moved closer together. Maxine bared her throat and Robert nibbled and licked its bump, which was like a soft plum. He breathed in the taste of turps in her hair, and the hot, subtle musk between her breasts.

Her knees jack-knifed and her moist little tiger's muff bucked in the air, even though his forearms were tightening around her rib cage, and holding her there. She gurgled with pleasure, and his face rested for a moment on her shoulder, so he could hear gurgles echoing through her skin and bones. He pushed hard, to catch her out. There was a lot of give.

'Oww,' she laughed, '*oww*.'

Was she serious? There was blood, bright pink blood. They stopped and stared at it. His prick depressed slightly.

Oh fucking hell, she thought, what's wrong with them? She took him in her hand, and massaged him into life again, slipped him in, drew her legs around his hips.

She kissed him. 'I was bleeding before...'

'Mmm...' he said.

'Then it stopped. The fucking just churned it up.'

He slid into her again, and was working again. She pulled herself away so only her crotch and legs touched him. They finished and Robert stroked the hollow of Maxine's neck with his knuckles. The flow hadn't stopped. It was splashed on them, matted between their legs.

They went to the bath, where the water turned pink, and poured jugs of water over each other.

'Ablutions,' she said.

'Ablutions,' he laughed.

She flung a towel at him.

They dabbed each other dry with the towels, carefully avoiding trouble spots. They checked odd areas where the blood had strayed, all with the nifty precision of monkeys checking each other for nits.

There were two dots of blood on the wall, still. Maxine gazed at them before turning off the light, and thought she might leave them there for a while, as a memory, a memory of someone who loved her. Robert squeezed her as he went out in the morning, and Maxine stirred in her sleep, smiling and thinking blood flowers.

18

Lydia, bored with her functions, had stuck four notices on the *Macro*'s walls:

SMILE AT YOUR WAITRESS - SHE IS HUMAN TOO.
NO TANTRUMS PLEASE.
DRINK YOURSELF SILLY BY ALL MEANS, BUT
DON'T TAKE IT OUT ON US.
PLEASE TURN YOUR WATCH ALARMS AND
MOBILE PHONES OFF.

Marcus, back from a day's leave, read them all and ripped them down.

'We've got backers in and out. What - you want them to think we're some dozy hippie outfit?'

'Backers,' said Lydia. 'Where? All I see is customers. Don't walk away when I'm talking to you…'

'Marcus…' said Janet.

'The notices,' said Marcus, 'are dumb.'

'I can't stand mobile phones. People act really annoyingly when they're speaking to them. Complete *arseholes*.'

'Up to them isn't it?'

'Marcus…' said Janet.

'You're a singer Lydia, stick to that.'

'What's this music?'

'House '92,' said Marcus. 'Alright?'

'It's shite.'

'I like it.'

'You used to let me handle *that* at least. I thought we were a project.'

'Someone's got to be in charge. That's me alright?' Marcus stood in front of the mirror, and slapped his face. 'Good new shaver, this.'

'Contribute ideas. Do it how we want.'

'Only if they're good ideas.'

'Marcus…' said Janet.

'For Christ's sake!' he yelled at Janet. 'Can I do one thing at a time?'

Janet returned to the kitchen, muttering.

'And you decide what's good or not?' said Lydia.

'Yes,' said Marcus. 'We're running a business, not trying to adjust the world to your karmic level.'

'Business,' said Lydia. 'Yeah everything's run like a fucking business. It's not exactly original is it?'

Maxine had observed most of this argument. The place was run on tighter reins now. She used to do drawings on the blackboard menus, and she didn't bother any more. She was the designer now, and she'd stopped being interested in anything else. She was with Marcus on this one, but pretended she wasn't.

Or at least, she stood beside Lydia with her arms folded and a grim expression aimed in Marcus' direction.

'You busy after this shift?' she said to Lydia.

'Kind of.'

Maxine could tell she wasn't really.

'I've just remembered a painting I've got to collect. The one we did at the Community Centre. I've got to have it.'

'So…'

'I've been phoning them up for ages, the Council. They're not answering. I thought we could just go round and get it.'

Lydia sighed. 'Are you mad? What if they're closed?'

'We could break in.'

Lydia looked at the ceiling.

'I've bought a chisel, and there's a window I could climb through. I checked it out.'

'We *can't*.'

'Oh *come on*, it won't take long.'

'It's a Community Centre,' said Lydia, biding time.

'I've bought us some Cava and some of Mickey's most excellent grass.'

They walked to the Community Centre in their most anonymous clothes.

'Didn't they *pay* us?' said Lydia.

'Oh maybe,' said Maxine, 'but not much. Expenses. A Travelcard, something like that.'

It was rough justice. About a year ago, she and Lydia had offered their services to the Centre as local artists. They had gone in one afternoon and Maxine had done an improvised painting while Lydia stood at the side, performing her vocal contribution to Martin Grimshaw's *Deptford Traffic Jam* - syncopated screeches and her banshee voice. The women assembled for the event spent most of the time trying to pacify their children. They didn't compliment them at the end, nor ask one sensible question. Maxine and Lydia had decided that the experience had been awful. It was all very patronising, taking arts into the community. Nobody really valued anything unless they'd discovered it themselves. Arguments of that kind had easily settled the matter, and curbed any further impulses like that.

They arrived at the Centre.

'Okay, it's locked,' said Maxine.

'Did you see that vicious looking Doberman on the way in?'

'Oh c'mon they're not pit bulls.'

'Be quick about it,' said Lydia.

She gave Maxine a leg up and Maxine set to work with her chisel.

'I'm not really sure if this'll work,' she said.

'No,' said a man behind them.

Maxine's balance slipped and Lydia grabbed her ankles. Maxine fell into Lydia's shoulders.

'You've ricked my bloody neck you clumsy cow...'

'Well?' said Maxine. 'Who are you? The caretaker? Plain clothes police?'

'No.'

'You know how to do this?'

'Don't ask me,' he said.

'I've made quite a few wedges in the frame, maybe just

carry on with that,' said Maxine.

'Yes, you're probably on the right track,' said the man.

Lydia looked at her watch. 'I've got a rehearsal at five. Give it a hard bang and get it over with.'

Maxine got out a hammer from her overalls, got a leg up again, and smacked the hammer on the frame. The window crashed into the Centre.

'That's done it,' said the man. 'Watch yourself on the glass. Rehearsal?' he said to Lydia. 'Rehearsal for what? Are you an actress?'

'Singer,' said Lydia, bored.

Maxine heaved herself up on her elbows, and climbed in.

'Much obliged for your interest anyway,' Lydia added. 'She's collecting a painting she donated. We improvised here a while ago, you see.'

'Oh yes?' said the man. 'Got a cigarette?'

Lydia handed him one. They both stood there, smoking. Lydia stared into the distance.

'Terrible to have it locked up like that,' said the man. 'Art needs freedom. How else can it free people?'

'That's very true,' said Lydia, and flicked her cigarette.

'Do you want to buy a TV set?' he said. 'Very cheap £100.'

'We've got one,' said Lydia.

He ambled off without a word. Shortly, Maxine's canvas was thrust through the window. Lydia took it. Maxine climbed out, brushed herself down, and looked at it. 'Rooster, yeah,' she said, 'the strokes need going over. No texture is there? Very thin. Still, I did it in an hour didn't I? And it had to be simple for the audience. It's not bad.'

'Can we go?' said Lydia.

'Just one from Casa Nostra now, and that's it,' said Maxine. 'I'll take the car.'

They walked on.

'Oh I forgot to tell you,' said Lydia. 'The Council towed it away.'

'What?'

'They towed it away. It was unroadworthy. They thought it was abandoned. There's nothing we can do.'

'Oh great,' said Maxine. 'Oh that's *fantastic*. What? Didn't we even get an MOT?'

'No,' said Lydia, 'we couldn't. It wouldn't have passed.'

When Maxine went out again, Lydia was sitting having a quiet cup of tea with Syd, calming him down about their late rent. Why bother? She'd just got a bank loan to help with the exhibition. They could just pay him off. Maxine even got sick of Lydia and the musicians now, at it all night when she was trying to sleep. Lydia banging a bottle of beer on the table and throwing a cork at someone, first thing in the morning when she was trying to think. Lydia did so love living the life, which was presumably why she got so little done.

A mailout of slides had resulted in one enquiry from Delia Jip, Style Editor of *Phantom* magazine. Maxine had laid three of her fun sculptures on boxes over old tablecloths, and got in Darjeeling and Rose Hip teas, four cans of Budweiser and one of Badoit.

A busy apparition with an acorn face and short, sticky

orange hair pulled up in a lime Ford Capri. She tore up the stairs like a herd of buffalo, looked around dazedly and sniffed deeply.

'I might be moving soon,' said Maxine.

'God it's heavenly!' Delia exclaimed. 'So atmospheric. These are the fun sculptures are they? Yes.'

She touched the white fur, and admired the orange-wigged head. 'Very angry. Very ugly. Fantastic. Maxine - uh - do you have any *cocaine*?'

'Um. No.'

'My chap's just been sent down for seven years. Fucking disastrous, and pretty bad luck for him too. I mean, I'm not desperate but it's actually frightfully good for headaches and I could do with a top up.'

'I'll remember that,' said Maxine.

'Get headaches do you?'

'No,' said Maxine. 'There's a chance my flatmate might have some speed.'

'Oh no! Look listen, if it was that bad I'd just go to the corner shop here and get myself some Vim alright? So - we'd better get on. You look suitably rugged don't you? Could we put these sculptures by the bed, then you can languish on it. Where the fuck's Pierre?'

She marched to the window while Maxine re-arranged the room.

'Now look that's my car. It's not going to get vandalised is it?'

'We had a car,' said Maxine, 'it didn't tend to get mucked about with during the day. Except the schoolchildren, and they're not due out yet.'

'What about that man downstairs? Is he one of the famed mentally ill?'

'Just generally miserable. Doesn't like his customers much. Nothing to do with us.'

'He won't nick my car?'

'I doubt it,' said Maxine. 'He hasn't had a licence for years.'

'God it was a shame about Bobby though,' Delia tugged at her hair. 'You know I had a little flingette with him, which makes it all the more poignant. He used to wake me up by hitting me on the head with my teddy. He didn't *hate* me for having a career - I mean *pain au raisin* and my espresso machine were just fine with him! He didn't have to make sarcastic remarks before gobbling it all down like all my other so-called working class - oh ha bloody ha! - media scumbag friends! Wouldn't hurt a fly. Seven years, just for that. How absolutely fucking ghastly!'

She began to cry, then stopped.

'Would you like a beer?'

'Alright,' said Delia. She followed Maxine into the kitchen. 'I was thinking of sending him a card, but I don't know where he is. Wandsworth? Winchester? Where are the prisons Maxine?'

'I think there might be one in Wandsworth.'

'Wandsworth right. I'll write that down. Pen?'

Maxine handed her one. Delia scribbled.

'If Pierre's been delayed by trade again that's it he's fired,' she muttered.

Delia threw the pen down, strode around, and went to the window again. 'It's not so bad around here, is it? Not really like a slum at all. I ventured out to Clissold Park the other day. They've got these deer. Fashion shoot. I must say I thought those antlers on the males would make a jolly nice hat. Still, better off on the animal probably. Oh here he is.'

A swarthy faced man came in with one solitary camera, and didn't say anything.

'Naughty, naughty!' Delia smacked him on both cheeks of his bottom.

He regarded her with a look of sustained hatred.

'To work, Maxine. Yeah? Ready? Stand there. Serious. Don't smile. Sit. Lie. Further. Good. Sort of Theda Bara. Could you manage a pout? No don't bother.'

The camera clicked. Pierre put the camera down.

'I'm supposed to be the photographer here.'

'Look - no displays of temperament, okay?' said Delia. 'I've had enough of you for one day. Right Maxine, sideways on. Head up. C'mon Pierre, hurry up. God it's a shame we couldn't get a shot of your bum isn't it? Never mind. Push your shoulders forward. Look moody. Terrific. That's it then. 'Bye.'

She leapt down the stairs and Pierre followed slowly. They got into the car and were off. What a strange woman, Maxine thought. She was glad she had gone.

The Casa Nostra was already crowded and the smoke stung Maxine's eyes as she went in. She had to press herself through the crowded bar, and waited a long time for Señor Martinez. Her painting was stuck in a small corner, ill lit and largely unseen. So much for public space, so much for publicity.

'Yes?' he said. He was small and squat and his face didn't hold much promise.

'My painting. I want it back.'

'It's mine,' he said. 'I bought it.'

He poured sherry into two ornate glasses and handed Maxine one. She wet her lips with it.

'You signed an agreement.' Maxine produced a thinly photocopied sheet. 'It's mine, my painting. *Quisiera...*' she jabbed her finger at the corner, 'that.'

Señor Martinez shook his head. 'Enjoy your sherry,' he said, and walked off.

But it's mine, she thought, it's mine. She looked at the thin sherry glass and wanted to chuck it at the wall. Julius had already sent *Motorway* back, properly cleaned, tightly packaged. A real gallery owner. She got a rankling feeling she'd been doing everything wrong.

She called Daniel at work.

'Daniel Foster, helew.'

'Eh?'

'Oh, it's you.'

'I need someone with fluent Spanish, to collect a painting.'

'But I'm working,' he said. 'I'm working all day.'

She put the phone down, glanced through a Spanish dictionary, then remembered something. She picked up the phone again.

'Consuela?' she said, in her most confidential voice.

'It's Maxine, we met.'

'Yes?'

'I've got a bit of a problem. I need someone who can speak

fluent Spanish. I need to collect a painting and...the Council's towed our car away.'

There was a pause. 'That's terrible,' said Consuela. 'Do you want me to come now? I could come in an hour. It would be easier if I brought my car wouldn't it?'

Yeah it would, Maxine thought.

Consuela greeted Señor Martinez warmly and spoke and gestured very precisely. Lovely flamenco wrists. Maxine tried to imitate her demeanour. Señor Martinez looked at her more severely.

Consuela turned to her. Her eyes had become larger and more doe-like. 'It's okay,' she said, 'you can bring it back when the exhibition's finished.'

Señor Martinez took the picture down and handed it over.

'You didn't say you wanted it for an exhibition,' he said. 'You just said you wanted it back.'

Consuela drove her home.

'I would have thought that was *implicit*,' said Maxine. 'You were brilliant,' she added.

'It's very striking,' said Consuela. '*Goldrush*. What's that? History?'

'No, just a sensation,' said Maxine.

It made her even more perplexed now. Deanna and Claire. They pulled up outside Maxine's place.

'Thanks very much, thanks so much,' Maxine said, 'and look, this thing Deanna's got going with Claire. I don't know what's got into her. I mean, when I saw you both that time you seemed perfect together. She must just be going through a phase, Deanna.'

Consuela rolled her hands over the steering wheel, and repeated 'thing with Claire'.

'It can't last can it?' said Maxine.

Consuela shrugged. 'Life sometimes gets like that.'

Lydia came in earlier than expected, while Maxine was still cleaning up the painting. Go away, she thought.

'Cava's in the fridge,' she said, 'rest's in the kitchen drawer.'

'Marcus has turned into a real bossman, hasn't he? He thinks he's a bloody celebrity chef,' Lydia said, lingering, 'I just can't stand him any more. He gets more and more pompous by the minute. Janet's thinking of leaving him.'

'He's always been like that,' said Maxine, 'you just didn't notice. And Janet's always been a bit of a doormat.'

Maxine opened the Cava and poured them both a glass, without their usual ceremony.

'Your shoulder still hurting?' Maxine said. 'I'll do it with some oils later.'

'He's a jerk. It's not the same.'

'Nothing stays the same.'

'I'll give it till the end of the year,' said Lydia. 'You know we could make more waitressing in town? Less hassle, less commitment.'

'*We?* Who's *we?*' Maxine thought.

'You want me to do that shoulder now?'

Maxine massaged Lydia's neck with the marjoram oil and stuck a joint in her mouth. They sipped their drinks. Just shut up, Maxine thought. Calm down. Go to sleep. Don't bother me now.

'Is it helping?'

'Yeah,' smiled Lydia. 'A bit lower…yeah there, lower.'

There was a crash on the landing.

'Oh not now,' Lydia moaned.

'Stay where you are,' said Maxine.

Syd barged in, looking worse than he had last time they saw him. He always did.

'Here's Keanu Reeves,' said Lydia. 'Our lucky night!'

Syd ignored her.

'Oh that's a nice picture!' he said, looking at the girls. 'And you've got some more!'

'We've just collected them,' said Maxine, digging her fingers into Lydia's back, 'for my exhibition.'

'Yeah. Heard you both making a bloody racket,' He pulled some fluff from his cardigan. 'Oh - a great big *cunt*!' He spluttered, looking at the relevant picture. 'You two really fancy yourselves don't you?'

'Thank you and goodnight,' said Lydia. 'He doesn't understand,' she added, to Maxine.

'Don't offer me a drink or a smoke then.'

Lydia passed him the joint so automatically, Maxine sneered. 'Lydia…'

'Leave it,' she whispered, 'might calm him down.'

'We bloody live here,' Maxine hissed, 'we pay him.'

'Not lately,' said Lydia.

'What's all this about then?' said Syd.

'I've got an exhibition,' Maxine mumbled. 'I just said.'

Lydia pulled her kimono around her, got up and stood in front of the canvases.

'Oh don't worry,' said Syd. 'I don't want to *touch* them! You didn't invite me then? Suppose I'm not good enough?'

'Have a wash and you'll be very welcome Syd,' Maxine smiled.

'You bitches only think of yourselves!'

'Unlike Mother Theresa here!'

'She didn't mean it like that Syd,' said Lydia.

'This is getting really boring,' said Maxine. 'You get rid of him or I will.'

'Ssh,' said Lydia.

'You didn't invite me to your bloody singing did you?'

'You wouldn't like it, Syd.'

'Snotty fucking cunt bitches.'

'Let's get him out,' said Maxine.

Syd looked around.

'You don't keep this place up to scratch do you? Fuck the pair of you,' he said. 'Fuck the pair of you,' and left.

'See?' said Lydia.

Maxine went to the door, bolted it and kicked the laundry basket in front of its hinge.

'I'm leaving Lydia.'

'Leaving?'

'I can't stand this any more.'

'No,' said Lydia. 'Well I'm going on tour soon, briefly,' she laughed mirthlessly. 'Might as well pack up altogether.'

Maxine rolled another joint. They dimmed the lights and played ambient music, sitting very close together, locked in thought. Lydia crashed out and Maxine lay beside her, stroking her hair, trying to lull Lydia into a deeper sleep, so she could get on. It was really a pity. Sometimes things had been perfect. It was going to be such a shame, to leave Lydia.

Soon they were both fast asleep, on Maxine's bed. The laundry basket was still in front of the door. The only sound of life outside was an odd cough, and the distant noise of tired traffic, making its way home.

In the morning Lydia found Maxine in the kitchen, wearing full make-up and a royal blue dress. She was tidying up, fast. Maxine kissed her and then disappeared. Robert stood at the kitchen door.

'Hi,' said Lydia. She hid under her hair. She hovered in the kitchen while Robert went to Maxine's room to collect the last painting, watching them. She just stood there.

Robert was at the kitchen door again. Lydia had never liked him. Maxine smiled conspiratorially and Lydia offered an amused smile back, but Lydia had to turn away first as her expression began to disintegrate.

'Well!' said Maxine, watching Robert disappear down the stairs. 'Off we go, then.'

She turned to Lydia and looked around the kitchen.

'I liked it here, you know. I must be mad.'

'Yeah,' Lydia said. 'You must be.'

19

Deanna thought they'd sorted this out last night. Now she felt another sulk coming on. She took Consuela in her arms.

'For godsakes Claire means *nothing*, nothing. She's nothing to do with you.'

Consuela extricated herself. 'So why do it?' she said, looking injured.

'I already said. Fascination, something. She's straight. We've known each other for years. I was restless. We might have done a book together…'

Consuela looked at the wall. 'Is that how you get to do a book here? Fuck the publisher? Your explanations - they're all over the place.'

'Well it doesn't matter now. It was before you in any case. I've already blown her off. Claire's *married*.'

'Blown her off,' said Consuela, sitting on the bed. She was warming up again. 'What's that?'

'What you do to show someone you're not interested without saying it in so many words…'

'What you do,' Consuela smiled. 'Very English. Very round and about. Just another person. 'Blow them off.' Thought it was exciting. You are funny. Come here.'

Consuela threw Deanna back on the bed and pinned her wrists above her head. Deanna's back arched and she squealed as Consuela jammed her knee between her legs.

'You're mine now,' she said.

'I know...,' said Deanna. 'I know...oh!'

'You're mine, you're mine...'

'I know...'

She cupped Deanna's breasts and pushed them to their optimum cleavage. She sunk her lips in them, moving her knee. Deanna moaned and arched again. They had an hour before they were due to collect Jonathan.

'I'm going to get a tarantula,' said Consuela, afterwards.

'There are limits sweetheart.'

'As a houseguard.'

'Okay.'

Consuela leaned and picked up a postcard by Deanna's bed:

> *Dear Deanna,*
> *At the lunch we had recently you very kindly*
> *offered to drive me to Maxine's exhibition. Would*
> *you do that as my car's fucked again?*
> *Best regards*
> *Jonathan*

'He's confused too,' said Deanna, 'like Claire.'

'Oh fine,' said Consuela. 'I guess I'm getting the hang of this now.'

Consuela opened a map in the car, pointed to Canary Wharf, threw the map on the floor then fell asleep. Deanna completed a very thorough tour of Docklands side streets before she found Jonathan's block. He stood to attention outside his flats like a prop from a stage set. He looked at Consuela thoughtfully, then scrambled in. Deanna seemed in a much better mood than last time.

'You're difficult to find,' said Consuela, waking up, 'it's like another planet here.' She looked at his block of flats, then his suit. 'You're a yuppie,' she said. But she made being a yuppie sound cute.

'Yes I am,' said Jonathan, sticking his head between the front seats, 'excessively.'

'You didn't have anyone you wanted to bring?'

'Too busy working,' said Jonathan, 'for that.'

Deanna crunched her gears.

'Forgiven?' said Jonathan. 'Am I?'

'Forgiven?' said Deanna. 'What? Did I complain about anything?'

Claire arrived earlier than expected and sat impatiently in her fuggy car. The area was dead apart from the gallery sign beckoning malevolently ahead. She didn't want to go in yet. Stuck behind the wheel, dressed with frantic elegance, she tried to make herself comfortable, and couldn't. She saw Deanna's car pull up and huddled into her seat. Deanna, another woman, and Jonathan got out, loose and chatty, very much with each other. Something about Deanna's way with the woman convinced Claire that they were lovers. She felt bleak.

Maxine stood in the corner of the gallery and cracked her finger joints, one by one. She looked like someone who didn't quite know how they had got there, and wanted to go soon. The pictures were hung as well as they could get them, and felt bigger than she ever did, but their standing here was more precarious than at the *Macro*. Janet had arranged the food and drink and having no takers, started re-arranging it again. Robert looked at the paintings. Tim had returned to his office on the unlikely pretext of making more phone calls.

Maxine knew that in watching the guest's faces, she'd see their judgments too. She was frozen on the spot and wished it would start. She put on a tape, one of Lydia's. Lydia hadn't shown up yet. She didn't at the moment know where she'd find the energy to do another body of work like this.

Tim strode out with a silky walk and greeted someone in a white suit. Deanna and Consuela were there. Oh. Claire stood beside them, limp as a dishrag. So that was it. Maxine felt a faint wave of pity following hot on the satisfaction. She didn't really care any more. Daniel had arrived with Paul. They were beside themselves with each other. Old friends and associates she hadn't seen for a long time entered. The paintings were regarded, everyone seemed pleased to be there, and now she was glad too, glad that they'd be here for her. Glasses were filled, exclamations paid tribute to Janet's black bread and grapes. Julius arrived and presented Maxine with a bottle of calvados. Maxine said hello to everyone, less nervous.

'So!' said Deanna to Claire. 'Did Miranda get in touch?'

'No need to yet,' Claire replied. Her voice was brittle. 'But yes, when the proofs come in…' She looked away. Her neck was tight.

'I don't see,' said Consuela, steadily, looking at Deanna, then more warmly at Claire, 'why anyone has to pretend. Not on my account. How are you today Claire?'

'I'm very well,' said Claire.

Deanna wished Consuela was Paula, just then. Paula was English. She'd understand. Understand that some things were best left unsaid, a little coldness saved on real explosions.

Julius touched Claire's arm. They stood facing a painting of an erection peeping through rose petals, in various pinks.

Julius smiled. 'She's very funny isn't she?'

'Oh yes,' Claire said, 'quite hilarious.'

She saw Jonathan out of the corner of her eye. He looked across at her. His eyes and lips were very thin. He wasn't going to come over, he looked as if he could wait. His blond hair was slicked expertly over his forehead. He was older now. He lifted his glass to toast her.

Maxine was happier now. Judith Bowen was at the door and she was bald. Piers van Damme followed behind, looking concerned. He nodded at Maxine and went and stood in front of her crossed pricks painting for half an hour. Judith stood beside Maxine, their backs to the wall.

'He posed for that one,' said Maxine. 'Piers.'

'Yes,' said Judith, 'he likes to work in the nude.'

Judith didn't seem in a hurry to look at anything. Maxine chose to take this as a gesture of faith.

'How do you cope,' she said, 'with Piers never saying anything?'

'Tantric sex,' said Judith. 'It's the only way. We prepare a special room, light the incense burner, dress in diaphanous robes, and imagine each other as the Divine. We wash each other's genitals, mingle the waters, then drink. All very slow.'

'Oh,' said Maxine, 'oh.'

'Well you know,' said Judith, 'we haven't got much money and it helps pass the time.'

They stared at the crowd, who were doing more talking than looking. Maxine was suddenly too important for anyone to approach her.

'I had another reason for coming here,' said Judith. 'We're going to start a chapter of Guerrilla Girls. Combat in the art zone. Interested?'

Maxine stretched her neck over a row of heads.

'Yeah,' she said, 'definitely.'

'That's me, you and Tiggy and maybe Tin Tin then. Maybe Jocasta Martin - you know, she does nursery rhymes...'

'Yeah...' said Maxine.

'The Black Clothes, White Drugs lot have got a show at The Cataract. Alice Schwartz'll get us in. You heard of her?'

'Rings a bell,' said Maxine.

'She's into psycho-sex, anal sex, decapitation and the unconscious. Does two installations a year, then spends three months in The Willow Clinic, W11, trying to come off heroin.'

'Oh right, right,' said Maxine. 'I thought she was just maybe someone they'd invented, you know, to save face.'

'No,' said Judith, 'she's real. Only one who's gone right

down that road though.' She sighed. 'It's the Leonora Carrington syndrome all over again. I'd kill for that lifestyle though. You know I wouldn't mind being smacked out of my head most of the time but I had to take that DSS job to pay off my fuckin' student grant.'

'Well,' said Maxine, 'suppose it gets difficult once it gets to that stage.'

'Are you kidding?' said Judith. 'She buys her dinner in Pret A Manger. But you know, fair enough, she's on our side. Nice little exhibition this, not too *beige*.'

'You're on,' Maxine said. 'And thanks.'

Tim was talking to someone whose clothes and demeanour breathed money. Only the slightest air of boredom and twitch of discontent told her that this wasn't the man from Saatchi's, as promised.

'My drug dealer!' Judith continued, catching the whiff of disappointment, 'who does she think she is? I don't think 'drug dealer' I think 'dear friend'. Maybe it's just a class thing.'

'What?' said Maxine.

'Friend Alice,' said Judith.

'Oh.'

Tim looked at Maxine and jerked his head.

'Off you go then,' said Judith, 'he looks nice and ripe.'

She made a circle out of her thumb and forefinger and winked. Maxine returned the gesture.

'Yes it's brilliant!' declared Daniel. 'We've got Greek art, *Measure for Measure*, The PragMATiks - I did that myself, and a play about date rape!'

Jonathan overheard this and flinched, remembering Patti's cousin. Then he remembered it had only been a thought - he hadn't actually done anything. Still, it was obviously a common occurrence. Happened all the time. They did art about it. It was an issue. Other people did it.

Claire wondered why Daniel sounded like an automaton. She thought she was being made fun of, but he seemed perfectly frank. She didn't know why she'd leapt at the chance to get him a job. Maybe some kind of futile attempt at imitating Anthony. Had she known then what she knew now… The man who was evidently Daniel's new boyfriend was dressed almost identically. Together they looked like Pinky and Perky. The boys turned to Maxine's box of objects: hothouse poppies, pubic hair, a contact lens, bits of rock it looked like, and a picture of a supermodel.

'She's certainly got a way with toenails!' Paul said.

Daniel laughed.

So that's what they were, Claire thought. She felt bitterly at a loss. The boys watched Tim pass.

'I bet he's adventurous,' Paul whispered to Daniel.

One man wore a T-shirt saying 'Will you be my experiment?' Claire looked around for Deanna and couldn't see her. Another man wore one saying 'Leave Diana Alone!' He was saying to someone else: 'I've always liked the idea of being whipped but don't think I'd like it in real life.' Claire blushed. Her own thoughts exactly. Paul had just announced to someone that dinner parties had gone out of fashion. She caught another speech: 'Brew some frozen peas in chicken stock, add lots of black pepper then blend it. Makes a fantastic soup.' History had it in for the likes of her. These people - they wouldn't even want her life. Yet it connected her with something she wanted to know about now, as a life raft, the only one left. Jonathan's eyes were aimed at her. She remembered something Maxine had said. He sent me hate mail. Of course he did. It made sense now.

Daniel knew Jonathan was looking at him. He felt slightly ashamed of touching up Paul at every opportunity. It was mainly for Jonathan's benefit. He just couldn't help himself. He looked across at Jonathan to try and gauge a reaction.

Jonathan stared at Maxine's *Hurricane*. He liked the scraped colours in deep blues, and the wounds and scars worked into the paint. But this event wasn't doing for him what being at her place had done. Not the same, the production and the display of it. These people were no different from those at work, except in a different style - a more subtle style, but it was the same thing on a low budget. The sums he was dealing in just amounted to more. Claire was nearer to him.

Claire stared very hard at the paintings. She had to have something to concentrate on to divert her from Deanna and Jonathan. But she found an apocalyptic feel in the painting that met and chimed with something in her. They had no doubt, these paintings. She looked at *Earthquake*. It was about destruction, and loving it. She liked that. Yes, she thought. Do it. Jonathan was beside her.

'How are you?' she said. She couldn't look at him.

'How are you Claire?'

She knew he'd done it. She knew he'd been at the cottage.

He was changed. This place was a safe haven, away from old associations.

'We have to talk, about Anthony,' she said. 'We really do.'

'Sure,' said Jonathan, 'sure. Old Uncle Anthony.'

Claire felt sick.

'Are you going to do anything else, to us?'

The 'us' sounded wrong.

'Not until we've talked,' said Jonathan.

Priscilla had arrived and had already looked at everything. She recognised the artist as the kind of girl who might, on another occasion, maybe in another time, have dressed herself up like an old-fashioned doll. The type of girl who had no grasp at all of her value, except the unnecessary things she alone considered important.

'Well,' she said to Daniel. 'I suppose it's kind of muted Jackson Pollock meets Anselm Kiefer with a load of feminist stuff thrown in.'

She really can be very unpleasant at times, Daniel thought. 'How did you get *that?*' he wanted to complain. But he wasn't at work now. He moved towards Deanna and Consuela.

'How's your niece then?' he said. 'How's *Boo?*'

'Oh my niece,' said Deanna. Her face was blank.

'Niece in name,' she added, to Consuela.

Consuela bit her lip, and took in Maxine's *Snowstorm* as she looked away. 'Before me,' she said, 'I guess.'

'I'd like to buy *Hurricane*,' said Jonathan to Maxine.

Maxine was stunned.

'Should I pay for it now?'

Claire watched Jonathan write a cheque for £800. There

was a lump in Maxine's throat.

'Fabulous painting,' said Claire, 'fabulous.'

Maxine wanted to pinch herself. Jonathan smiled at the greed in her eyes as he put his signature to the cheque and underlined it.

'I'll deliver it,' said Maxine. 'Are you okay, Claire?'

'Yes.'

Jonathan smiled at Claire, and Maxine, and left.

Priscilla spotted Robert as someone she recognised. She went up to him, asked what he did, and told him all about her house. To Robert's famished ears, this sounded very interesting. For the first time all afternoon, he felt wanted.

'Pity is,' Priscilla said, 'there's no one else living there now. Anwar, my husband, is in the Far East. Dull dull dull.'

Marcus had been at the market with Janet, and she made a lot of jokes at his expense with their regular traders. He now arrived late, freshly washed, clothed and perfumed, with the intention of making overtures to the most glamourous woman in the room. He grabbed two drinks and charged towards Consuela, who jumped at his proximity.

'You an artist too?' he said. 'You look like one.'

'No, I decorate. I'm a decorator.'

'Fantastic,' said Marcus. 'I have a restaurant.'

'Oh, nice,' said Consuela.

Robert sidled up.

'She's a decorator,' declared Marcus, eying her up and down. 'Anyone we know, perhaps?'

'Omega Projects,' said Consuela. 'A women's firm, all women, you know.'

Deanna appeared, also carrying two glasses. 'Alright, gentlemen?' she said.

Marcus and Robert retreated.

'Bloody women,' Marcus muttered. 'I mean, it's not that I mind taking out the rubbish, popping down to the shops or putting plug tops on or whatever, but you know, I like to be asked not told - know what I mean? It's when they get you buying their tampons *and* the condoms - I think there's a hidden agenda there don't you?'

'Yeah,' said Robert, trying to fathom what was going on at the opposite end of the room.

'It's like 'welcome to my reproductive system'. Eh? Yeah, Janet wants a baby. I've got her number.'

'Mmm,' said Robert. He watched Claire and Priscilla pause disconsolately over a pile of sticky cotton buds. They looked like a pair of candlesticks.

Priscilla yelled '*Brasted?!*' and Claire nodded.

'You lay and you pay,' said Marcus. 'Everything going okay here then?'

'Seems to be,' said Robert.

'Want to go to the pub then?'

Janet saw them leave. 'Here we go,' she said to Lydia.

'He's really not worth it, Janet.'

Syd arrived with Lydia and approached Claire.

'They're my girls,' he said, 'my girls.'

'Got to go,' said Priscilla.

'Oh really?' said Claire.

'I'm their kind of patron.'

'Patron?' said Claire. He stank of sour booze.

'I give 'em low rent. They produce beauty and truth.'

She was drinking in gulps now. The man's cardigan had holes. Claire looked at Maxine and drew herself up to her full height.

'What precisely do you mean by that?' she said.

'Well look at them,' said Syd, 'her and Lydia. It's not as if they couldn't pass in regular company. They do it for a purpose.'

'Yes, yes,' said Claire. 'I see.'

It was nearly over. Only 6pm. The festive air that had infiltrated the texture of Maxine's thoughts had dwindled and started on its last, hopeful gasps. She could hear the hum of the air conditioning now. Tim was ushering out the last dealer, who said he would think about it. He looked at Maxine and threw his hands in the air. She had sold three paintings. That was it, five years' work. It was anyone's guess who would come and view it now.

Robert came back and put his hands around her, and she forgot he'd been and gone for an hour. She put her hands on top of his, feeling better.

Robert looked up at Maxine's *Thunder*, the one he thought was about him, and was glad it hadn't sold. Now he had her - and the way she sucked up the atmosphere of any environment she inhabited and exhaled it infused with something of herself, suddenly making it seem special. He wanted her to be with him. He was sick of hiking over to an inaccessible part of town, where places opened and shut at erratic hours, where people were bad tempered with poverty and the fact that their clothes didn't even fit properly. She would live with him and he'd have her all to himself. Love was too difficult and disturbing when it was always done on the run. He wanted to keep his hands free, and still have it there on tap. If they could combine her art with his utility. Boom, boom, he thought.

Later, having turned off the TV because nothing in the world was as interesting as them, Maxine and Robert lay against each other on the floor, drinking Julius' calvados, and Julie London, who filled the air with ease and white luxury. They thought they were in heaven, they thought they were in paradise.

Lydia had left the exhibition early and come home in search of a 'life sucks, fuck it, I'm better off on my own' song that she might play a few times to get everything into perspective, then perform on stage that night. She sorted through a large selection of such songs - women, men, old, new, there was plenty of choice - then gave up.

Maxine's attitude to love was painful to witness. She didn't know where it came from - except that exposure to *Wuthering Heights* and the works of Patti Smith at an impressionable age had obviously done its worst. She wondered if Maxine and Robert would get married now? Probably not. Or if they did, it could only be to assuage Maxine's desire for an exhibitionistic wedding dress.

She was glad she was working tonight, because it reminded her that there was one thing in the world she could do. The Drachma Club had cut their dates, and cut their musicians. The audience was thin, she wasn't singing her own songs, but it didn't matter. It would do. Tonight, she was happy with something impersonal.

She picked herself up off the floor at the side of the stage where she'd been sitting, legs apart, smoking a cigarette. She removed the boiled sweet she'd been rolling around her mouth to make it moist and supple, and then she was ready. She clicked her fingers, the drummer banged and splashed, and Paul started up on the piano. Lydia shook her hair out of her way, and shut her eyes, so she could just focus on the essential sensations.

Daniel watched enchanted from a table at the back, knowing that the pianist with effort engraved on his face would be going home with him that night. Paul played the piano as if he was born to it, spent other parts of his time offering his hands as a sweet convalescence to bodies ravaged by chemotherapy and childbirth, and could, Daniel knew already, stroke a shy sphincter into heaving submission. Unlike everyone he met in Italy, Paul had been the one who stayed over, and didn't seem in a hurry to snatch his clothes and bolt off as soon as possible.

Daniel was dreamily contented to have spent all day in the company of friends who could do things, even on a small scale like this. It made him feel part of a charmed race. You did not have to invent excuses as to why anyone should like it.

Lydia's voice glided over the phrases like melted butter. The songs were vaguely familiar, although not so familiar that they forestalled attention. He watched the audience breaking off conversations to watch her. And he watched Paul, who cast him the odd glance as he added pretty frills to his accompaniment, which Daniel thought boded very well for later.

Lydia was relieved that the drummer had simmered down now, and she realised he had only been noisy at first to grab her attention. With Riccardo unavailable, it looked as if he was going spare that night. Alright. She knew they'd go home together for comfort, not passion, but she'd already decided to be gregarious this summer. The tour was soon, and she was happy to think there would be someone around for her.

The song changed, and the drums whispered seductively - he knew he'd got her now. Paul's piano chords went oh-so-quietly into the gut. It was only that and her voice, rising up somewhere from just under her lungs, and she could ride it. It didn't matter if anyone else was listening now.

> …*Thrill has gone*
> *The thrill has gone away from me*
> *Thrill has gone*
> *The thrill had gone away for good*
> *Done me wrong*
> *Baby you'll be sorry some day*

She left the stage to a smattering of applause and washed of the misery she had arrived with.

Their skin was a bit waxy in the heat, but what she and the drummer had just done was as good a preliminary as any. She saw Paul join Daniel at his table. He looked and acted differently with other men than he did when he was with them - more relaxed. She'd done good work tonight, and was pleased that at the moment, the drummer would be going home with a singer, not just a poor girl who lived above a comic shop, whose best friend had just deserted her.

20

'Out.' Jonathan couldn't quite believe what he was hearing. 'Out.'

Then again, he'd half expected it all along. He and Charles stood in front of a big desk with three heavy faces staring back at them. They were lost for words. They weren't the first, and they wouldn't be the last to go. Anthony's pay-off had just run out.

'Out. Now.'

They loved doing this, these old men. They were sick to death of tykes like him and Charles swaggering around, thinking they were the only people in the world who had ever done anything. Ugly bastards. It was an ugly world. You did all this for me, Anthony, he thought, but you didn't want me in your own world, not really, not your own territory. He wanted not to care. He wanted to sink to his knees and scream. No references, no fucking clock.

Hours later, he and Charles were still in a quiet bar-cum-hamburger joint, getting steadily drunk.

'Wasso odd,' Charles slobbered, 'is that Ginny's I Ching woman said things were about to look up.'

Jonathan considered this for about a minute, his eyes fixed on an empty chair. 'Well that was a load of crap wasn't it?'

There were a few things, there were a few things, he could put straight now.

'Maybe...maybe they'll rehire us,' said Charles.

I just got something back, Jonathan thought, just a little compensation. He had known it would end. He looked at Charles' blubbery face and despised him for thinking everything could be alright, forever, that anything riding on luck like that could last forever.

If You Don't Know Me By Now was playing. It sounded like the thirty five minute version. Jonathan and Charles had shrunk from men whose actions were laws to two boys skiving off from school.

'Just goes on and on this song,' said Charles, 'never stops does it?' He stared into his drink. 'Fuck.'

The video machine hanging from the ceiling was playing a Stones tape with the sound off.

'Hey-argh!' Charles waved at the barman. 'Any chance of getting any sound up on this one?'

The barman slid over the counter, stood on a chair, fiddled with the machine, banged it, shrugged, collected their glasses and brought them more.

'No,' said Charles. 'Like those guys up there, they had some job security, right?'

'Yeah,' said Jonathan, 'yeah. So has the barman, maybe.'

'You can lip read this,' said Charles. 'It's *Sympathy For The Devil.*'

'Really,' said Jonathan.

'Yuo,' said Charles. '*Woo woo*,' he went.

Fuck's sake, Jonathan thought. Had it come to this? They ordered chopped steaks. The food bore as much resemblance to steak as a tin of dogfood, but they wolfed it all down anyway.

The streets were very dark by the time they left, the air harsh on their flushed skin. Tall grey buildings seemed to be caving in on them. There was hardly any sky to be seen. Away from the big talk, the pips, the glares, and public announcements, there was nothing here, and they were nothing. They staggered back to their old office, and pissed enthusiastically over its doorway, making noises like machine guns. Charles slapped Jonathan's back, and Jonathan slapped Charles' back. They weaved on, and started singing:

> *I'm Jake the Peg diddle-iddle-iddle-ee*
> *With an extra leg diddle-iddle-iddle-ee*

'Hey yeah ba that would be discri-' Charles tried again, 'discrimination wouldna it now?'

'Yu?' said Jonathan.

'Discrimination for je disabled.'

Jonathan thought about this, long and hard, as they ploughed on down the very long road.

'No one,' he said, 'no one has *three* legs do they? *Pillock*.' He pushed Charles. 'No one has three legs ya cunt. Can't fuckin' count can you? Two legs. You get *two*. That's yer lot. No more. Never. No one's gor three legs.'

Charles pushed him back. Jonathan took a slug at him and

missed. Charles turned to punch Jonathan, and got him in the chest. They both fell onto the pavement.

'Here here!' Charles got up, lost his footing and fell down again, waving at a passing car. Jonathan crawled over to him, punched him down, then picked him up.

'We lost,' Jonathan whispered in his ear, as they fell into each other and tried to work out where they were. 'We fuckin' lost. Nothing we can do about it, mate. We're *fucked*. We're out.'

It was nearly morning. Jonathan's thoughts were running in blood. He left Charles at an empty taxi rank and went to the river by a wall made of granite bricks with no particular view, where he could sit and just be quiet for a while.

The air was cold in his lungs and when he inhaled everything was heightened. He felt his blood coursing through his veins and was conscious of his flesh and bones. He rubbed his legs. He was going, slowly, from complete tunnel vision to seeing things. He had sustained Anthony's impositions, he had got this far, now he could take anything. His body could take anything. He was still alive. Thirty seconds used to be a long attention span. Now he had all the time in the world. Five minutes passed and it seemed like hours. The river slapped against the stone walls. There was no decency. None. He rocked back and forth. He didn't want to take up too much space. He opened his wallet, took out all but one of his credit cards, snapped them in two, and hurled them into the river. His last two packets of pale powder were carefully unwrapped and sprayed in after the cards. The wind whistled around him. His outsize bully suit was all he had left of his former glory. He stared at the river and wondered what he'd do now. I'm more than a telephone, he thought. Much more than that.

He passed a video shop and numerals in the same print as the dealing room's printer told punters that the shop would be open again in a matter of hours. This was it, this was real.

The next day, he bought three bottles of Absolut vodka and stood them on the mantelpiece in his flat. Just in case anyone came round. Not for him. He was clean now. This was something he could offer to other people. Well... He dialled Buzz Snag's number. He hung up as his mouth filled with saliva. He remembered the dealer's face - disbelief and loathing. He'd be abstinent from now on.

The chaos came slowly. He kept hearing things that weren't there. His empty ears picked up on every sound and distorted it. He used to predict things on his instincts. Now there was nothing to predict. He called his horoscope:

> 'Hello Leo. You're in a generous, good-natured mood at the beginning of the week. You need the co-operation of others at the moment, and the expertise of a colleague could prove invaluable! The Sun moves into your sector of relationships, so maybe now's the time to pursue that special friendship! A clash with Mars on Thursday could mean a slight setback but Mercury turning to forward motion will pack you off into horizons new. Don't forget to ring me next week to hear more! Thanks for calling Leo!

It was so nice when she talked to you like that. She really seemed to care. But her remarks on his life seemed pointless since he didn't have a life now. Just one drink, then, to calm his nerves.

The next morning he woke up in a raddled sweat. Two of the Absolut bottles were empty. Liquid streamed from every orifice and his front room looked as if wild beasts had been tramping through it. His hair was matted with blood where he had crashed into the wall. The carpet was stained with blood too. Oh well. Rome wasn't built in a day. He put *Abwegige Leidenschaft* on top of the bloodstain. That covered it. He got out his gun. Finish it now, then.

He ran it alongside his cheek, he tried it on his chest, he put it to his head, and he sucked it, long and slow. The steel was very comforting. Nice and cold. Then he remembered - Maxine was coming round. He rubbed the gun lasciviously in his palm, and stowed it away.

He examined his face in the bathroom mirror. His tongue was coated with a white substance and he scrubbed at it angrily with a toothbrush. He picked around his teeth with a silver instrument, and extracted some evil smelling scum. His skin was flaky and dry. The sides of his lips were browning and chapped. I'm rotting from within and without, he thought.

Maxine arrived and saw Jonathan's car, and paused to look at it. She wondered how he managed to drive around town without acquiring dents and skewered wing mirrors. It was a very handsome car. She ran her hands down its flanks. It was a piece of genius, this machine.

Jonathan looked a mess. She unwrapped the painting and laid it against the wall.

'There.'

'Great,' said Jonathan. 'Great.'

He regarded it from various angles. From a distance, close up. She regarded him warily.

'How did you do it?'

Maxine sat down, cautiously. Keep him talking.

'You start with the drawing,' she said. 'Well I do. Then go on from there. That's what I did here anyway.' She got out her sketchbook, and selected a new piece of paper.

'You really want to know?'

'Yes.'

What was this, an inquisition? Then she settled down.

'You just have to work out where the source of energy is, in an object.' She drew, very rapidly.

Jonathan was surprised she could draw things properly.

'It's not creation,' she said, 'so much as recognition.'

'Why do you do it?' he said.

'It helps things make sense.' She put the sketchbook down. 'And it's the only thing I'm any good at. The only thing I've ever been any good at ever.'

So, he thought, she was an innocent after all.

Maxine got up, looked around at Jonathan's furniture, the expansive view out of the window, and the clocks. Her eye fell on *Abwegige Leidenschaft*.

'Oh I like his stuff,' she said. 'I haven't seen this one.'

She went to pick it up.

'No leave it alone…'

'I only wanted to look...'

'No leave it alone. I'll lend it to you when I've finished with it. I'll bring it round honest. Don't touch it.'

He looked very peculiar. Ruffled, but determined.

'Whatever...' she said. 'What are you going to do now? Will Anthony find you something else?'

'No. Not Anthony,' he said.

She seemed pleased with this, and didn't say anything else.

Fear, everyone lived on fear, he thought. He didn't have anything to fear any more. He was in a no man's land. So was she, in her way. He was among the damned now. He didn't care. He was glad. He felt violently empty. He watched Maxine go, from his window, and banged on it to re-direct her on the right path. You and me both, he thought, watching her go - trying to make out our time's fought over.

He drove to Claire's. Same old house. He wanted to burn it down. He presented her with a Limoges perfume bottle - navy porcelain finished with gold. She dropped it as she unwrapped it.

'I'm so terribly terribly sorry.'

'Yeah.'

'You didn't have to buy me this. I... You must realise...' Her fragile spine re-asserted itself. 'I had no idea.'

'No,' he said, 'no.'

'I really didn't.'

She looked at him, pleadingly. She was scared of him and also, somehow ravenous for him - to make amends, to be comforted. Her language and voice didn't seem so clipped, now he'd seen her like this. He was coming round to Claire.

'What do you want to do?' she said.

'Ladies first, Claire. What do you want to do?'

His smarmy gentility was something she'd have to put up with, for the time being. The opposite of Anthony, but somehow Anthony's legacy also. What would he have been like otherwise? They'd never know.

'Oh,' Claire said, 'I want Anthony out of my life.'

'Right,' he said, 'right.'

'You want to come into his study? There's things there…' She took a deep breath. 'Diaries, photos. They're yours by rights. It's up to you to decide what's done with it.'

'Good,' said Jonathan. 'And I'll sleep here tonight.'

Claire was clearly alarmed.

'Here?'

'Anthony's away isn't he?'

'Yes.'

'Demons,' said Jonathan, 'to get rid of my demons.'

Claire nodded.

Jonathan slept in one of the spare rooms and dreamed of a glittering summer party in a park. A gallery of the great and the good, in evening wear. Some of them looked like film stars, but no one he could place. A van of police appeared, and rammed a car. They leaned out of the van and cheered, and kept ramming the car until it was flat as a pancake. Everyone stood there watching them do it. They turned around and murmured to each other, as if nothing had happened. As if nothing had happened at all.

When he woke up and explored the house he found Claire

sitting at her dressing table, in a white silk gown, clutching her hair. He kissed the back of her neck, she held his wrist briefly, but firmly, holding him at a distance, but tightly.

'Okay,' he said. 'Alright.'

Anne was sitting on the steps outside, smoking a cigarette.

'What's the matter with you,' said Jonathan. 'Haven't you got a home to go to?'

'You're going about this completely the wrong way you vicious little sod,' she said.

'What?' said Jonathan. 'I beg your pardon?'

'Smashing their clock and all that. Pathetic. You could take Anthony to court. You could fix him. I've got newspaper contacts. That's the public spirited way of doing it. Not all this crap, whatever it is.'

'Mrs. Brasted,' said Jonathan. 'I have no idea what you're talking about.'

He returned to Claire. She got up hurriedly.

'Old bag Brasted,' he said, 'pay her off.'

Claire nodded.

'And destroy the evidence, all of it.'

'Who else knows?,' she said. *Who else knows?*'

'Maxine,' said Jonathan, and smiled, 'that's all.'

'Oh,' said Claire. 'Maxine. Yes.'

It would be. Of course. She should have known.

21

Daniel stood in Arts Inc's huge and deserted toilets, where a metallic version of *Telstar* was playing. He'd had one too many Slivovitz's with the Czech dancers at lunchtime, and now forgot why Priscilla had sent him in this direction in the first place. It would come. Back at the office, the tabloid newspaper's headline shouted at him from Priscilla's desk:

PC PLAYWRIGHT IN GAY ROCK ROMP

There was a picture of David Brasted looking suitably baffled and implausible in a duffel coat and woolly hat.

'I should really stop getting drunk with that Jack Pallack,' said Priscilla. 'It's not as if he ever gives us any sensible coverage. Then again,' she added, 'there's already been a bit of a fillip at the box office. Not sure if this is quite the thing for the crossover crowd. Still, never mind. Fancy a drink?'

The bar was emptied of staff and it was too early for any of the public to have appeared. Priscilla sat at the table and wrapped her ankles around the chair. It was clear Daniel was expected to play the man on this one.

He fetched two glasses of white wine. When he came back, Priscilla was staring into space.

'Look - *Brasted*!' she whispered.

'Who's the woman?' said Daniel.

'Looks like his mother. Yeah it is. Look - you can see the likeness. She's with him in his hour of need - oh bless her, oh *sweet!*'

Mrs. Brasted approached them.

'Whatever you do,' muttered Priscilla, 'keep a straight face.'

'You're Daniel aren't you?' said Mrs. Brasted.

'Friend of Claire - the publisher? I've seen you at her place?'

'Yes!'

'Can we have a word?'

'Now?'

Mrs. Brasted looked at Priscilla. 'Later, I'll call you. I'll call you here.' She left.

Priscilla's hands were over her face. She removed them, and recovered.

'Oh dear! Claire's gay friend. She wants to talk to you seriously.' She dropped her tone. 'Discuss David's dilemma. Oh *no*. Poor sausage doesn't realise that in our world we really don't *care* about that kind of thing!'

Daniel laughed now. Our world, he thought, feeling sultry.

'She's Claire's cleaning woman - that's it! I remember!'

'Oh!' cried Priscilla. 'She's not is she? Oh God!'

'What shall I say?'

'Oh just tell her - y'know. Being Gay's Great. Or - The

Filthy Tabloids Have Got It All Wrong. Make something up. Reassurance. I don't know! I mean it isn't as if Claire wouldn't reassure her! God!'

'But he's not is he? He's not gay?'

'Not now,' said Priscilla, recovering. 'I suppose. If ever. Who cares?'

She swigged her drink, so did Daniel.

'I was wondering…' he said.

'Yes…'

'When I might get, you know, an actual contract.'

'Contract?' said Priscilla. 'Contract? Oh. There's no *contract* is there? As such,' she added, slowly. 'You're on a work scheme.'

'Work scheme,' said Daniel, 'work scheme.' No wonder the salary was the start-up type.

'Yes. There's one of the American students taking over next month. Oh God Daniel. You didn't *know*?'

Her hands flew to her face. 'Oh God I feel *awful*. Didn't Claire…'

Daniel shook his head.

'No. Maybe I didn't make it clear. Didn't you read *Future Policy Documents*?'

'Uh-no.'

'Look, now, um, drink up…' She waved at the barman. 'Emergency, Eric, thanks. Yes, we've got one Paul Rabinowitz coming in. It's just a scheme, you know, to get a little experience, marketing the arts. Bit of a con really, but…thanks Eric. Drink up. No - there's him, then it goes up for grabs, as an actual job. That awful girl Bella from

Personnel has already applied.'

'Bella?'

Priscilla nodded. 'She's been doing a marketing course on the sly. At which stage I bail out, I think. She's got a lot of people on her side and a cast iron case. I've already applied for something with British Steel. I've worked in the arts for years, so they'll think I'm really gifted. Hope so. Oh dear. Oh dear. Sorry!'

'It's alright,' said Daniel. 'No it's fine.' There was a great big hole in front of him.

'You know I shouldn't tell you this,' said Priscilla. 'But Bella's been putting this rumour around that you've been doing some informal dope dealing.'

'*Whaat?*'

'Daniel,' Priscilla held her hand up. 'I saw the Board today. I said to everyone...'

'*Everyone?*'

'...look, he's really not the type. He's always very alert, I said, you know, in an appropriate sort of way, and as for any slip-ups. Well, it's only what we expect...'

'I could be arrested!'

'Oh, you won't be.'

'Do I get a reference?'

'I don't see why not.'

'Would there perhaps be any openings in *Shakespeare in Tuscany*, or *Greek Drama in Greece*? I was a tour guide.' His voice had changed.

'Well,' said Priscilla, 'you could certainly apply!'

'How long before that gets off the ground?'

'Difficult to say really. Eighteen months. Two years?'

Daniel returned to his soon-to-be-vacated desk. He turfed over the papers, and discovered a complimentary ticket to *Challenging Cultural Norms* at the University of North Barnet. Might as well go. It featured names that vaguely intrigued him. Get some experience, at what, whatever it was he was supposed to have been doing here, investigate, check it out. He had nothing else to do. Nothing else at all. He was still in shock.

When he finally found the campus, then the right block, and room, two of the speakers were already there, planted on wooden chairs on a raised platform with CHALLENGING CULTURAL NORMS chalked behind them on a blackboard. The audience's chairs were arranged like pews. Daniel sat down next to a couple of androgynes.

Professor Alun Crikshit held the Transgressive Chair at North Barnet, sponsored by Tizer. His most notable works were *Exploring Diversities*, now a set text, and *Tension and Extension in Edmund Spencer*, a wily dissection of oppositions. He was joined by Dr. Ruth Bush, who wore a sharp bob, a serious expression and a grey Chanel suit. Old feminist/new dyke, and strict disciplinarian, Ruth preferred her lovers to be 25 or younger, and straight before she met them.

She was author of the pioneering *Gender & Class*, followed five years later by *Sex, Class & Race*. The most drastic change to date in her personal life prompted a further volume: *Sexuality, Gender, Class & Race*. In the late 80s, she branched out with *Sex, Class, Race, Sexuality, Shopping Malls and All That Jazz*, but this had been somewhat preempted by the publication of Clover Crass's less eclectic *The Virtual & The Feminine*, in the same week.

A wash of layered pastel silks, waist length blonde hair and Eau Dynamisante cued Clover's aromatic entrance. She and Ruth greeted each other in a girlie fashion, without warmth. One did journalism, the other didn't.

Dr. Maurice Blanche arrived, suited and bespectacled. He wrote mostly about Marx and Hegel.

'Okay I think we're ready to start now,' said Alun. 'Clover, would you like to kick off?'

'Thanks Alun,' said Clover. 'I'd like to start just by stating my own position clearly. First off, there's my name - Clover - a plant, a flower and a symbol. Then 'Crass' - a kind of ironical joke at my own expense, also etymologically related to the Hungarian adjective 'krasseveriet' meaning 'basic, true, abrasive, an irritant', which is how I see my role as a feminist writing and appearing to, for, and on behalf of women in various high profile spots...' she leaned forward and peered at Ruth, who stared furiously at the floor, '...in a male-dominated media. My roles are varied - writer, teacher, mother, confidante, rebel, lover - mother to Aureole and Piggy, lover to Rick Stitch, lead singer and lyricist of Just Red, daughter of militantly un-bookish working class parents, middle class more by education than disposition, half Swiss on my grandmother's side...'

Add grated cheese, Daniel thought, season to taste, and bake in the oven for 30 minutes.

'...choc addict, Gemini, survivor of anorexia, PMT, date

grope, Freudian psychoanalysis, a near-mugging and one water birth. As a woman in post-modern society I'm not, of course, above flashing the Switch and scoring a stash of Body Shop goodies, dabbling in soft drugs, getting rat-arsed on Stoli, sucking off boyz in the back of cabs, if that's what I feel like doing at the time, taking a spin in Rick's manager's Jaguar, stuffing the old Wonderbra with Kleenex or slamming on a workout tape in times of stress but…'

'Excuse me Alun,' said Dr. Ruth, 'do you have an introduction or what?'

'Headings, endings - they're mere formalities.'

'So you're not going to introduce it?'

'Don't go all teleological on me Ruthie.'

'You're not? But you're chairing it?'

'Yes, Ruth,' he turned to the audience and opened his arms, 'No - we all know why we're here, right?'

'Fine,' said Ruth.

'I forgot my notepad,' Alun mumbled. 'Audience?'

A woman dressed and coiffed identically to Ruth stood up and spoke in a soft Home Counties accent.

'I'd like to address this issue of the possibility of straight people or recidivist gays going around claiming a Bent identity. This might work adequately in terms of some of the voyeurs that crop up at venues like this, but what about your normative nuclear families in Cheam, or whatever? What implications does this have for Bent Art, and how do we distinguish what we do from the petit-bourgeois, suburban, essentially reactionary shenanigans featured in *Fiesta* or *Razzle*, Larkin-style spanking mags or, for that matter the kind of glossy, ironic materials favoured by so-called New Lads?'

'Yes,' said Alun, 'interesting points. Someone else?'

A woman put her hand up. 'As a lesbian previously engaged in heterosexual practice, me and my - ahem - peeresses have been surprised, sharing our experience, at how many straight men in our collective pasts requested anal stimulation...'

'You're not the only ones!' smiled Alun, raising his eyes wistfully to the ceiling.

The audience laughed and some of them clapped. Clover pulled a face.

'Is there not an ontological difficulty here?' the woman continued. 'Are straight men, in this case, not so different from gay men? Are they Bent men, in fact?'

'Could be,' said Alun, 'but that's a bit problematic, and dare I say it, essentialist. Go with that insight and we're exposing ourselves to the term 'Bent' being reduced to the meaning 'likes anal sex'. What we're driving at here is a wide range of sexual practice, and *malpractice*, combined with political activism, across a wide force-field of identities and potentialities. So let's not be too promiscuous with our definitions here.'

'Right,' said the woman. She shrugged at her friend and sat down.

'Following on from that point,' said a worried looking man, 'as a straight man who greatly enjoys cunnilingual activity with women, one on one kind of thing...'

'What does he mean - 'on'?' said a woman behind Daniel.

'...does that mean I could pass as some sort of a lesbian?'

'Uh - no,' said Alun.

'As usual,' said Dr. Ruth, firmly, 'we are eliding socio-economic determinations…'

There were murmurs of agreement.

'Right, Ruth - yeah, I think we should bear that in mind,' said Alun.

Plum Duff, budding pundit, swathed in black leather, stood up. 'I think we need a bit of flexibility here. We all know that, currently, sexual relations with men is a very *dykey* thing to do.'

'Speak for yourself!' yelled someone.

'I wasn't speaking personally,' replied Plum calmly, 'fact is, we know it *happens*!' She sat down.

'Good point,' said Alun.

'I'd've thought fucking men for penetrative sex was a pretty lame excuse,' said a quiet spoken woman in jeans, ' if you want to still call yourself a lesbian or dyke, given the range of dildoes now available.'

'Maybe they can't tell the difference!'

'And what,' cried another, 'if you don't want to sell into the pink pound?'

'I think it's about time,' said Ruth, 'that we extended this discussion beyond merely sexual matters.'

There was a long pause.

'Anyone?' said Alun. 'Yes? Over there?'

'Sorry I was just trying to find a tissue…' a ginger haired man blushed crimson.

A young woman waved.

'Alun…'

'Trudi…

'I thought your paper *Challenging Cultural Norms* was very thorough - fantastic in fact. But you say Bent people make up 23% of urban dwellings. If all the Bent people tried to persuade, rustle or set examples to the Boring people to adapt to a broadly Bent lifestyle, then by 2025, 60% of the population would be Bent. But that's positivist, isn't it?'

'Not really Trudi,' said Alun, thinking ex-students were always the worst. 'I meant it provocatively rather than a statement of facts or probability, as such.'

'Oh I see Alun, sorry,'

Stupid cow, he thought.

'Just to return to sex per se, before we get all high theoretical about this,' said a boy, 'let us after all not forget that some of us spend so much time trying to screw tuppence out of the DSS, or sending out 300 CVs for jobs we don't even want, we can't sit around on our arses all day going through Durkheim and Derrida with a fine tooth comb. In fact we often find ourselves wondering if reading all this stuff for 3 to 6 years was actually even *valid* in the first place.'

'Uhuh,' said Alun, 'so what's your question?'

'I've lost my drift now,' said the boy, 'but it was something to do with AIDS and safe sex.'

'Well that's one huge topic in itself,' said Alun, 'thanks.'

'I think it's important to distinguish between 'AIDS',' Ruth gestured with her forefingers, 'and 'sex' as such. Otherwise we play into the rabble rousing assumptions of the right wing tabloid press.'

'Quite so,' said Alun.

'Is anyone going to address my point about accessing Bent Art?' said Judy.

'Clover,' said a pale man, 'I was really hurt and angered by your failure to mention sewage workers in Tobago in your piece on the Minimum Wage.'

'I only had 800 words!' said Clover.

'But it was such an obvious hook wasn't it? It was just disappointing that's all.'

'I'd like to pick up Plum's point just for a moment,' said Ruth. 'For example Alun - have you ever had sex with a woman ever in your *life*?'

'Uh - not really,' said Alun.

'Are you fully Bent yourself then? It seems clear that men follow a more phallic trajectory in their sociosexual orientation. Women, being more amorphous and flexible, are more *intrinsically* Bent. Maybe at the end of the day we're all born Bent. But some are more Bent than others. Men have it too easy.'

'Right!' said Clover, and folded her arms.

'You know what I did the other day?' said Alun. 'Played some of my old records. In the Elvis Presley track, *Don't*, he goes '*Don't...don't...don't...*'" His Presley impersonation was fair, and the room went all quiet. 'Which in fact in the context of the whole song, actually means '*Do...do...do...*' There's,' he twisted his wrist back and forth, 'a little dialectical twist there.'

'You mean,' said Clover, 'it's challenging the axis of desire and denial?'

'Partly,' said Alun, 'also, on the same album, I was struck

by a line in *Jailhouse Rock*: *'if you can't find a partner use a wooden chair'*. Could that be a reference to onanism perhaps?'

'Oh come off it Alun!' cried Clover, I don't think you can construct a political *or* cultural strategy out of having sex with your furniture!'

'I think you're missing the point a bit there, Clover,' said Alun. 'Chairs are particularly pertinent in the avant-garde panorama at the moment. Take Phillipe Starck's chairs, for example. On the one hand, they're objects to sit on, on the other hand, they're much more than that - more like statements of libidinal intention. And take Ruth's defensiveness, for example, at my refusal to come clean about *chairing* the seminar just now...'

'He was in and out of hospital in his post-grad days y'know,' whispered someone near Daniel. 'Involved in some of RD Laing's initiatives.'

'...so there you have your metaphorical alliance, then there's the direct one. *One Night*, for instance, could be construed as a euphemism for cottaging...'

'Then surely Alun,' said Ruth, 'the song would be entitled *Ten Minutes Or Thereabouts*, not *One Night*...'

A couple in sports clothes who hadn't said anything got up and left.

'The political and the aesthetic are like an illicit affair,' said Alun, 'never fully consummated, but always tensely on the verge...'

'With the greatest respect to the contribution deconstruction and psychoanalysis have made to political debate,' said Ruth, 'I think that if you go too far down that road, you can end up sounding brain damaged.'

'As a drug user,' someone shot up, 'I resent that reference. Could we cut the judgmental, biologistic crap and talk of mind alterations, or mind enhancement. It's a minor point, but, I'd say, an important one.'

'Fair enough,' said Alun.

Someone clutched their throat, rushed out and had what sounded like an epileptic fit in the corridor. Everyone felt guilty and embarrassed about not knowing what to do.

A young man with a spiky haircut and holey top jumped onto his chair. 'You fucking bastards make me want to PUKE! Sitting there in your bloody Nike TRAINERS and pathetic casual wear feeling really pleased with yourselves even though you screwed EVERYTHING UP in the Sixties!' He ground his teeth. 'Someone out there's fuckin' DYING and what do you care? WHAT do you ever DO? Read non-existent meanings into crappy old records no one's ever heard of ANYWAY when L7, TV5 and Salad are out there SAYING it all OUT LOUD!' He burst into tears. 'My nan died last week,' he said, and ran out.

His girlfriend stood up and wrung her hands. 'I'm really sorry Alun, he's had a lot of problems lately. It's not him speaking, it's the speed.'

'We've had words Helene,' said Alun. 'If he's not sorted by the end of term, he's out of the course, basically...'

She dashed out.

'Were you going to say anything?' said Ruth to Maurice Blanche.

Maurice cleared his throat. 'I'd just prepared a short presentation on the relationship of *The Phenomenology of Spirit*...'

'Oh Gawd,' muttered someone, 'not that old warhorse...'

'...to everyday life and the role of religion within multiculturalism.'

'Let's be having it then,' said Alun.

Daniel closed his eyes and his thoughts swarmed. Who was he? An out of work ex tour guide tentatively employed in the mainstream arts. A had-been or never-was in that field already. Lover of Paul, he hoped, pianist and healer. They'd had four dates now. Twenty eight years old, prone to slight asthma. Fluent Italian. So-so French and German. Abba fan. A Taurean. Lives alone. Was the kind of porn he liked the proper type? Were he and Paul doing sex right? Was his being gay a choice, or a genetic accident, or something worse? What would he have told Mrs. Brasted anyway - about her son's sexual ambiguity? Who was he to talk?

He'd only had one girlfriend - Sandie Sort, when they were both seven. They'd inspected each other's bottoms and marvelled at the differences, snogged in lawnmower cuttings with their mouths shut. But it had not been sexual. Or had it? They were drawn together by a shared admiration of The Monkees. What did that mean? Where was she now?

After that it had been quite straightforward. Or had it? Was he a secret misogynist? Was it as simple as that? The boys at the holiday camp, but not at school, had noticed the differences before he did. Was the bullying he experienced such as to make him a pitiful victim, or was he a survivor of rampant homophobia in the under-tens? It wasn't what he remembered most. He remembered being a Pontin Prince and his Princess being grateful that he didn't go 'yuk' when he was asked to kiss her. He remembered charming the Bluecoats, Uncle Roger and Auntie Nancy with his own uninhibited version of *The Twist*. He thought they were alcoholics. He remembered being ill after too many Wagon Wheels, near the chalet's washbasin, and his mother, wearing powder blue slacks, leaning over him and saying, 'Cough up chicken'. Why hadn't he become a Bluecoat anyway?

He had liked being a tour guide, being entrusted with everyone's most precious part of the year. Holidaymakers looking to him to make the difference with something small - a restaurant, a bar, a route, emergency contraceptives. It made him feel useful. He enjoyed getting them to sing on the coaches home from day trips, and doing his Wham! dance for them. They liked that, or at least the women did. How did you get a job like Alun Crickshit's? What was he going to do with his life now? He'd have to tell Claire. Did Claire know it was a work scheme? He wondered how he'd ever imagined that jobs that anyone would actually want to do just dropped out of thin air.

'Thanks Maurice,' said Alun. 'Any questions? No. Good. I think we can wind up now. Let's eat, drink, dance, relax, yeah?'

Maurice Blanche had recently fathered two children by his second marriage. He had become quietly excited by a new book he had in mind - *Poo As Metaphor* - which indeed would be a departure for him. He wondered if this audience would have been more interested in his random thoughts on that, rather than what he actually said. Packing up, alone, he concluded they probably wouldn't have been.

Everyone else marched down the corridor to the student bar, where a friend of Plum Duff's was to perform cabaret. Clover and Alun headed the procession.

Ruth talked to one of her students. 'I mean it must be awful being a journalist mustn't it?' she said loudly. 'All that work and basically it's just tomorrow's cat litter.'

'Alun,' said a young woman. 'As a 21 year old Grrrl who is not entirely committed in terms of sexual orientation, I'd love to help. But how? Say I pop into Our Price to buy a CD. Do I say to whoever's behind the till 'I'm Bent as a three bob note - whatcha gonna do about it?"

Alun, now off-duty, snapped his head round. 'Try it, why not,' he replied. 'T-shirts and badges can often act as a useful bridge.'

The crowd sat down in the bar, which was dark except for a red spotlight riveted on one of the chairs from a classroom. Bare lightbulbs hung over four messages:

DON'T MASTURBATE!
NO TALKING.
DISRUPTIVE ELEMENTS WILL BE EJECTED!
DEFINITELY NO CAMERAS!

A bald woman, head bowed, wearing only a studded harness, came on holding a tube of lube and a cucumber. She straddled the chair, stuck her bottom in the air, and rubbed herself and the object thoroughly with the lube. There was much squelching onstage, and held breath in the audience, astonished at the expanded and lightly pulsing spread of her buttocks. They watched as she pushed the cucumber up her arsehole, and twisted it around and back and out again, and in again, and out again, and in again. The cucumber broke.

Daniel felt weak, his eyes watered. Whispers of arousal were happening below the waist, while his conscious mind was mortified. Was there a funny smell or was it just his imagination? A tape played a chorus relaying the lines 'A thing of beauty is a joy forever', over and over, in a computerised voice.

He went to Paul's. He couldn't stand to be alone at the moment. If Paul wasn't there, he'd just camp out on his doorstep all night. He rang the bell and looked at Paul's weed garden. What an adorable thing Paul was, he thought.

'God, what happened to you?'

Daniel barged in. 'I've got the sack. Well - the job - it never really existed. I went to a talk at the University of North Barnet. They were…analysing everything. There was a woman with a cucumber. I feel kind of horny now but very very agitated…'

'Camomile tea? Drink?'

'Need something stronger. Have you got any of your serious drugs?'

Paul went to the bathroom and unwrapped a monthly gift he got from a medic friend, in return for moules frites at somewhere middling good. The morphine was for him. He selected another cocktail for Daniel. See what that did.

'Do you want your pressure points done too?'

'Oh yes yes...' said Daniel.

'You never liked it there. You were moaning about it the first time we met.'

'Oh I did!' Daniel cried. 'Oh I *did* like it! How long does this take to work?'

'Keep still.'

'Do we count as Bent do you think?'

''Course we do.'

Paul left him, dozing off, wrapped in a blanket on the sofa. Daniel stirred a couple of hours later. He didn't want to disturb Paul. His eye fell on a video he hadn't noticed there before - *Strangers in Paradise*.

The camera ran over a wet, tanned torso and fixed on a stubborn erection. A hand appeared and pumped it. The man came in a whoosh. The camera lingered and then drew back. The owner of the hand was Paul. Daniel played it back again. It was definitely him. Oh well, he thought, nothing's perfect. He felt quite proud of Paul. There were many ways to keep body and soul together. It aroused him, this cheap flick. Which was more than could be said for most of the products shifted through Arts Inc.

22

Marcus banged in drunk one night when Robert was still working at home.

'Janet's left me. That plumber. You remember him?'

Robert didn't.

'They're hoping to get into organic farming. They'll be lucky, there are very few openings. She told me on the *phone*. Got anything to drink?'

Robert gave him a beer. Marcus looked at it sorrowfully, so he gave him vodka as well.

'One clog left beside the bed,' said Marcus. 'I was wondering if she might come back for it. Otherwise I'd take it round. But I don't know where she is!'

'She'll come back.'

'No.'

'She hasn't been gone long. How long were you together?'

'Years. Years. We worked together first. Then we set up the place together. Seven years.'

'She's bound to come back. She'll come back.'

'No,' said Marcus. 'No. Oh God - I'm such a useless bastard!' He collapsed into tears.

The weeks rolled on.

Robert had produced models for the new building. He tried to interest Marcus in these in the evenings, but by the fourth drink, efforts dissolved into listening to Marcus reminisce about the *Macro*'s opening night, and the red dress Janet wore, their trips abroad and the new ideas for recipes culled there, the time they went into the wood and ate magic mushrooms - 'We were like…trees…and the grass or whatever it was we were lying on was all crunchy. She had a little hat and flowering dress that moved all about.' He went on and on about how they used to work together - 'poetry in motion'. He mentioned sundry sexual details.

'She had fantastic knockers. Did you ever notice?'

'Yes,' said Robert. 'Well you know…'

'Like freshly risen bread,' said Marcus, mistily. 'Oh maybe we didn't do it enough. Maybe I could be a bit brusque. It's not easy, running a restaurant. Everything's on the hop. The trouble with her was - she had no bloody *vision*!'

He fell off the chair. Robert picked him up. Maxine served up some leftover, raggedy cabbage soup. Robert propped Marcus over it with a spoon, thinking this kind of thing was really Maxine's job.

'So - she's with the plumber right, in a squat with some travellers. I said how can they be travellers if they're in one place? No answer to that! No phone either: 'If I have anything to say I'll write to you Marcus.' That's it. We can't meet up or anything. Her and the plumber - they're planning a *child*. A child. I mean, I would've liked one - it's just the timing was wrong, tricky. Honestly. Couldn't we have talked about it? I don't think a squat's the ideal place to have a child to be honest. I think she's being a bit reckless.'

'You know the other Sunday?' Marcus said, later still. 'I got all the old clothes Janet left and took them to bed with me, and had - y'know - a snooze. I thought - oh Marcus, this is weird, weird stuff, but I felt better afterwards. The clothes smelled of her. Hay and rosehips.'

'We're seeing the backers soon aren't we?' said Robert.

'No mate. Not yet. They've got a bit cagey. And it's difficult, at the moment, with Janet gone. Kind of spoils the package. I can't think about that, not now. It's enough keeping this place going. Hey - look though, we're going to have customer investment.'

'What?'

'They put in some money. Then they get free meals in the new place. £1,000 in, free meals for a year. That kind of scale.'

'How much have you got so far?'

'£400.'

'£400. What's the minimum investment?'

'£100.'

'Maximum?'

'No maximum. Hoping for £1,000. But look - we'll get your models in. That'll jack up interest!'

Robert's models stood on a table, under Maxine's *Goldrush*. Robert felt anxious about leaving them there, night after night, gathering dust. He looked around the restaurant and wondered why it had seemed such an oasis of hope. Right now, it just seemed like a dingy room that served food. He looked at Maxine, who was working extra hours, and doing some of the cooking with a mean temper. She'd led him down this blind alley, and he'd followed like a dumb mutt.

The food wasn't as good as before. Marcus commemorated the Fridays and Saturdays when he and Janet had cooked together with dishes of enormous complication - a *Moulion of Swede and Turnip with a Puff Pastry Lid, Celeriac Mould with a Pumpkin Coulis* - which he served with a heartbreaking air of penitence. The customers who looked moneyed didn't seem to appear any more. Robert went there most nights, it made him feel involved still, and helped clear up. He thought he should keep half an eye, at least, on what state of disintegration Marcus was in.

'Hey - this is great,' Marcus said to him and Maxine. 'A true co-operative. Everyone sharing the load. You know there's this theory that just doing one thing destroys the animal spirits? We're all doing a bit of everything. Fantastic.'

Not. Robert looked at his models, he looked at Marcus. The connection was impossible.

'It's not going to happen is it?' he said to Maxine, one night, 'he's pissed all the time.'

'Not at lunchtime. He's not pissed then. It'll be alright. The restaurant's running fine.'

It was not. It was shut on Mondays and Tuesdays now.

'I did two litres of Citrus Hollandaise the other day...' she rambled on, 'he can still manage to slosh that on anything. It's just the time's not right. You work too much to timetables.' She made this sound despicable, then duffed him on the nose with a gesture that seemed so cutely at one with what drew him to her in the first place, he wanted to throw her out of his flat on the spot.

'I pay the fucking rent!'

'Not on the *Macro*.'

'I do, here.'

She looked very steadily at him. 'I'm so terribly sorry about that, my love.'

The next day she called up everyone she knew to try and secure studio space. She phoned three Housing Associations. She sat swearing over unlikely grant applications, until he begged her to stop.

'You're too impatient,' she said, once her mood had improved, 'if you want to do something your way, it always takes longer. I've had designs for menu cards and furniture that have been lying around two years,'

Menu cards. Furniture. Did she know anything about furniture or anything practical? She started muttering about Tim knowing someone who commissioned murals abroad. In Berlin. She was living in a playground.

At least he still had a job. He was working on a team to build an old people's home. That wasn't without interest, he kept reminding himself. He found it interesting - well it was - to think about how that might work and what old people might need and want. He was relieved to work within specifications and limitations, and with other people who seemed to know what they were doing. He performed his most routine functions with a rigid tenacity that helped him to hold onto something concrete. Colleagues he'd imagined he'd slyly had one over for months were greeted respectfully as markers of what structure, function, status and sanity he actually had left.

Marcus perked up after going home, one night, with one of the customers.

'Had to get rid of her friend. Hope I wasn't too rude. Still I flattered the other one, gave her gooseberry champagne. You learn a lot about human psychology, working in a restaurant.'

Yeah, Robert thought.

'Anyway I know she really liked me because she opened a fresh packet of Crunchy Nut Cornflakes. *And she already had some open!*'

'She made you breakfast?'

'Cornflakes, yeah.'

'Maxine doesn't.'

'Yeah, well, you live together don't you, now? Janet never made me breakfast. Never made me any food at all, come to think of it, apart from what we had here. Like living together do you?'

'It's alright,' said Robert, 'it's alright.'

'Alright,' said Marcus. 'Yeah. You really miss it once it's gone. Maxine's a very nice girl. Very nice girl really. I know sometimes she seems a bit of a fucking *twat*, but she and Lydia are very nice girls. They really made this place what it is. I love them both dearly. It'll be great once Lydia gets back. Maxine - yeah - she's *deep!*'

He laughed, for the first time in ages. Robert didn't.

Maxine was hardly ever in. She was at the *Macro*, or at Julius' gallery, or at her exhibition, which she invigilated herself, when she could, in a manner Robert thought amateurish. Otherwise, she was in the spare room at his flat - he couldn't quite call it their flat yet - looking through her scrapbooks and pictures, occasionally moving to the sitting room to stare at a video for hours on end, and scribbling in sketchbooks as if this constituted some kind of activity. She wasn't producing anything, nothing specific, as far as he could see.

'Have to re-charge my batteries,' she explained.

He realised her sartorial charms were just spirited breaks from the collection of coverings - overalls, T-shirts and leggings - that she stamped around in normally. She worked, or said that was what she was doing, looked at him, if at all, as if he was a bug, then went all girlie when she wanted sex.

That wasn't too often. She usually came home exhausted from the *Macro* at midnight, and wanted to be fucked - just that, nothing else - when he was on his last legs. She fondled his cock distractedly, as if it were a boring and aged household pet. He felt used, he felt neglected.

She was just an ordinary woman who left coffee dregs in the sink, a ring round the bath, and got through an inordinate quantity of bog rolls. They rarely went out. He looked at her puddingy curves and concentrated face that refused to work itself into any appeasing contours for his benefit, and decided he could probably do better.

Priscilla, Claire's friend, rang Robert at work - 'Helew, how are you?' Just her voice and his memories of what she looked like reminded him of good Italian white wine, decorative underwear, and - years back - scooters screaming down foreign streets, when the windows were open at nights, when he was younger, when he was a student, when he had great plans, and nothing he ever did had any consequences.

They met up at the kind of restaurant he hardly went into, with linen napkins, heavy silverware, and main courses that didn't start under £15. Priscilla looked at him with a bored, doe-eyed adoration that was only two degrees away from sarcasm. The building of an old people's home was hardly a seductive topic of conversation. He rattled on about the *Macro* plans, and she looked at him as if he was demented. The bill came to £88. She offered to pay. The taxi was a tenner. He tried to see it all in a scintillating light, but there was no real connection.

He sat on her pink and white checked sofa, having been shown her house. She didn't reply to any of his comments on its technical features. It was nearly midnight. He was deflating by the minute. She was a part of old aspirations that were now lost. She'd gone all cold, and he didn't know if he had the will or the means to do whatever would initiate the thaw, and carry the evening to its logical conclusion.

He couldn't think of anything to say about Shakespeare or Tuscany, abstract artists, or the soul diva she'd just put on - '*mynnnaaawahwah*'.

'Shall we get on with it then?' she said.

He was conscious of snagging her sheer black tights with his nail. Her skin was as chilly as her sheets. He performed his usual routine with a dogged air. She wasn't that pleased. She said nothing afterwards. Her husband was away and she was bored.

Priscilla decided that the next time she had a drought like this, she'd phone that agency her friend Carmel had told her about.

Robert left before Priscilla went to sleep, with a lame excuse. It was not a cordial parting and the evening wouldn't be repeated. He went home on the number 10 bus. He had a dream now, and couldn't forget or let go of it. Maxine was asleep and snoring when he got in. She groaned and pressed herself against him as he lay in bed. He clung onto her for dear life, hoping against hope that she and Marcus were right, and everyone else was wrong.

23

'Oh pleease Maxine, oh pleease…' said Marcus.

Thanks for buggering off now, Lydia, Maxine thought. Damn Janet too.

'You could hire someone else.'

'I will. I am. Yeah, I'll advertise. But you know the place, you know how it works.'

'Alright,' said Maxine, 'just for a bit.'

So she cooked the starters and the desserts, served them up, re-arranged her paintings on the walls, but that was all. She wouldn't deal with Marcus and his crisis. He'd brought it on himself. Robert came in late and they seemed to like talking to each other. She was quite pleased to see them bonding like that. She had enough on her mind, anyway, about what was going to happen next. Nothing much looked imminent.

Her exhibition had run its course. She'd sold eight paintings, and two were due to go into mixed shows. Good. But she had even less time for her own work. Being at the *Macro* nearly every day seemed to flatten everything out. The days passed slowly, through a veil. She thrashed the pots and pans and felt like she was sleepwalking through someone else's life. She couldn't seem to see anything properly any more. Little if anything had any kick to it - no charge, nothing.

She sat in the spare room in Robert's flat. Their flat, she amended. His place wasn't bigger than where she used to live, after all, it just let more light in. The palette she was using looked bleached out. She'd done *Blood Flowers* - in paint, in blood, and they looked terrible. This was a sign, a sign to stop. Perhaps none of it was ever as alive as she had thought. She was stuck for ideas. She realised she could give this up tomorrow, and no one would mind or care.

She had three press cuttings from the show.

'The New Spirit in Painting reaches its nadir in Maxine Kendrick's work. Feminine hysteria meets with elemental claptrap. Pretty much what you'd expect from the hairy armpit brigade…'

These Brian Sewell wannabes on the little magazines were getting completely out of hand. There was one from a woman's art magazine:

'Meaning is obscure, but meaning is nevertheless present. Solid shapes melt into dissolution, emphasising weight and force. Cyclical trajectories of theme replicate the cycles of nature in the seasons, harking back to the fragmented voice of the invisible Siren, and the inarticulable call of the semiotic. Mesmerising.'

That was a good review. Maxine wasn't sure if she knew what it meant.

Delia's short piece was accompanied by a photo of Maxine looking like a ghoul.

'Bad Girl Maxine Kendrick constructs her fun sculptures in a cosy studio near Crow Rd., Hackney. 'I suppose I'm drawing on my love of intimate, sensuous objects,' says Maxine. Girls just wanna have fun! Jip.'

Not much detail. Good old Delia, though. She read her comments book:

> Ace!
>
> Echoes of Brockley, but not enough emphasis.
>
> A sad reflection of the crushing of human nature to become puppets of unseen forces.
>
> Some of the sculptures are good. Then again, some are not v. funny.
>
> What's the blue one supposed to be? A flood? If so, the religious motif should've been more pointed.
>
> I like the dark ones best, not the others. Too rebarbative.
>
> 'Rebarbative' is the name of a film by Simon Kelly.
>
> It's about a man who sees God on his TV.
>
> Who is the pretentious soul above? Why use words to talk of art?

There was a drawing of a penis with splashes coming off it, and 'Part of Male Body!!!' scrawled underneath.

She turned the page.

> Good enough for me to tell my other half to come in the lunch break.
>
> On the bus on the way here the upstairs smelled of patchouli.

Not much there.

Now her exhibition had been and gone, it was as if it had

never happened. She picked up her tips at the end of an evening at the *Macro*, or wrapped up another painting in brown paper at Julius' gallery, and wondered if anything had changed at all.

She tried to get back to sources, looking at books, old sketches, films she remembered liking. Robert was always there, watching. He hung around, waiting for her to be with him. The back of his neck even accused her while she was reading. She didn't know how Lydia had managed to be such a discreet presence. Robert was at the *Macro* a lot too. There was no space to call her own.

It had been alright when he was still working on the *Macro* building. He worked, she worked, they paced up and down. Eventually, someone would give up, and do some food, late, to the accompaniment of burned fingers and muttered curses. Now he had stopped or paused, and seemed to think it was her fault. She couldn't understand the naivety of his imagining it would all happen overnight, and his defeatism when it didn't. He was there, all the time she wanted to work, or just be by herself. She'd get studio space, in time, but that wasn't the problem. She wondered what his expectations of her were, and realised that one of the reasons for her being there was so she would be there for him, whenever he was in. Not doing anything, especially, just being there, paying attention to him, although he didn't seem to feel any pressure to be there for her, not in that way.

You, she thought, *you*, make me feel dead in all the places where the important things happen.

She threw herself into any form of study to avoid him

draining her more. She began to feel abnormal, being a waitress, with no actual project in hand. When Judith's Guerrilla Girls postcard floated through the letter box, she greeted it like the cavalry coming in. It at least reminded her of having a stake in something.

The Zoom Bar, W1, was the venue where the gang gathered to plot their act of cultural terrorism; Judith, Maxine, Tiggy, Tin-Tin and Jocasta Martin. They congratulated each other on how nice they each looked, and were on their third jug of Margaritas. Tin-Tin was pregnant. Tiggy was in full flow:

'There's no doubt about it - my fanny's long. They really have to dig around with the speculum to get anywhere near my cervix.'

'Yeah I have that problem too,' said Maxine.

'With me,' said Judith, 'they have to put out an order for the longest speculum in the district, when I have appointments.'

Tin-Tin cleared her throat. 'When I was - you know - like this, except without a bump, I could lie on a beach - face down - and read a dirty book and come without touching myself.'

There was silence.

'What was the book?' said Tiggy.

'*Zelda's Dungeon,*' said Tin-Tin.

They all made a very firm mental note of *that*.

'Anyway, to conclude what I was saying earlier,' said Tiggy, 'he said the other night - 'it's not easy living with an alcoholic'. I said well you'd better piss off then hadn't you?

Seeing the solicitor Tuesday. He has the bloody nerve to say my sweet sculptures are silly. He spends all his time doing special effects if you please.'

'Oh it's awful,' said Judith, 'those kind of things are just there for people too insensitive to respond to anything that isn't an explosion.'

'No that's not strictly true,' said Tiggy. 'Special effects have an honourable place in the cinema. It just happens that the ones my Malcolm does are all completely banal. No wonder I drink. It's not possible to live with someone you can't respect.'

'What are you on Tig?' said Maxine.

'Opal Fruits and Maltesers. You know - separate.'

'You're still alright being pregnant Tin-Tin?' said Judith.

'Alright,' she replied, 'but Nige's got all bossy since the pregnancy. And he's trying to stick his nose in about my medical treatment. Sent loads of letters because I'd been given iron pills when I didn't need them. I wish he'd shut up…' She grew tearful. '…the GP's threatened to strike us off her list. Doctors can get very vindictive if you don't pretend you think they know what they're doing…'

'What's he doing tonight your Nige then? Writing more letters?'

'Staying in and watching television,' said Tin-Tin. 'He'll probably have a wank too. He'll definitely do that. Hasn't touched me since, y'know…hence - the beach an' all. God I'll be sorry to lose that faculty.'

'That's great isn't it?' said Tiggy. 'Knocks you up then that's it. Charming!'

'Things working out with you and whatsit?' said Judith to Maxine.

'Alright,' said Maxine. 'Except I haven't seemed to be able to work properly since I moved in with him.'

Tiggy groaned. 'You're living at his place and working there too?'

'Yes.'

'Bad move.'

'Seemed like a good idea at the time.'

"Course you can't work can you?' said Tiggy. 'If he's there. I'd make him go out and stuff...'

'My general level of invention has definitely taken a nosedive since I got involved with Michael,' said Jocasta. 'It went right up at first, then it sort of stopped.'

'Same here,' said Maxine.

'Men come in two types,' declared Tiggy. 'The boring ones and the exciting ones. The boring ones, well, they're boring. The exciting ones, well, they drive you mad too.'

Everyone frowned and considered what category their partners fell into.

'Yes,' said Jocasta. 'Men are boring. Especially if you're in a relationship with them.'

'No,' said Tiggy, 'it's just the word. Being married's *worse*.'

Alice Schwartz appeared. She was only wearing one false eyelash, and her hair was a bit of a mess. Apart from that she was bearing up splendidly. Tiggy wobbled across the room with two more jugs of Margarita.

'Oh God,' said Alice, sitting down, 'it gets worse. Black Clothes White Drugs are going down the toilet.'

They all leaned forward.

'You know they're really going to dig up corpses in graveyards now?'

'They're actually going to do it?'

'Yep they're actually going to do it. Chosen the spot, everything. I said - okay - it's illegal - good. It'll attract the usual amount of publicity. But you know, they'll be dead bodies and they're a bit of an unknown quantity. You could get quite ill if you didn't know what you were doing with them.'

'Bastards,' said Tiggy.

'Of course,' continued Alice. 'Richard Pidgin's read a lot of horror and one medical textbook and thinks he knows it all.'

'Yeah,' said Tiggy, 'well I suppose the bodies they're planning to dig up are all *women's* bodies are they?'

'They're still deciding,' said Alice. 'Their *Beverley Allit Virtual Porn* project is probably worse. They've got these dolls and...Oh God...and what they do is...'

'Just popping out for a breath of fresh air,' said Tin-Tin.

'Well never mind,' said Alice, 'it's made me think twice about my tribute to Lorena Bobbit...'

'Oh come on,' said Judith, 'that's completely different.'

'You think Bobbit's valid?' She put her cigarette out and lit another one.

'Oh yes Alice!' they all chanted.

'What I couldn't understand about her case,' said Tiggy, 'is why chop off the best bit? I'd leave the dick and chop off the head!'

Everyone agreed.

'The essentially arbitrary nature of the body in crisis was what I was trying to get across in my *Body Count II*,' said Alice. 'Any of you seen it?'

They all went 'um'.

'It's back at the Arnolfini in August,' she said.

'Sorry I didn't mean to sound so wooden. Done too many grant applications lately. Anyway, if that's not bad enough my fabulous peer group are getting in a complete state about this new sect that's just started up - Nice 'n' Normal - heard of them?'

'Yeah, some of the PragMATiks lot are involved in that,' said Judith. 'What are they going to do - try and wreck their event?'

'They're going to firebomb it,' said Alice. 'Well, are we going to this thing or not?'

'Peers and contemporaries,' said Judith, 'we as women artists inhabit a particularly despised space. We work without the pressure of success, we are labelled 'feminine' come what may, we are not embarrassed by the epithet 'genius', we do not suffer the dubious merits of being hyped or overpaid...'

'Well some of us do,' said Alice.

'Alice,' said Judith, 'just for the sake of argument.'

'Okay.'

'And let's face it, you're only there by the skin of your teeth, and it doesn't look like you'll be with Black Clothes White Drugs much longer.'

'Do we have any actual contact with New York?' said Jocasta.

'No.'

'Have we got gorilla suits?' said Maxine.

'No.'

'Masks?' said Tin-Tin, having returned, looking bilious.

'No, but we've got a couple of banners.' Judith unrolled two scarves on which the slogans EAT MY PUSSY and BIG BOSOMS RULE had been painted.

'Guerrilla Girls NYC are with us in spirit!' cried Judith. 'Let's go!'

They stormed down the streets, waving the banners. Alice paused to take a slash over a drain - 'No it's alright, I don't mind the public catching a load of my privates - oh alright look just stand around me till I've finished...' Then they stood outside the gallery and watched an elegant crowd enter. The artists passed, with friends in tow. There were critics who somehow never made it to their own shows.

'So what now?' said Maxine.

'Oh!' said Judith, suddenly quiet. 'Whatever you like!'

'We could - um - make those Red Indian noises like they did at Greenham Common,' said Jocasta.

No one seemed too keen on that.

'We could - maybe - just stand here and - um - wave the banners?' said Maxine.

'Shades of Grunwick,' said Tin-Tin, 'and we're not picketing it, are we? Or are we?'

'Yeah, and it's a bit nippy out here,' said Tiggy, 'we should go in - that's more of a presence, and have a nice drink each.'

'We could go in and smash the place to pieces,' said Tin-Tin, 'I've got a lot of aggression inside that needs letting out.'

'We wouldn't get that far,' said Alice, 'security's really

tight. And it's philistine. They'd think we were religious maniacs or something.'

'What was ACT UP'S last stunt?' said Jocasta.

No one could remember.

'We could, like - go in, and just make really sarcastic remarks?' Tiggy looked at them all, eyes gleaming.

They nodded sadly.

'We're slaves of irony,' said Alice, 'irony's lost babes. Silenced by our own embarrassment. Well what the hell - I didn't particularly want to fall out with them anyway.'

They went in, got a glass of wine each, and regarded portraits of rapists, serial killers, dismembered organs, instruments of torture, cut up dummies and paeans to death with an identical degree of idle detachment assumed by everyone else in attendance. They looked across at each other, in case someone started some action. No one did.

They gathered again at the drink's table.

'Okay,' said Judith, 'well we've made our presence felt. No one important's left now - just the artists. Now let's go to the party and see if there's anything worth pulling. I thought that bloke with Nicholas Farago looked kinda cute!'

Alice yawned, a yawn in which the remark, 'He's gay you prat' was only half audible.

Maxine felt inspired. A quick fuck with a near stranger was just the ticket, and she didn't like to go home now without some sense of accomplishment. One chocolate wouldn't do any harm.

'Oh I'm not sure,' said Tin-Tin. 'I'm sick of blokes getting all weird around me just because of my condition.'

'You stick with me then,' said Alice. 'I'm not feeling desperately sociable at the moment.'

The room at Ratso's was very dark. They were offered Daze Cakes and cider. The cakes were dainty and round with pink icing and hundreds and thousands on top. Just like their mothers used to make. Maxine thought she saw Janet but could have been mistaken. Alice and Tin-Tin settled in a corner, for an intense discussion of matters medical.

'Doctors are the pits,' said Alice, 'they confiscate all your good drugs and then give you some lousy cocktail of their own devising. Still, that's enough about me. Is this your first?'

Judith saw Piers van Damme and dragged Jocasta off to the toilets. Tiggy yelled at the barman, 'Haven't you got anything stronger?' and Maxine made a beeline for Paul Dart, hiking her skirt up, her top down and fixing him with an intense stare. It didn't matter much as his eyes were shut. He opened them.

'Oh it's you. What are you doing now?' he murmured.

'Abstracts at the Espina and...'

'Oh yeah I saw a flyer lying around about that somewhere. Managed to sell anything yet or get it placed? I'm on death. Death. The will to destruction. The nihilistic will to Thanatos. We're all dead meat. We're all übermenschen in the viscous swell and inevitable rotting of our organs...'

He still looked quite nice, Maxine thought. Incredible, considering.

'Oh yes Paul? That's interesting,' she said settling down.

'It's been a year of death. Moretta had a miscarriage. Roger got put in the bin. Suicide attempt. I nearly got run over myself, by a motorcycle messenger - no an articulated lorry at Cambridge Circus. Death, death. That's all there is. You put on the news. People have died - air crashes, cars, starvation, Bosnia. There's life and then there's death. I feel like I'm dying now. I'm going to sign up for one of those BUPA tests.'

'Part of life though isn't it, death?' said Maxine sulkily, realising that a casual shag was probably out of the question. This was compounded by the fact that a bomb had just gone off in her head.

'Have you heard Nick Cave's new thing?' said Paul. '*I'm sorry sorry sorry.* Yeah it's great. Sorry sorry sorry. Complete story of my life.'

'Yeah I feel like that sometimes Paul.'

'*Sorry sorry sorry. I'm sorry that I'm always pissed I'm sorry that I exist* - yeah, right Nick, I am, I really am very sorry indeed about that. *I'm sorry for things I cannot even mention*…yeah, yeah…*Sorry I've forgotten how to fuck* - yeah, fair enough Moretta but we could try doing it mornings…*Sorry sorry sorry*…' - he shook his head like a dog - 'oh I'm so fucking sorry all you bastards…Love's always having to say you're sorry. Yeah, yeah. Remember that film - Love Story? Yeah, I bet you saw that in your local fleapit didn't you, Maxine, all that time ago? A good old 'AA' film. Life was so hygienic then wasn't it? Like someone always ran a J-cloth over life's skirting boards didn't they?'

She felt like a cloud. The blue light from the ceiling penetrated her completely. Paul's face was a skull, then assumed the comical contours of a Dali watch, then it was like a weasel, and he had a tail too. Her head was ringing and everything was blurred.

'I don't really want to firebomb anyone really. I think it's just a bad idea. I don't like *hate* as such. I don't like hating. It's just it's this fuckin' *stuff* in my head...'

'Don't talk about violence Paul.'

'Yeah I'd like to be nice 'n normal, on Sundays at least. Trouble is I'm not wasn't ever nor ever will be now too much has happened...that psychiatric ward...'

Maxine lay on the floor, giggling. Paul watched her.

'Yeah it's hilarious. You really are a bitch. Maybe you'll have a miscarriage or some brush with death...'

'My legs are paralysed,' said Maxine. 'I can't move. I CAN'T MOVE PAUL!'

'No no no no no no no,' he said. 'No you're not paralysed. That's impossible. It's the drugs. It's not you, it's the drugs. It's not you, it's the drugs. Christ I should have a fucking tape made on a loop of this. It's not you, it's the drugs. You alright now?'

'Yes thanks. Hey - that's great! My legs are alright! And I could get up if I wanted to...'

'No hurry,' said Paul. He stuck a cigarette in his mouth and walked off.

Maxine hugged herself. She felt vindicated. Then she felt all dead. It was great.

Tiggy dance alone, ecstatically, the protest scarves wrapped around her head. She was dancing to a particular phrase in the mix. It was Parker from *Thunderbirds* going:

Yes Milady

Yes Milady

Yes Milady

Yes Milady

Alright, she thought. That bastard at home's going to do what I want from now on! She danced, on and on, enthralled.

Maxine got up off the floor and saw Judith at a distance, sitting down, with Piers' unconscious head pinning her to the spot. She looked as if she was chewing tacks. That was probably what she was doing. Chewing nails or something like that. She was definitely chewing something, maybe the cud. Her face was bright red and she had little wings. She bumped into Alice outside the toilets. Steam was coming off her face. Then Tiggy was at the top of the stairs, clutching the purple shirt of a man she'd just met.

'Want to share a cab?' said Alice.

'Oh yeah, yeah,' said Maxine. She looked across at the crowd. They all looked so pretty, we're all like ghosts, she thought, lovely ghosts.

They were on the street.

'Could we just stand for a minute?' said Maxine.

'Oh sure,' said Alice, 'never touch hash myself. You never know when it's going to creep up on you. Like you can just feel your synapses *conking out*. Sorry don't mean to be frightening. Got plenty of nibbles at home have you?'

A car pulled up and Tiggy's husband got out. He dragged Tiggy out of the venue and back to the car.

Tiggy pushed him away and went back to the party.

'Yellow light, that's us,' said Alice.

'What's the traffic lights?' said Maxine.

Thank God I'm really living again, she thought as she stepped gingerly to her door and fitted the key in the lock on the seventh attempt. There was nothing to beat a great girl's night out. Her heart was full of vaporous joy for Judith and Alice, Tiggy, Tin-Tin and Jocasta. Just the fact they were doing it made her feel alright. She brushed her teeth very thoroughly with her soap-free facial wash, thinking that she'd never noticed before what a fantastic feeling and taste that was. She fell into bed. She woke up and threw up. Robert had gone out without saying anything. It was nothing to do with last night, the sickness. She had a funny feeling that it wouldn't go away until she'd checked it out. She'd been feeling diabolical in a very particular way before last night. She called in sick to Marcus, then rushed to the chemist's.

The kits processed you in five minutes. She would have preferred hours, or days, but she had to know. She peed into the tray, used the dropper, and left the bathroom. She counted the seconds of the minutes and stepped into the bathroom, afraid of what she'd find there.

The blue line was unmistakable. She was up the spout. Oh thanks God, she thought. Just what I need now. Thanks a fucking bunch.

24

Consuela hadn't been so understanding about Boo. She and Deanna saw each other once a week, and it was touch and go. Every time they met up Deanna felt like she was completing a round of auditions, ones she'd passed, just, when they went home together. Consuela hadn't liked the way she'd dealt with Claire. Really mean and cold.

'She's married,' said Deanna. 'She didn't pursue me in any case.'

'Who would?' said Consuela. 'You were like a fridge. You wouldn't even *talk* to her.'

'I was with you. With you. The time wasn't right. Anyway if I hadn't taken Boo on, where would she be now, eh?'

'You didn't take her on. That was an accident. I'm not worried about Boo, especially,' said Consuela. 'I'm worried about me.'

'But I'm crazy about you,' said Deanna, weakly.

'To have sex with people like that…' said Consuela, 'all of a sudden. You had to be a bit crazy about them, at the time. Otherwise you wouldn't have bothered. Or maybe you were just crazy for it, not the person.'

Deanna sat in a café, staring at her *Under An Hour* proposal in a hopeless limbo. It had received three rejections so far. Maxine came in. Deanna observed her long enough, before being noticed, to realise that Maxine's private face was several degrees more sober than her public one.

Maxine sat down. 'Just collecting some orders.'

'For paintings?'

'Food.'

'Food?'

'The *Macrobiotic Speedline Café* - where I work.' She didn't add 'part-time' because it wasn't any more.

'You work in a restaurant?'

'Yes.'

Deanna had never known. She hoped Maxine was a manager, or something.

'Look,' said Maxine, 'I hope I didn't put my foot in it, mentioning Claire to Consuela, and all that...'

'Oh it doesn't matter,' said Deanna. 'Daniel put his foot in it worse.'

Maxine's eyes flared. 'I'm pregnant!' she said.

It sounded like a yelp, but Maxine's face was pursed and firm, and she was presumably just wanting some congratulations. So demanding, straight women.

'That's wonderful!' said Deanna. 'She'll be a redhead just like you! You can teach her to paint! You must let - um - me and Consuela borrow her at weekends!'

Will that do? she thought. Maxine seemed a bit winded. Perhaps that was something to do with what it did to you physically.

'Do you know what's happened to Claire? She's wasn't in her office today. Left, they said. I haven't tried her at home yet.'

Maxine shrugged. 'No idea. Must go.'

Maxine went round the corner, close to tears. Deanna nipped out and bought ten Marlboros and sat there smoking one after the other in long, slow drags. She had never known Maxine that well, but already felt her retreat into obscurity. Her career, such as it was, would be back-dated by five years, at least, and old friends would be allowed to drift away. All this might have happened anyway, but it was a real shame Maxine couldn't have made it as a painter.

She had that sinking feeling she got whenever someone she liked put their hand over their glass after the second refill of wine, refused coffee at 10pm, or anchovies or chilli sauce or any other highly flavoured thing. The queasy feeling she got when no dessert was undertaken without the ohhing and ahhing and wriggling that by rights, should only accompany the sampling of crack.

It was a similar sinking feeling she got, at work, when she adjusted brand goods to a respectable level of blandness, or threw out innovative designs for something that was enough like everything else to be guaranteed to push the product. What awful rule dictated that at a certain age, you had to shift your entire lifestyle to fit the tastes and constitution of a five year old? Consuela didn't think or act like that, but in her backing-off, there was an indication of something similar.

On the train to Derby she frowned over information sheets

about vitamins and enzymes and diets. But her mind wasn't there. It was with Paula - *You're only going to flog them yoghurts*; with Boo - *You only like having sex when you're drunk*, and Consuela - *Maybe you were just crazy for it, not a person.* She was filled with a sense of being entirely hollow, a suspicion that she'd never made any difference to anyone.

She stood with her suitcase of firm's products outside a school identical to the one she'd attended. A yellow bricked building done on a stern design, flanked by muddy playing fields and a soggy netball court. She knew whatever happened, she'd never want to go back there again. She remembered acres of empty time, having to learn about how the weather worked, learning sheaves of information off by heart, hanging around waiting for your real life to start. Then she thought of Boo's escape - its punch drunk courage, the determination not to wait any longer, to drop yourself right in it, and see what happened.

She never had that kind of guts. She took a slow climbing route. And she wondered if she really was that interested in the work she did, or if that was just the excuse for other deficiencies.

A woman in reception in baggy trousers and a sweater rose to greet her. She wasn't unlike Paula. Someone who had given over her life to the futures of other people. Someone who stayed in school all her life.

'You're between the Police and the woman from the tampon company,' she said cheerfully. 'Do you mind if I sit in?'

They walked down the corridor. Deanna remembered her

immersion in studies, the ones that would get her somewhere. She would never have thrown herself at someone in a bar, then. She wouldn't have even known where to go. She sat it out with tactful social evasions, embarked on the appropriate number of affairs, and only stepped into her true self once she'd created the means for it, and the steps were well secured.

They were in the science room. There were worn bunsen burners and other items of basic, junior equipment dotted round the sides, and a series of benches seating 13 year old versions of herself. They were all girls. The jocular speech about nutrition she'd prepared suddenly fell apart. She laid out her wares, thinking of stolen glances, notes passed in the back of class, and rulers springing under unsuspecting bottoms.

'I'm here to talk about food, but basically, eat what you like. Fussing about food is a waste of time. Counting calories is tedious. Diets are useless, they hardly ever work. You don't have to look or act like anyone else. You only have to feed someone else if you want to. You're all very beautiful and precious and don't let anyone else tell you otherwise…'

Thirty pairs of eyes were staring at her. She cleared her throat.

'Ignore most things you read in magazines. I spend a lot of time trying to dream up images to sell products, that's all it is - ways of selling things. Consume what you want, not what you think you need. You are not a product yourself. Suspect everything that's dressed up as the truth about how you're supposed to be. Women's stomachs are round. If people won't take you as you come, then fuck 'em…'

Deanna paused briefly for breath.

'Don't live in other people's minds. Don't chase other people's rainbows. Just say no to other people's expectations. Don't be frightened of anything or anybody. Your own fear is the only thing that can hurt you. Express yourself. Love yourself. Make your conflicts external ones. If anyone tries to torture you with their customs or ideology, remember that fashions will have changed in five years, and your time will come, and your first instincts are often the right ones. Don't put up with crap sex. Choose lovers who give you what you need, not just what you think you want. I've - er - got some samples from my company if anyone would like any...'

The teacher accompanied Deanna back down the corridor. She felt as if she were under armed guard.

'Most interesting...' she said.

'I'm sorry,' said Deanna, 'I don't know what came over me. It just seemed to come out of nowhere.'

'It's a bit of a shock,' said the teacher, 'being face to face with a roomful of much younger people. I suppose I'm used to it.'

'Do you think it was true? What I said?'

'Yes,' said the teacher, 'in a sense, yes. It would help if more people felt a bit like that.' She gave the smile she gave to all visitor's from outside companies.

'I should've put in some nutritional information?'

'They get it all from their magazines,' said the teacher. 'I know about that stuff anyway. I teach Biology, geography and physics,' she added, 'which reminds me I've got to go and have a quick peak at the book during the break.'

'Thank you for this opportunity to flog them some merchandise,' said Deanna.

She and the teacher shook hands. Deanna doubted whether Macy's would hear of this. She grasped her filofax and A-Z and went to the house where Boo's caravan was based as if guided by an invisible spirit.

It was a tired terrace with misty white curtains, but there were a clutch of new shoots in the front garden, on a recently cleared patch, which Deanna guessed must have been Boo's contribution.

She rang the bell and it chimed in response. Two heads shot from behind the door. Mr. & Mrs. Pickle. They were pale and thin from an excess of scrupulous self denial.

They invited her in. The hallway was dark and the front room was small and impeccably polished. There was one red sofa, a dining room table with two stout chairs, a piano, a Bible on top of it, and a picture of Christ Our Saviour, done in ecstatic lemons and powder blues.

Boo was summoned. Mrs. Pickle went to prepare tea and brought it in on a tray. Mr. Pickle's eyes shone at Deanna.

'Valerie's Good Samaritan!'

'Oh,' said Deanna, 'it was nothing.'

Boo appeared. She seemed to have aged about two years. Her face was more in charge of itself. She seemed only mildly pleased to see Deanna.

'Valerie has a job as a motorcycle messenger,' said Mrs. Pickle.

'Yes, I know.'

'An active life is the best life,' said Mr. Pickle.

'Start low, aim high, but always serve,' said Mrs. Pickle.

Boo smiled. 'Hallelujah!'

Deanna smiled.

'I'm moving soon,' said Boo, 'to a house in Streatham.'

'Four women!' cried Mrs. Pickle.

'Lovely,' said Deanna. 'Oh that'll be nice, yes.'

'And how did you cross Valerie's path?'

'Oh I told you,' said Boo. 'Deanna's local Quaker Meeting House.'

'Do you know how we came across the caravan?' said Mrs. Pickle.

'No!' said Deanna.

'Our friend Irene was widowed,' said Mr. Pickle.

'We said you won't have much use for the caravan will you Irene? Now someone else could make use of that.'

'You've let it run to seed, Irene, we said.'

'We were quite persuasive.'

'We took it off her hands later that day.'

'Didn't take long to get it shipshape did it Roy?'

'Now it's being used by Valerie here!'

Deanna took a breath. 'If only more people were like you!' she sighed. 'Nice tea,' she added. The teacup shook on her knees.

Mr. and Mrs. Pickle looked at each other and beamed.

'Like to have a look at it while you're here?' said Boo.

It was small. Deanna's and Boo's knees virtually touched as they sat down. Rain plink plonked on the roof. Deanna thought of the mild rages she'd had in her head about work on the way. *I predicted vegetarian fast food...I expanded virtually the whole of fizzy drinks…* None of that seemed very important here. Boo took her hands and examined them.

'I could probably improve on these.'

She got out her equipment.

'I'm glad you're moving,' said Deanna, as Boo massaged hand cream in, 'you're clearly in moral danger.'

'Hardly,' said Boo. 'Sister Wendy Beckett lives in a caravan, so there you are.'

She pushed Deanna's cuticles back.

'We can use my car, for your move.'

'Let's go,' said Boo. 'There's not much stuff to take.'

'If you hadn't met me that night,' said Deanna, 'would you have gone off with anyone?'

'Probably,' said Boo. 'I went off with you. Polish?'

'The amber one.'

Deanna tried to remember what eighteen felt like.

Boo's brush glided over her nails, skilfully avoiding any skin.

She wasn't wrong. Boo's small collection of possessions didn't need a whole car - three changes of clothes, a cassette radio, a few tapes, two glasses, two cups and saucers, her biker gear. Boo blow-dried Deanna's nails then Deanna helped wrap Boo's things in newspaper, as if they were precious gifts.

'Are you alright?' said Boo.

'Oh fine,' said Deanna. 'Is this place furnished or what?'

The house was Victorian, and almost forbidding outside. Indoors it was bright pink all the way through, with gold moons and stars decorating the walls. The noticeboard in the kitchen showed a riotous devotion to the scene. Boo had landed in paradise.

A woman in a long white smock descended the stairs. This had to be Aurelia, the landlady. She looked about forty-five, and had long hair and searching eyes. Deanna wondered how old she was when she got divorced. Aurelia opened a bottle of claret while Boo put her stuff in her room. She poured the wine into purple goblets decorated with stones. A pregnant black cat came in and rubbed itself against Deanna's leg. Deanna wrote out a cheque for Boo's deposit.

'We'd prefer not to ask,' said Aurelia.

'Oh it's okay,' said Deanna. 'She's had enough problems.'

'Oh - what? Like you dumping her?'

Another woman was mauling a nectarine by the kitchen door.

'Kate...' said Aurelia. 'PMT,' she whispered, to Deanna, as Kate disappeared.

'Like your cat,' said Deanna.

'Splosh,' informed Aurelia.

'My company - Macy's - have just revised our cat food - Tuna & Salmon, Duck and Liver, Spicy Beef, Heart & Kidney, Spring Chicken - that's the new one.'

Aurelia smiled and took the cheque. 'Our pussies,' she said, 'prefer Hills.'

Kate returned.

'You've left your car unlocked.'

'Oh?'

'It's alright, I'll lock it for you. Keys?'

'Uh - thanks,' said Deanna, handing them over.

'There,' said Aurelia.

Boo came back.

'I'll leave you,' said Aurelia. 'You must have a lot to talk about.'

Boo was doubly animated, now. She looked like a fairy on top of a Christmas tree, with the lights flashing.

'Fantastic isn't it?' she said. 'A real family. Aurelia said I could do the manicures next to her altar.'

'How's that going, as a business?'

'Not bad at all. I'm doing blokes as well now.'

Boo's voice dropped. 'Just for information…Kate had an affair with Petra, she lives on the top floor. BT Engineer. Petra is one of Aurelia's ex's. Now Kate's peeved with Petra and Petra's in a bit of a bind. Then of course Sally was involved with Kate and one of Petra's ex's. We have an agreement though…'

'What?'

'We don't discuss it in the kitchen.'

Deanna had always thought that this kind of arrangement would be like being locked in an airing cupboard. On this evidence, she was right.

'Me,' Boo continued, 'I prefer to keep my domestic and private life separate.'

'You've got someone?'

'Oh!' said Boo. 'Oh Barbara - yes!' She punched the air with her fist. 'We do everything together. We're queens of the town!'

Deanna realised she had just taken on the status, for Boo, of an aged, lost and lonesome aunt.

'You know,' said Boo, 'you know I wasn't in love with you or anything when I was staying over…'

'Oh yes. I mean, no. Yes. Sure. Plenty aren't…'

'I needed a roof…'

'Obviously. Of course. Yes.'

'And that was the only way I could do it…'

'Yes. Of course.

Something inside Deanna howled.

'Not that it was like any problem oh no I'd…'

'It's fine,' said Deanna. 'It's fine…'

'You still having trouble at work?'

'Yes.'

'That's all going to change soon.'

'Oh - how?'

'We did your Tarot. And we've been casting spells.'

'What?'

'Aurelia said you had a good aura. Many in your position would've charged rent…Don't worry. It's white witchcraft. Nothing nasty. No way. But Aurelia said you were troubled too. All that career stress. Trying to be like a man and so on…'

Fuck off, Deanna thought.

'You won't be so stressed soon. And things'll work out okay with a dark-haired Latin woman…'

'You've been…'

'Gossiping yes. But Aurelia's psychic as well, she has special powers. She can't help it. She's off to study female bonding systems in Turkey shortly.'

'What does she do anyway?'

'She has a private income. She reads an incredible amount. Just wait and see. You're going to come out on top.'

The next morning Deanna was bellowing at a wholesaler on the phone. Miranda came in with a grave expression.

'Laurie's just been rushed to hospital.'

'Oh brilliant,' said Deanna. 'Oh, *brilliant*.'

She rushed to the computer and pushed the button for sales print out. It was as she'd expected. Sales were down. Later that afternoon she was offered her old job back. She told them she'd think about it.

Deanna arrived at the private hospital, clutching a bunch of flowers. It wasn't hypocritical, it was being professional. Laurie sat up in bed, perplexed. He looked much friendlier like that. He was bantering with the nurses like he used to banter with Miranda. He saluted Deanna.

'I'm a bit of a medical mystery,' he exclaimed. 'The consultant said my powers of recovery were phenomenal!'

'How long will you be here?' said Deanna, with concern.

'Oh a few weeks,' said Laurie. 'They're keeping me in for observation. I'm very particular. They've never seen a case like this before!'

'Much pain?' said Deanna.

'Curiously no,' said Laurie. 'It's just I'm strangely incapacitated.'

Deanna arrived home. There were two messages on the ansafone.

'Hi. Consuela. It's the anniversary of our afternoon in the park on Saturday. I've booked a table. Call me soon. Please.'

'Hi, s'me. Just some news. Splosh is the proud owner of a

— 300 —

brand new litter! You can have one if you want. They're lovely. Black and white. Bring it round Tuesday, alright. Aurelia says you could use your firm's goods, for feeding, but she's a little concerned about Spicy Beef. Maybe have a word first. See you soon. Oh and by the way I dropped off an envelope for you earlier.'

Deanna found the envelope:

Please come to a Roman gathering
Wear toga or other suitable garment
RSVP
Aurelius

Deanna burst into tears.

The doorbell rang. It was Paula.

'Well I'd expected a slightly more enthusiastic welcome than that! I've got us Pimms. You got any oranges and lemons?'

She's found someone else, Deanna thought.

'Yes I've got oranges and lemons.'

'What's the upset?'

'No upset, just emotional, generally. Happiness. I'm glad to see you.'

She cried again. Paula gathered her up.

'That's alright then isn't it?' she shook her, 'if you're *happy*? Look, you fix the drinks, I'll find us some music.'

'I completely ballsed-up my first schools presentation.'

'Oh don't worry,' said Paula, 'they almost certainly weren't listening.'

Paula put on Connie Francis. Bright sunlight suddenly poured through the windows:

> 'Lipstick on your collar
> Told a tale on you-oo
> Lipstick on your collar
> Said you were untrue-oo
> Bet your bottom dollar
> You an I are through
> Cos lipstick on your collar
> Told a tale on you!

'Our story,' said Deanna.

They clinked glasses.

'What's her name?'

'Tell you later,' said Paula.

So they'd stay friends. Their affair, after all, had been that inconsequential. Deanna took her shoes off and threw them against the wall. Paula's shoes followed suit. Maybe all you had to do was believe in magic. She'd believe, for the moment. She looked into Paula's love-touched face. She hoped she wouldn't leave too soon.

26

Maxine sat in her local GP's surgery, looking at everyone else there and wondering what was wrong with them. She flicked through a few magazines, scan reading coarsely related and photographed tales of personal catastrophe. She upgraded her selection. There was an article on the importance of being playful. 'Eyebrows are arching higher and higher this season', another said. There was a table in a box:

ARE YOU A GIRLIE OR ARE YOU A FEMINIST?	
Girlies	*Feminists*
Wear Wonderbras and no knickers!	Wear dungarees
	Hate men
Make the first move	Don't like sex
Slap on the warpaint	Whine on about stuff no one can do anything about anyway!
Give great blowjobs	Have pc sex!!
Have careers	Have crappy jobs/are New Age housewives
Hold their liquor	Drink Ovaltine
Are now!!	Are history!!

She couldn't decide, at the moment, where she fitted into all of this. She had spent the last few days watching Robert for a glimmer of recognition and, finding none, had decided to go it alone. She was close to panic. With things as they were at the moment, she could go ahead and end up stuck forever. She sat there and waited. And then she realised that she couldn't recall the date of her last period any more than she could remember other, less important, dates.

She knew this would be the place she'd visit in future, for more objective procedures: smears, routine checks, holiday vacs, other things she hadn't encountered yet. It wasn't right, she wanted somewhere anonymous. She went home and phoned the number in the directory, and then she called Claire.

Claire suggested a coffee shop in Marylebone. She looked very tired sitting there among the marble tables, beside pristine glass counters containing delicate pastries that could have been shipped directly from France. This wasn't the kind of place Maxine usually visited. This was, also, pleasingly anonymous.

'Well?' said Claire. 'This is a surprise.'

The coffee was very good indeed.

'I'm in a bit of trouble Claire.'

Claire was relieved. 'Oh?' she said.

'I'm pregnant.'

'Is it Robert's?'

'Yes.'

'You don't want it, presumably?'

'No.'

'How much to get it fixed?'

'£350.'

Claire wrote out a cheque on the spot. It wasn't what Maxine had expected.

'I have a scheme,' said Claire, detaching the cheque from the book, 'that might interest you. I thought of acquiring studios, a large building, maybe in your part of town, setting up bursaries, so artists could work…uninterrupted, for a year maybe. They'd be selected. You'd be eligible, naturally. You could help me run it. I've talked to other people who'd like to get involved. Julius said he would. Well? That would be rather helpful to you, wouldn't it?'

Claire looked away. Just for your eternal silence, she thought. Just for that. Please.

Maxine shook her head, in disbelief, not refusal. Claire's precious manner of speech, which used to drive her nuts, had just acquired real charm.

'Oh don't think I'm being kind or nice or anything. The accountant said it might be a good idea, something like that, to offload…it would make sense. Anthony and I are getting divorced. I need a new project. I want to sever all links with the past.'

'Is that anything to do with Deanna?'

Claire laughed. 'No, not really. Maybe she was just some kind of catalyst.'

'You and Anthony?'

'Irreconcilable differences, you might say.' Claire laughed again.

'That's all?'

'Yes,' said Claire, 'that's really all... Jonathan might like to also be involved.'

'Oh yes?'

'Oh yes, I think he would.'

'Sounds good.'

They need each other, Claire thought - how wonderful and how terrible.

'Right,' said Maxine, 'okay Claire.'

The coffee shop was very soothing, bathed in peach light, with twinkling chandelier style wall lights. Everyone sitting there looked as if they had power showers and lots of fresh clothes. Impressionist prints on the walls reminded Maxine of books she'd read years ago about artists nurtured by benign patrons, and what an incredibly satisfying way of life that had sounded until she realised it was beyond her. Yet she could do with some help from an only slightly ignoble source. It would be a bridge to the next thing. It might flatten her sense of independence, but that had been flattened anyway, like it or not. She had a dependence on Robert that she wanted to ditch as soon as possible. Claire would be better, more distant. It was either this or be on her own completely. She didn't fancy that. She ordered a raspberry tart and Claire had a madeleine.

'Okay,' said Maxine, 'that sounds a great idea, Claire. That's marvellous. But why art?'

'Why not?' said Claire. 'There's money to be made, isn't there?' She sipped her coffee and crossed her legs. 'It's something I know about. I can use Anthony's connections. I hoped you'd come in. I hoped you would.'

'I might be going to Berlin,' said Maxine.

'Why run,' said Claire, 'when you only have to walk?'

'Just for a couple of months. Murals.'

'Really? It won't interfere with this…?'

'Not at all,' said Maxine. 'Not at all. As long as we get started soon. Get ahead of it.'

Claire pushed the cheque across. 'As soon as you've dealt with the mishap.'

'Yes,' said Maxine, 'yes. I'll do it. Consider it dealt with.'

Claire watched Maxine leave, wondering if anything would have turned out so differently if Maxine's mother, Maria, hadn't died like that. She looked at Maxine going through the door, seeming as lonely as Claire had always felt. Well, they'd be together now.

The building was at the end of a tube route, white, solid and old, set behind trees; plush, concealing trees. Maxine would never have to visit this place again. She signed in, put on a smock, and took the injection. The nurses' faces were hard and glazed with foundation and make-up. She supposed this was how they had to deal with it, doing this on a daily basis - be detached. It made sense. She appreciated the art of it, managing this, making it easier.

She went down in a lift. She was suddenly unconscious. She woke, hours later, numb as a bone and liking the sensation.

She sat on the train in the deserted station, fired with hope. She felt refreshed by the blood sacrifice, and the power to give life and take it. The bleeding was a mess but wouldn't last. She bore it, at the moment, with pride, like a war wound. Now she'd done this, she could do other things. Life had moved on.

And Lydia was back. She had to see Lydia. She had to talk to someone who would understand. Maxine remembered her own mother's response when she had announced, as a teenager, that she wanted to go to art school. Her mother was fearful. She wanted to protect her lamb from pain and disappointment. Bollocks. She'd stuck it out this far. Claire was made of sterner stuff. So was Lydia. Her true allies, comrades in arms.

It was a cool, dark basement that was one of their old haunts. It had stone alcoves. It was a place no one else knew about. Lydia was already there, and had ordered a bottle of wine and two glasses. Lydia never did follow the convention of indifference.

'How was the tour?' said Maxine.

'Fine,' said Lydia. 'Nina Hagen wanted to meet me, but we never got it together. You didn't call me out to talk about that. So?'

Slow down, Maxine thought. Chrissakes.

'I was pregnant. I had an abortion.'

'Does he know?'

'No.'

'Oh - oh good. Well done. You want my approval?'

'Something like that.'

'You've got it.'

'It wouldn't have worked out - I mean, he wouldn't really have wanted it. There'd have been - arguments, and difficulties like that and…'

All this prepared spiel came trickling out. Maxine knew it was something she'd prepared for Claire, and saw Lydia's face flicker with impatience, because it wasn't necessary, but she couldn't stop it now.

'…really for the best…'

'You've got no principles have you?' said Lydia. 'I've always admired that about you.'

'Thanks. Well you know,' said Maxine. 'If you don't like the rules as they are, you just have to invent new ones don't you? Was that my notion, or yours?'

'Yours I think,' said Lydia. 'I never forgot it.'

'Robert doesn't understand that.'

'No,' said Lydia, 'he wouldn't.'

'And he's not happy really. I can't seem to hack it.'

'Oh?' said Lydia. 'Isn't he? That's a bloody shame isn't it?'

They ordered. Just snacks.

'Really swamped you under hasn't he?' said Lydia. 'God Almighty.'

There was a slight air of triumph. Maxine ignored it.

'I wouldn't worry about Robert,' said Lydia, 'he'll look after himself.'

'That's not true of everyone.'

'It's true of him.'

'Maybe.'

'It is.'

'Yes.'

'He's got you.'

'Yeah.'

'Hasn't he? I'd call it a mixed blessing, you know. But you're there, aren't you? It must have been what he wanted. You don't have to fix everything for him.'

'It's love,' said Maxine, 'it's still there somewhere.'

'Love?!' said Lydia, and laughed. She emptied the bottle into the glasses. They forked their food.

'Love. God. Love. A bee in your bonnet. Some misplaced maternal instinct. Someone who believed in you. The *Macro* project…'

'So love kills does it? That's it?'

'I wouldn't know,' Lydia said, 'I gave it up years ago. I just wonder about your terms. You did this for love of yourself, not him, or you both. Didn't you? Better believe it. Just as well you did.'

'Yeah,' said Maxine. 'Yeah. Anyway,' twirling the stem of her glass, 'that's the last time he fucks me when I'm asleep.'

Lydia's mouth dropped open. 'Oh dear,' she said, epicurean touches gone out the window? You don't even like *that* about him now?'

'Oh I like that…' said Maxine.

'You'd better,' said Lydia, 'you moved house to prove it.'

Maxine picked her teeth with a torn off corner of matchbox.

'He wants the freedom without having to give up what security he's got,' she said. 'He blames me for all that - the wanting it, wanting the freedom. He wishes he'd never got involved.'

'How long did it take you to work all that out?' said Lydia.

'It's only just happened.'

'Didn't you see it coming?'

'No.'

'I did - a mile off. So did Janet.'

'Oh well - thanks, Lydia. But you know - the *Macro* building, all that stuff. It wasn't original. He just dragged up old plans and wanted to do them better.'

'Outrageous,' said Lydia, and laughed. 'And you're going to keep quiet about it are you?'

'Oh yes.'

'Oh yes.'

'No, I will. I'll start painting again. I'm going to Berlin, I think. Get a bit of space there. And if I don't get that I'll try and get to go somewhere else.'

'Good.'

'Work again, properly. Are you going back to the *Macro*?'

'Not if I can help it. I went in earlier, just to say hello. There are two new people, full time. Janet insisted. She wrote him a letter about having nurtured him too much....'

'Alright...'

'And she wants a kid, a proper one, not just him.'

'Oh right. Well, whatever...'

'No it wouldn't be my choice, but she likes all that stuff. She set up a dope house, they were busted. So Marcus really thinks she's someone of note now...'

'I might have sampled one of Janet's wares,' said Maxine, 'seems I've been away for weeks...'

'Well,' said Lydia. 'It's her choice. But it looks like you're off the hook. Oh *look* - you had to create all the business because you couldn't work. Robert was just the spur, the excuse. You had to get out and put me in my place. You weren't convinced you wanted to leave. You had to get yourself into a place so you could be pushed. It doesn't matter now. I'm still there. You'll know where to find me. I suppose we'll always have a mattress.'

'You didn't move out?'

'Not in the end, no. Riccardo took it over while I was away. Now he's there most nights. That'll do, for now. Anyway, there are more important things.'

'Oh?' said Maxine.

'I just heard Solange Dekarti's latest record. I'll never be that good.'

'Doesn't matter,' said Maxine. 'Who's to know?'

'I was thinking of getting a proper job.'

'As what?'

'Don't know.'

'That's crap,' said Maxine. 'You can't give up. You don't like doing anything else.'

'No,' said Lydia, 'no, I don't.'

'So there you are.'

'Cheers,' said Lydia.

'Did you get it together with thingy after all that?'

'Oh yes,' said Lydia. 'It was a bit push-me-pull-you, but he was fun. He's gone back home now.'

'Where's that?'

'Canada.'

'You don't fancy getting really wrecked tonight?'

'I would,' said Lydia, 'but there's a photocall in the morning. Another time.'

'How's Syd?' said Maxine, suddenly sentimental.

'Oh, same as usual. Yeah Syd's alright. He'll carry on forever. I think the grog just *pickles* him.'

There was nothing to do but go home.

The *Macro* was thrumming that evening and Robert knew something had happened. Marcus was bouncing around, seeing to the customers. He wasn't wearing kitchen clothes. Janet came out, uncorked two bottles of wine and offered Robert an exuberant smile. He felt nauseated, he felt envious. She and Marcus *worked together*. The food looked more inviting. A new light had been placed beside his models on the table. They looked like living and breathing objects.

'Oh hi,' said Marcus. 'You'll never guess what Janet was up to? Only set up a dope house. No - we used to do those things together, in the old days. She must've been thinking of me all the time. She and the plumber fell out. She's going to get pregnant. It's great you know - lots of fucking. The plumber can't have been much cop in that area. Anyway. Makes me feel great. I think I'm pretty good at it.'

Janet came out again. Marcus beamed.

'Alright love?' He looked around. 'We're seeing the backers Friday fortnight. That alright with you?'

'Yes,' said Robert, 'yes.'

'Maxine should be in on this one too.'

'Is she here? Is she coming?'

'Haven't seen her for a few days. Been sick, hasn't she?'

It was the first Robert had heard of it.

'What about Crunchy Nut Cornflakes?'

'Oh she,' said Marcus, 'was living with someone else as it turned out. It wouldn't have worked. Plum wine, love? Yeah just coming…'

The place was turning over like clockwork. There was nothing for Robert to do. He went to an exhibition by a Spanish architect. The classical building off Kensington Gore didn't fill him with despair as it might have done before; the high ceilings, the precisely arranged exhibits, slipped him back neatly into notions of his own possibilities. He belonged in this place. He made buildings too. He peered at catalogues and read technical details and realised he understood how things worked.

He recognised someone from Maxine's exhibition. That seemed a natural sighting. Consuela. He said hello. He remembered she was Spanish.

He talked about the Barcelona development by the sea. She knew all about it. Neither of them had visited it. She talked about the square kite someone had been flying outside. They stalled on that, pretty soon. She couldn't think of anything to say. And then she remembered, of course.

'Congratulations,' she said.

He didn't know what she was talking about. She can't have seen the small item in the architectural journal about the Rotterdam project, at work?

'Congratulations!' she said, 'you're going to be a father. Wonderful! Deanna told me.'

He balked. He stared at her. Then he smiled.

'Congratulations! Wonderful!'

He knew women never made mistakes about things like that. He left in a hurry. Was that what Maxine was doing, calling off sick? He went home. She wasn't there, of course. He went to the late shops for food. He wanted wholesome food that nourished every faculty. He wanted to get her back. He put the food down in the kitchen, tenderly recalling their better days, when they used to kiss and fuck at the same time. He left the food, and started sorting through her things with the thoroughness of a detective. Then he had a terrible feeling that she'd already dealt with it.

There was one message on the ansafone when Maxine came back home. Deanna. Well that was nice. It was half past midnight. It could wait until tomorrow, or the weekend.

The place was warm, the lights were on, Robert was in. She had the strangest feeling that he might have left, on the way home. But she remembered - he didn't have anywhere to go any more either.

He was playing some very old blues records, full of sex and vague contempt. This wasn't unlike how she was feeling, now - time worn and time wearied. If they made him feel better she'd go along with it. She started to hum along.

The door of the spare room open and she went in. Half finished sketches, books and notes were more or less as she'd left them. The women's health book she'd recently consulted was in a different place, she thought. Oh.

He was in the kitchen chopping vegetables, an uncharacteristic stoop in his shoulders. He cut the food into quarters, which told her he had learnt to cook a lot later than she did. People who learnt when she did cut them small.

'Hello,' she said.

He didn't answer. She wouldn't mention about him being in her room.

'Can I have some?'

'Yeah.'

She picked a piece of Stilton off the breadboard and he slapped her hand away really hard. Ouch. Right on her knuckles. He threw the knife down, turned around, and then she knew that he knew. Now it's started, she thought. It won't stop now until something big has happened.

'Why did you do it?'

'It was for the best.'

She never lied, and now she was tearing his heart to pieces.

'And you're the only one who decides that?'

'Yes…No.'

'Why did you do it?'

'You shouldn't have looked in my room,' she said.

'It's my fucking flat!'

My fucking flat, she thought, and suddenly knew she'd been right to take care of her own responsibilities. He looked at her as if she was a madwoman. Then he saw her hair swept back over a moist café au lait hairline, that he used to like to kiss, sweet and slow, when he saw her less often.

'I'm not leaving,' she said.

'No, nor am I.'

Then he broke down. All that was left were the soft, boyish things about him, since she'd deprived him of all other functions. She threw her arms around him. She was shaking now.

'It's alright, it's alright, it's alright,' she said. They couldn't split up over this. Not something so practical. Her timing had been off, but she wasn't wrong. In a few months time, when things started looking up again, he'd know she had made the right decision. They held each other tight, knowing their days together were numbered. But not yet, not yet, not while they still had a joint project going.

'I do love you,' she said, 'that's why I did it.'

'Yeah,' he said. 'Yeah, yeah, I know.'

And she knew it was over.

27

Daniel dozed on the sofa, *The Guardian* careers supplement spread lightly on top of him. He was woken by the repeated honks of a quiz show buzzer. He put the paper aside and pressed the remote. A woman with a tea towel on her head. He pressed again. Someone doing something artisanal to the accompaniment of windpipes. He pressed the button. Russian puppets doing *The Winter's Tale*. Oh no - please, not *that*.

He pressed again. A couple of gonk things were knocking around:

'What would the strange one want with the train?'

'Wee! Oh not that Mr. Nobbly!'

'NO NO NO!'

He was at Paul's flat. He liked being there because it lent him a feeling of transience. Having exhausted Paul's selection of videos - the last one featuring a robotic adolescent getting it in the neck from a chainsaw-wielding maniac - he now tried to find some music he liked.

It was consoling that while music was what Paul did, he had still acquired exactly the same items as Daniel had. Talking Heads? Too chilly. Pet Shop Boys? Too much of that and you felt like an android. The Weather Girls? Whatever happened to them? *It's Raining Men*. Well - all lies, as it happened. He tried a compilation tape:

Hey hey hey
Move it, get on up
Go go go
Move it, get on up

Not at the moment. The supplement was full of jobs he wouldn't get, couldn't do or wasn't qualified for. He could do one of two things - raid Paul's stash again, or get out of the house and do something constructive. He persuaded himself to go for the path of virtue. The way he was feeling at the moment, he could be holed up here for weeks. He had no alternative but to go back to what he'd worked at before.

He rang the bell on the worn brown door of an office in Wardour Street. Oh be in, For godsakes, be in, he thought. The door unlocked with a crunch. Maggie was behind her desk. Good old Maggie, he thought.

'This a social visit?'

'Not exactly. Anything going in Italy?'

'This time of year?' She cackled. 'You'd be lucky. Arts job didn't work out then? I'm not surprised. That's a posh girl's job.'

'Anything in Europe at all?'

'Depends,' said Maggie. 'You were the one who left in the first place. I might be able to get you some trips to Leeds Castle. Day jobs.' Maggie caught his eye. 'Make yourself a cup of tea if you like,' she said.

'It's alright,' said Daniel. 'Oh c'mon Maggie, you always had a soft spot for me.'

'Huh.'

'What about gay tours? Anything with them?'

'I don't know any of them.'

'Great idea though don't you think? Gay Tours. That would be good wouldn't it? I think that would be my true niche.'

'Doubtless,' she said. 'But what are you going to launch it on? Air?'

Daniel went home. There was a sinkful of washing up he hadn't got around to. Condom wrappers littered the bedroom floor, from his and Paul's last bout. A tube of Paul's homeopathic toothpaste lay on his washbasin with its top off. There were a few things to be thankful for.

The phone rang. Work, he thought.

'Hello. It's Jonathan.'

'Jonathan,' he said. '*Jonathan!*' he thought.

'I got the sack,' said Jonathan.

'So did I,' said Daniel.

'Want to come over?'

Daniel jogged along on the top deck of the bus, caressing a bottle of Beaujolais in its green tissue paper. He was about to enter one of his fantasies. He looked out of the window. He had thought about this place so much, had imagined what it might look like. He'd imagined this meeting so vividly. How would it turn out?

He entered Jonathan's flat expectantly. It wasn't so

different from his, except bigger, with more expensive furniture, all new. There were a lot of clocks. He was pleased to see that they shared a few books in common.

Jonathan was talking to an investor on the phone like you'd talk to a lover. He put the phone down and regarded the friendly lust on Daniel's face, and realised he would never tell him anything of importance. He felt remarkably serene in that knowledge. Jonathan poured them both a large glass of Absolut Citron, with ice.

'I was going to do that thing Claire used to do - *Lapin Recteuil*...' said Jonathan.

For me?! Daniel thought.

There was an ineffable air of sadness about Jonathan as he went on, '...but I don't know what a *chavronnier* is. Do you?'

'No,' said Daniel, 'haven't a clue.'

'You have to fill it up two thirds,' said Jonathan, bewildered. 'We can send out for something instead.'

Talk to me, just talk to me, he thought. And Daniel did.

He told him about Arts Inc and how Claire had made a mistake.

'Typical,' said Jonathan, 'silly bitch.'

'Did you know David Brasted's mother was Claire's cleaning woman?' said Daniel.

'No,' said Jonathan, 'no I didn't. Mrs. Brasted, eh? That's right. I remember now. What's he - writer or something.'

'Yes - but she wanted to talk to me...' said Daniel.

'Oh?' Jonathan looked up. 'What about?'

'I think it was about her son being gay,' he giggled. 'You know, he was outed, a while ago. Tabloids.'

Jonathan smiled. 'Oh right. How silly,' he said. 'That's really funny.'

'I think she might be a bit naive,' Daniel added, portentously.

'Yeah - expect she is,' said Jonathan. 'Silly old noodle.'

'I suppose I could always give her a ring.'

'Oh,' said Jonathan, 'I wouldn't bother.'

'No - maybe not,' said Daniel cheerfully, 'maybe she's come to terms with it now.'

Daniel told Jonathan about how nothing Arts Inc did seemed very interesting.

'No,' said Jonathan, 'doesn't sound like it. Never did.'

He said how much he missed tour guiding, how he longed to get back to it, and Jonathan heard him out. He told him about his Gay Tours idea and Jonathan took it seriously.

'I need a new project,' Jonathan said. 'That might be it. Would it be difficult to set up?'

'Not at all,' Daniel said. Fingers crossed.

They talked about whether they were old souls or new souls. They talked about past lives. They demolished people they used to work with. Jonathan put on some old Tamla Motown hits and they got very drunk. They started some inconclusive kissing and fumbling - passed out - and completed it in the morning. Daniel was starry eyed.

'You want to go to Paris?' said Jonathan. 'I've never been. We could do it now. We could use it as the template for our new business.'

Daniel lay in Jonathan's bed while he called the airlines, sinking his head into the soft, huge pillows. That would be good, that would be fine. Paul's explanation for his porn video hadn't entirely satisfied him. And there was Jonathan, Jonathan. He was here. He was in Jonathan's bed, and going with him on a romantic weekend in Paris. Was this really happening?

There was a chill in the air, but the enlivening kind, the sky was a lovely shade of blue and everything in Paris seemed sprinkled with silver light, so Daniel didn't see why he wasn't more delighted. He spoke French, he was in charge, maybe that seemed wrong. Jonathan was like a child. He had just exclaimed 'God - that's beautiful!' for about the twenty third time. Yet the views and sights they were seeing - Jonathan for the first time - were so firmly photographed in Daniel's mind from previous visits, that being here seemed an irrelevance. Remember this, treasure this, he thought. But it wasn't happening. Something essential was missing. He'd come to Mount Vesuvius, and it didn't bubble. Two pears had come up on his one arm bandit, followed by a lemon. He missed Paul.

'Couldn't we just…hang out?' he felt like saying. But Jonathan was relentless.

'How you've got to do it, this Gay Tours itinerary,' he said, half way up the Pompidou Centre's escalator, with a crêpe each, 'is pay attention to what I'm getting off on, and then sort out what the London equivalent is…Charles and Ginny came here once…'

'Oh?'

'My friends.'

'What? Oh - yes.'

'You got the itinerary? Good. You think there's too much shopping in it?' he asked, as they paused over a cup of hot chocolate with liquor in its at the Palais-Royal.

'No,' said Daniel, savouring the chocolate which felt like marshmallows in his mouth. Where's the fire? he thought. They piled off to the Louvre, and Daniel didn't like to say that anything pre-18th century bored him rigid. Well, that was love, Daniel thought. This was business.

Then, at night, once they'd finished having sex - might as well, they'd both thought - Daniel woke up and saw Jonathan's silhouette on their balcony, buried in his absurdly expensive thick bathrobe, chain smoking and sobbing, he could only tell by his shoulders. He was holding it in, so as not to wake Daniel, concealing griefs too large for Daniel to imagine. Daniel pretended to sleep, glad, just a little, that they were flying back Monday morning.

'I used to think beauty was evil,' said Jonathan, on the plane. 'I don't any more.'

Anyone's guess, Daniel thought. Who knew what he was on about? They were friends, they were never meant to be anything else. Now they were business partners. That was all.

They arrived at Heathrow. Daniel watched the conveyor belt. Jonathan had already gone off to make phone calls. Daniel's feet were twitching. He couldn't find it in work, he couldn't find it in a relationship. He hoped he'd be okay. He hoped he could work it out. He hoped, somehow, there might be some escape route.

Jonathan dropped Daniel off and sped up the motorway, to the little market town where Anthony was staying. His head was remarkably clear. His heart was full of sunshine. He stopped off at a service station and had crispy mushrooms and chilli con carne - both tasted very good and nourishing. He parked his car at a distance and walked, and stood opposite the house with the plump bay window with the light on. He had the gun. There were two bullets left. That was enough. He only needed one. He got out the keys Claire had given him, and let himself in.

There was Anthony. Shocked, like he'd once been. Fear on his face, a perfect reflection of how Jonathan must have seemed.

'Hello Anthony.'

'Jonathan,' he rose. 'What are you doing here?'

Then he saw the gun. Jonathan grabbed him - 'No'. He was quite a frail old man now really, easily handled. Put the bastard out of his misery. The shot rang out. Jonathan's arm whiplashed and a sure emission of gas burned his hand. He clutched himself against the pain, then smelled Anthony's blood, saw the state of his face, and gagged. He staggered towards the body with a tightened face, wiped the gun then wrapped Anthony's hand around it. He let the gun drop. He wiped his hands again, staring at Anthony. He felt terrible, violently awful. It was done. But it wasn't good. It didn't look good for him. His hand still burned. He stepped backwards out of the room, slowly, having just done what he had always wanted to do.

Paul had prepared a celebration breakfast for Daniel's homecoming from his business trip. There were chocolate croissants and scrambled eggs - Daniel's favourite. Paul brought it in on a tray, and got back into bed with him. Daniel looked at the paper. A small item told him that Claire's husband, Anthony, had just committed suicide. There were no suspicious circumstances.

'Poor Claire,' said Daniel. 'Well - he was always quiet.'

Paul sympathised. Daniel was secretly gratified that something real had happened to Claire, at last. He turned the pages. He liked to know what was going on in the Arts, still. He looked at the bulletin. A couple of lines informed the world that David Brasted's next work was a no-holds-barred examination of child sex abuse amongst the upper classes.

Later

A year later, the Dolorossa studios opened in a relatively accessible part of the East End, where the noise of the local Ring Road kept up a continual hum. Daniel wondered if the name was connected to the restaurant where he and Jonathan's oh-so-fateful reunion had taken place, all that time ago. But it was nothing to do with it. 'Dolorossa' was the name of an Italian countess to whom Claire fancied she was related.

It was the opening night, and while the general public would not be invited for another month, and those living in the locality might not appear at all, the place was busy. The benevolent scheme had attracted a lot of publicity, and somewhere down the line, word had got around that this was the return of old-fashioned patronage, and a true respect for the artists who were lucky enough to win places on Dolorossa's scheme.

Claire towered over the proceedings with all the fine airs and graces that used to attend the entertainment of Anthony's friends, and others she'd acquired in passing. The wine was very good, the canapés were excellent. Everyone agreed that no more delicious ambience could be created in which to enjoy art. And the great and the good who smiled and frowned on the borderlines of influence had to admit that Claire was quite different from the general run of gallery owners - more caring, less avaricious, more hands-on. Claire was very serene. Winning people round had always been an exceptional skill of hers, one that she used independently now, and in an excellent cause. At some point during negotiations for the premises, she had come to the conclusion that it was never sex that interested her, only power, and this kind of power - an iron fist in a velvet glove power - really suited her very well indeed, especially as she had only possessed any power by proxy for so very long.

Maxine was very hard and fast about who she wanted in, and who she didn't. Once the artists were in, though, she performed the administration of the scheme with an eerie level of consideration for everyone that had presumably, Claire thought, got her through her waitressing career. Claire sometimes wondered if every artist's little request had to be treated with such care, but no matter - Maxine kept an extremely firm eye on the budget, and her attitude kept everyone quiet, busy and happy, it seemed.

As for Anthony's unfortunate demise, she really didn't like to think about it now. At the time, Jonathan had been required to disappear for a while, of course. At the inquest, she had testified to Anthony's state of acute depression over a number of years, as had, much to her surprise, several other eminent people. These people had been keeping tabs on her husband all along, and in fact the whole business had been covered up so effectively, she found herself, more and more, believing the official story.

She rarely saw Jonathan now, and wondered at times if he was the victim of false memory syndrome, for he was clearly in something of a state. Financially, however, they had both done rather well. And Claire's name, at least, had not been disgraced. If Anthony had wanted to dispose of himself in that way, who was she to argue? It was a free world.

The ugly scene and exchange of cash that accompanied Anne's departure was also something Claire didn't care to think about, not now. Anne was furious. She made threats, until she was paid off, then on the back of more threats, was frightened into submission. Jonathan, of course, had been in perfect agreement with that course of action. It was just as well. Anne had even made some approach to Daniel at some point. Daniel had assumed it was about her son or something. Fortunately, he had left the job before Anne got to him. What an incredible cheek the woman had.

Claire greeted another set of arrivals, who were flattered to be invited, amongst them Deanna and her lover, Consuela. Claire was now as distant as she had ever been; Deanna, looking to her live-in partner for confirmation, realised she had been right to vanish when she did, and Consuela admitted she had perhaps been thinking of herself when considering Claire's plight, standing in front of this art-world doyenne whose smile acknowledged them but whose eyes were clearly fixed on some altogether different target.

Deanna and Consuela saw Robert, but luckily the Dolorossa studios were large enough, and the crowd big enough, for him to be avoided. Deanna had been surprised at the efficiency with which Maxine's pregnancy had been halted. She suspected that Robert insisted, and supposed that was what it meant to have a vocation. She only dipped in and out of this world now, and viewed it with the amazement and faint reservation of a social anthropologist.

Robert watched Maxine. She was hanging around Claire, and keeping an eye out for the man from the beer company, who was supposed to give them some money so they could then get commercial sponsorship. He never knew what it was between her and Claire, except they were closer now, and it wasn't just to do with work.

While Maxine was in Berlin, Robert had gone to Rotterdam, on the work project. They had worked on VR equipment which Robert relievedly came to appreciate as feasible rather than the dreams of organic building planned for the *Macro* - still a castle in the air, still needing funding. He and Maxine had moved to premises they could call theirs, not just Robert's, and now Maxine had a studio here, which she worked in, sometimes through the night.

They grew apart, but it was how it always should have been. Sometimes, especially when they didn't see each other much, it seemed as near perfection as either of them could be bothered to contemplate. The less they saw each other, the more their doing so seemed like a real urge. Their place was often deserted. Cloudy wine glasses lay around, that no one bothered to wash because there were more in the cupboard. Flowers shrivelled in their vases, and no one threw them out, because there were no fresh ones to replace them. Nothing grew. Pots of herbs bought when someone came round to eat lived for a week, then were turfed out with the rubbish. Yet they prided themselves on being together out of choice, more or less. And it slowly dawned on Robert that he was leading the life he had always wanted, with her, although he kept on having to remind himself.

He didn't understand most of her work now, he didn't know where it was coming from - canvases splattered with mashed carcasses and smashed eggs. But they got attention. 'Velocity' was a term of commendation that cropped up more than once. He thought they were terrible. There had been an installation for this event, entitled HOME SWEET HOME, featuring floral lampshades attached to branches, a bed with a paisley bedspread with a battlements motif, a dusty pink mantelpiece and a load of small floral print cushions with a stretched lace trim. He didn't know what it meant. He couldn't tell if she was a complete charlatan or the real thing.

Daniel arrived with a tour group. Claire greeted them. Only five of its members had taken up the offer of this optional excursion. The company hadn't worked out quite as well as he and Jonathan had planned; they had enough customers to run it for major festivals, though not through the whole year. Other than that, Daniel worked for Maggie. No news on *Shakespeare in Tuscany* yet, or *Greek Drama in Greece*. But Daniel had discovered recently that he wasn't really ambitious at all, not ambitious about work, in any sense.

Jonathan was weird, still. Daniel thought. One night when

they were out of it, he'd gone on and on about having killed Anthony. Then he had some idea that he'd raped somebody. Awful thing, thought Daniel, even having thoughts like that in your head. That's when Daniel had suggested that Paul get onto his medic friend, for something to calm Jonathan down.

So what now, Daniel thought, now most people had settled with a partner who would put up with them, now everyone had had a go with the handcuffs, now cherished teenage record collections had been solemnly converted to CD versions? He helped himself to another glass of wine, and dipped a prawn into a chilli dip. The tour group seemed to be enjoying themselves, and since he'd been removed from an arts environment, he found he had some liking for events like this. Better not to know how it all worked. He'd developed an avid interest in Chinese films, that Paul gamely shared. Paul would be coming later. It was probably for the best, although Daniel wondered wistfully what his chances would've been, otherwise, with the tall man from Seattle who was talking to Jonathan.

Jonathan had put his faith in a power higher than himself. He had handed his life and will over to the God of his understanding. He was working on self-actualization, being and becoming. *The Tibetan Book of Living & Dying* lay by his bedside. He read a chapter each night, over and over. He thought it was wonderful, he thought it was terrifying.

He had given up drink, cigarettes and caffeine. His complexion had never been better. His attachment to opiates had never disappeared, but now Paul's medic friend helped him out. Superb stuff. What lovely lovely people Daniel knew. He was so glad he'd met them. If it was real medicine, then it couldn't harm you. And this, he supposed, was the little bit of Anthony he'd always carry with him.

All he had lost, really, was the conviction that he was special, and somehow chosen. He had gained the realisation that this didn't really matter - the specialness he had felt when he was working in the City, and intermittently, when he had been with Anthony. He had applied for various other city jobs and got nowhere. It was if it had never happened, now Anthony had gone, as if it hadn't happened at all. He occasionally wondered if he'd killed the person who prized him most, because Anthony was a sad old bastard really, always was, much sadder than Claire, more vulnerable.

Yasmina Muradovic, one of the latest beneficiaries of a Dolorossa scheme, stood in a corner and watched the crowd. She had been put onto Maxine through an artist called Tiggy. She was glad Maxine was the link. She thought Maxine's work was okay, although she couldn't connect with it on any real level.

They were a strange clan, a strange dynasty. Half of them were supposedly related to each other, in a dysfunctional sort of way. There were some funny things to do with Claire, in Maxine's past, somehow connected with the man called Jonathan, who sometimes came in, that Maxine didn't want talked about. The whole party was peculiar. Black clothes and red mouths. All the men with soft, girlish hair, wearing mock casual clothes. Women in clothes that somehow sculpted them. All of them congratulating themselves on

Getting There on Their Own Terms and sobbing nostalgically over their Velvet Underground records. Ordinary kids who thought they were really kicking against something. That was alright for them, Yasmina thought. Or look at that slightly crazy man over there from the tour company, wriggling his bum around and waving his arms in the air.

That was very cute, she thought. Alright for some. No, she was glad of the opportunity now, no doubt about it. She could see a time, though - some time in the distant future - when she and people she hadn't yet met would want to be a part of blowing this house down.

Maxine was sizing up a dealer. She was more or less where she wanted to be, partly due to Claire and Jonathan, partly. There had been one time, a while ago, not so long after her abortion, when she went around to Claire with details of buildings without ringing first, and found Claire and Jonathan locked in some horrible intimacy, shortly after Anthony's death. Who knew what happened? Who cared? She didn't. It was good riddance, really, as far as she was concerned. Nothing could go on until the Anthonys of the world had been cleared out.

Lydia came in with her musicians. Soon, the only people left would be those who genuinely enjoyed each other's company - a handful, at most. The room was swamped in Nico's morbid tones and Druid drums, and Robert thought he'd leave quite soon. He didn't know if he'd be going home with Maxine tonight. She was still working, after all. He watched Claire holding a gallery owner's hand between her own with breathless sincerity, and Maxine's sweet red mouth forming itself into encouragements for the benefit of the man from the beer company, and thought how very strange it was how things changed, and then again, how nothing changed at all.